THE MAGDALENE RELIQUARY

GARY MCAVOY

LITERATI
EDITIONS.

Printed in the United States of America
Hardcover ISBN: 978-0-9908376-7-1
Paperback ISBN: 978-0-9908376-8-8
eBook ISBN: 978-0-9908376-9-5

Library of Congress Control Number: 2020919360

Published by:
Literati Editions
PO Box 5987
Bremerton WA 98312 USA
Email: info@literatieditions.com
Visit the author's website: www.garymcavoy.com
5.0

YOUR FREE BOOK IS WAITING

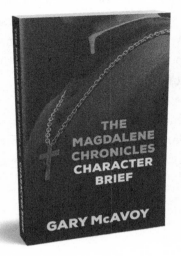

Download your free copy now of **The Magdalene Chronicles Character Brief**, containing brief backgrounds and other biographical details of all the main characters in *The Magdalene Deception*, *The Magdalene Reliquary*, and *The Magdalene Veil*—with my compliments as a loyal reader!

www.garymcavoy.com/character-brief/

PROLOGUE

CARCASSONNE, FRANCE – 1209-1244

Ten thousand of Pope Innocent III's most feared Crusaders had already swept through the Cathar stronghold of Béziers, killing twice that many men, women and children as the Albigensian Crusade ravaged its way through the Languedoc region of southern France. The next major assault would take place in the ancient, fortified city of Carcassonne, the jewel of the Occitanie province.

Word of the pope's troops drawing close to the city reached the ears of Raymond-Roger Trancavel, Viscount of Carcassonne, and in haste, he put into motion several defensive strategies. First, he sent all the city's Jews away, knowing certain death awaited them at the hands of the Catholic army. Then he alerted the Cathars, a small, influential mystic order considered heretics by the Catholic Church, urging them to flee the city. Few did, preferring to take their chances behind the strong defenses of the heavily walled city.

Long a discreet supporter of the peaceful Cathar movement, Trancavel tried to make accommodations with the approaching army to spare his city and its people, but the pope's commanders refused a meeting. His lands— indeed, his very life—were now at stake. But there was one last mission he had yet to accomplish in fulfillment of an oath taken years before.

Accompanied by loyal bodyguards and a small cadre of regimental troops, Trancavel arranged a secret visit with a trusted friend, Raymond VI, Count of Toulouse, carrying with him a small wooden box containing the legendary treasure of the Cathars. The ornately carved box was a sacred reliquary which itself had been handed down to him for safekeeping by Godfroi de Bouillon, conqueror and first ruler of the Kingdom of Jerusalem and Lord of Bouillon, France. Godfroi was of Merovingian descent, a bloodline traced directly back to Mary Magdalene, from whom the reliquary had been acquired after she personally carried it from Jerusalem to France as she and other apostles fled the Romans. Soon Trancavel returned to Carcassonne to stand with his people—and die with them —as the Crusaders waged their bloody war. But before he died, he gave the reliquary to his friend, Raymond VI, for safekeeping.

After Trancavel's death and the fall of Carcassonne, Raymond VI mounted several resistance campaigns against the Crusaders, only to lose Toulouse and suffer excommunication by the Church in the process. Years later he was able to regain his lands, but before he died, he passed on the sacred reliquary to his son, Raymond VII, who succeeded his father as Count of Toulouse in 1222.

Like his father, Raymond VII was sympathetic to both the Jews and the Cathars, and for his failure to suppress both factions, he too fell into disfavor with the Church. But war was again at hand, as the King of France sought to restore his rights in the Languedoc. Raymond VII lost his battles with the king's forces and was ultimately forced to sign the Treaty of Paris, ceding much of his property to the crown. To ensure that the holy reliquary entrusted to him not be acquired by the king, Raymond made secret provisions to transfer it to the Cathar leaders, devout followers of Mary Magdalene. The fabled sacred treasure was now in the hands of its final guardians.

IN THE ENSUING years the heretical Cathars continued to endure one defeat after another in the wake of the pope's Crusades, and the last of the movement's survivors, some four hundred souls, eventually resettled themselves in the mountaintop castle at Montségur, a fortified peak at the foot of the Pyrenees some fifty miles south of Toulouse. But their own days were numbered, as the Albigensian Crusaders blockaded the base of the mountain waiting for their moment to put an end to the scourge of this heresy once and for all.

After ten months of relentless sieges, in March 1244 the Cathars finally acceded to discuss the terms of their surrender with the pope's commanders waiting below. Unbeknownst to the Crusaders, however, four of the most capable Cathar soldiers known as *parfaits* had secretly descended the mountain, taking with them the sacred reliquary, which they eventually hid in a cave near Périllos, a day's journey east of Montségur.

Raymond VII, Count of Toulouse, had by now been

informed by one of the brave escaped *parfaits* of the secret whereabouts of the reliquary. To ensure its location would be known to future faithful collaborators, yet still protected, Raymond had enlisted the services of one of the renowned mapmakers of the day, Pietro Vesconte. He also dispatched a small, trusted group of soldiers to accompany Vesconte and the *parfait* to the cave site, and while the troops set up their base for a few days' encampment, Vesconte used the time to explore the entire cave and lay down on paper an intricate design of the cave system and the exact location of the concealed reliquary.

His mission accomplished, Vesconte returned to his workshop to complete the map on sturdy parchment and prepare it in the form of a shrewd puzzle so as to prevent the casual observer from understanding its solution, much less what its purpose was, without substantial effort.

Testing the design, Vesconte assured himself that, by folding and refolding the panels in specific ways, it would require great thought and effort to eventually arrive at the solution and ultimately reveal the secret location of the legendary treasure of the Cathars.

ONE

PRESENT DAY

S tanding in the center of the sprawling Cathedral cavern of the *Grotte de Lombrives*, the three young men geared up for their descent, echoes of their jangling gear the only sounds in an otherwise silent underground chamber.

Two of the three, Karl Dengler and Lukas Bischoff, were already expert cavers, their skills adapted during rigorous training as elite Mountain Grenadiers, the Swiss Army's equivalent of U.S. Navy SEAL teams. The third man, Michael Dominic, was new to the sport, and not a little intimidated by the massive subterranean labyrinth extending twenty-four miles deep into the earth below the Aude Valley. As a Jesuit priest working in the Vatican, the deepest he had ever been underground was in the basement of the Church's Secret Archives.

"How far back in are we going?" Dominic asked his

comrades, swallowing hard as pearls of sweat lined his brow.

Dengler, a blond, five-foot-nine, superbly conditioned athlete, sensed his friend's hesitation, but couldn't resist racking up the tension. "Not far, Michael. Only half a mile or so … deep, deep into the ground, beneath billions of tons of earth and granite and limestone. Exciting, isn't it?"

Dark-haired Lukas, six feet tall and a solid 190 pounds, stood looking at Dominic for his expected reaction.

The priest just stared at Dengler with a curious mix of tension and disbelief. "Thanks for the daunting optimism, Karl." He had accepted their invitation to try caving as a way to expand his horizons a bit, both of the natural wonders of the area as well as for a bit of needed exercise. Now he wondered if this fun excursion they had promised was a bit more than he had anticipated.

The largest and widest cave by volume in Europe, the Lombrives Cathedral is big enough to accommodate the entire Cathedral of Notre Dame in Paris, and then some. But this wasn't even the largest cavern in the extensive cave system snaking its way through the Languedoc region of southern France. That distinction belongs to the soaring Rule of Satan Hall, which is four times larger than the Cathedral.

A vast pool of stagnant, emerald-green water, brilliantly illuminated by shafts of daylight streaming in through open light wells in the roof of the chamber, formed a verdant natatorium for the pale salamanders and Iberian frogs native to the area.

Dengler and Lukas double-checked Dominic's gear before they made their way through the shallow underground lake and beyond the gallery, deep into the recesses of the cavern.

"I've checked the cave survey, and though this is mostly a horizontal vault, there are some tricky vertical passages. I'll take the lead. Michael, you stay close behind me, and Lukas will take the rear guard."

"*'Rear guard'?!*" Dominic asked with slight alarm. "What are we guarding against?!"

"Well," said Dengler, impishly, "horizontal caves are often home to animals seeking shelter from weather and predators, like bats and raccoons and bears."

"*'BEARS'?!*" Dominic cried out, the word echoing throughout the great chamber.

"Shh!" Dengler whispered. "You'll wake them."

Dominic took a deep breath, blushing as Karl and Lukas laughed.

"Don't worry, Michael," Dengler reassured him. "Cave bears are extinct in this part of France. You may find pictures of them on the walls, though, since these caverns once served as shelter for tribes in the Paleolithic era, some forty thousand years ago. And as for bats, well, nearly every cave has bats."

Wading through the ankle-deep water, the three men stayed close to the walls, careful they wouldn't crush any aqueous troglobites as their steps took them farther into the cave. Geological formations dating back millions of years struck the eye at every turn. Countless stalactites hung like massive icicles from the ceiling; tapering columns of stalagmites, formed by eons of calcified water dripping from above, rose intermittently from the floor bed; shimmering crystals and other minerals formed in nooks and crannies, beckoning those with an eye for natural treasures.

Emerging from the pool, their waders dripping with still water scum, the team slowly made its way to the rear chambers of the cave as the ceiling descended, narrowing their passage.

"You know," said Dominic, making conversation to ease his anxiety, "this cave is among those rumored to contain the Holy Grail, hidden by the Cathars in the thirteenth century. If I have to put up with you two lovebirds harassing me in some bat-ridden cave, the least you could do is to help me look for it while we're here."

Dengler and Lukas looked at each other, adventure in their eyes. "Holy Grail?" Dengler asked. "Are you serious?"

As they walked, LED headlamps on their helmets cast eerie shadows along their respective paths, giving the illusion of nebulous figures lurking in the dark. *The perfect time for a story*, Dominic figured.

He began to explain the historical heritage of the many caves in the Sabarthès region of France, renowned for their role in perpetuating oral traditions of the Holy Grail and other great treasures reputed to be buried here.

He told them about the legendary Cathars, a Gnostic sect of peaceful Byzantine settlers who opposed the Church of Rome's dogma and established their own Christian dualist movement in the nearby French city of Albi—for which they became known as Albigensians.

In 1209, vowing to crush the heresy sweeping the Languedoc during a brutal Inquisition campaign, Pope Innocent III launched the twenty-year Albigensian Crusade, perpetrating what many believe was among the earliest acts of genocide instigated by the Catholic Church. The Crusaders ultimately wiped out Catharism, along with the lives of hundreds of thousands of its followers.

A later revival of the Crusade in 1244 had, by then, virtually obliterated all bastions of Catharism, driving the sect's remaining adherents—a hardy settlement of some four hundred men, women and children—to seek refuge in a high mountain fortress known as Montségur.

Of the remaining men, some 200 had submitted themselves to the *Consolamentum,* a sacred baptismal ceremony whereby ordinary souls became "perfect" in the eyes of their Cathar brethren. Known as *parfaits,* these perfecti renounced the normal trappings of the physical world, embracing spiritual wholeness tempered by unyielding austerity.

The Cathars were also known to possess a great fortune in treasure, which, as their number dwindled, had been passed on to surviving members with one single objective —to ensure that the trove would never fall into the unholy hands of the Inquisition. But the real treasure of the Cathars was believed to be much more than just the gold, silver and precious gems they were known to have acquired over time. The true treasure was rumored to be something of great spiritual significance, not only to the Albigensians themselves but to all of Christianity: a reliquary containing the bones of Jesus Christ. Such a heretical belief was certainly one more motive behind the Church's efforts to wipe them out.

Straddling the summit of the impregnable mountain fortress presented a formidable challenge to the pope's Crusaders—an army ten thousand strong—and defeat of its well-defended peak proved nearly impossible. The Cathars had already withstood some ten months of unceasing assaults, but the tenacity of the Church's troops eventually wore down Montségur's defenders, and while terms of their surrender were being negotiated, under cover of darkness four of the most capable *parfaits* secretly descended one side of the mountain that was less guarded, taking with them the fabled holy relic. With the help of sympathizers waiting at the base of the escarpment, they carried the reliquary away from Montségur and hid it in one of the many caves of the region.

"*This* region," Dominic repeated pointedly. "And very possibly, *this* cave."

Dengler and Lukas were spellbound by Dominic's tale, visions of *Raiders of the Lost Ark* swimming through their minds as they pushed their way deeper into the cave.

Lukas cocked his head and said, "But that just isn't possible. Jesus was resurrected."

Michael knew that every priest, every Christian, would agree with this Swiss Guard. But Michael held silent. His discovery last summer of a papyrus manuscript secreted within the Church's Secret Archives had him privy to information he kept to himself consistent with the pope's expressed wishes. Yet the public still traded in rumors of such a reliquary, and Michael's compulsion for truth kept the fires of his desire for discovery alive. Others had speculated along these lines already, such as with the discovery of what was called the James ossuary which many believe to contain Jesus' bones, or at least his family's, in the Talpiot neighborhood of Jerusalem. But that discovery lacked the necessary provenance, such as he had found for the Magdalene manuscript. His Holiness had vowed Father Michael Dominic to secrecy and so it would stay.

Lukas squinted at the darkened corners. "But gold and gems, well, that alone would be worth burying in a cave."

"You would think others might have found something by now," Dengler said with a look of skepticism.

"Well, you don't think the Cathars would have just left

it out in the open, do you?" Dominic countered with a sly smile.

Approaching the first vertical pitch, Dengler free-climbed up to anchor a traverse line. For Dominic's benefit he rigged a ladder to prevent his novice friend from struggling too much on the climb, then extended the traverse out between the two walls before lowering the rope through a tight descending slot. As they made their way down, the pitch quickly widened to reveal the next rebelay point several meters lower, above a breathtaking shaft. A couple more rebelays completed the full descent, and they found themselves in another magnificent gallery, the light from their headlamps dancing off crystal formations jutting out from the gallery walls.

"So, what happened to the Cathars after they surrendered?" Lukas asked as they took in the splendors of the vast chamber, their headlamps dancing across the glittering walls.

Dominic's response was somber. "The pope's Crusaders had built a huge bonfire at the base of Montségur, and demanded that all *parfaits* renounce their heretical beliefs when they descended the mountain. Prepared for martyrdom, those who refused voluntarily walked into the blazing pyre, unrepentant, assured of a divine afterlife. The few remaining Cathars were allowed to go free, thus keeping alive the legend of the reliquary through later generations.

"It's been fairly well known, or at least widely believed among some scholars, that Mary Magdalene and her fellow disciples had spirited a reliquary, some say to be an ossuary containing Christ's bones, out of Jerusalem as they fled the Romans. Regardless of the real contents, it is believed something was secreted away and hidden. For centuries people have tried and failed to find the reliquary in these caves.

"But it's *got* to be here somewhere," he added mischievously, "so keep your eyes open."

Pointing to a large vertical crack between two giant boulders, Dengler led them forward. "Our route will take us up this chimney, which opens into a rift at the top. Just follow me."

At first, the crack proved easily climbable, but the rift soon led to an intimidating ten-meter drop, followed by a scramble down a descending passage. Dengler attached a rope to a couple of natural belays further up the rift, then placed two anchors over the pitch head to allow for a free-hang down the pitch. The others followed him dutifully.

The bottom of the pitch required a low, awkward crawl between two limestone slabs, and they squirmed through a few puddles along the way. After another ten meters, the passage widened at a trench, followed by a four-meter climb down to the floor of a small enlargement in the cave, though still too narrow to accommodate them all. So, one by one they crawled forward through a tight passage bending left, then right, culminating with a tricky sideways wriggle leading to another short drop.

The situation was becoming formidably claustrophobic for Dominic, as it might for most people unaccustomed to the confining rigors of caving. Although he kept himself reasonably fit with a daily run, the cramped, joint-bending crawl was taxing.

"Guys," he grunted as he struggled through the rift, the gear around his waist grinding against a sandstone wall, "this is a bit more than I expected. Are you sure we'll be able to get out of here?"

"It won't be a problem, Michael," Dengler said

cheerfully. "We'll just go back out the same way we came in."

"A pity I didn't bring breadcrumbs," Dominic replied.

They continued crawling, climbing, dropping and squeezing through the cave for some time until finally they came to an impressively large vault with several routes leading off of it—including an exit that led straight out into the lush forest from which they had originally come.

Seeing this easier path of escape from the tight confines of the earth, the expression on Dominic's face turned from worried to optimistic.

"Hallelujah!" he whispered to himself, then in a louder voice, "That was great, guys—hours of exercise punctuated by moments of terror. Did you two really have to do much of this training to be Swiss Guards?" he asked.

"That was nothing," said Lukas assertively. "Try rappelling down a rocky 300-meter cliff in a snowstorm."

"Pass," said Dominic simply, preferring his normal everyday challenges of translating ancient manuscripts in the civilized comfort of the Vatican reading rooms.

Coiling his rope and securing his gear, Dengler had a thought. "If you ever want to go looking for that Cathar treasure, Michael, count us in. It sounds like our kind of adventure, doesn't it, Lukas?"

Catching his partner's eye, Lukas nodded with a grin. "Let's get a move on. We've got to be back in the Vatican by noon tomorrow. I've got gate duty."

Their explorations done for the long weekend spent in France, the team made their way through the woods, around the mountain, and back to Dengler's Jeep Wrangler. Stowing their gear in the cargo bay, they all piled in for the twelve-hour drive back to Rome.

"No chest of gold or gems." Lukas sighed as he sat back, reflecting on their day.

Michael smiled, inwardly grateful for no discoveries today. The existence of a reliquary of Jesus' bones could be as damaging to both the Church and its legion of believers as his find last summer of the secreted scroll that stated its existence. As much as he sought the truth, he also preferred his quiet life as an archivist, and not to face another such dilemma.

Karl then piped in with a grin, "At least not this time."

CHAPTER
TWO

A s the mighty bells of Saint Peter's Basilica ended their sixth and final drone, the portly, bald monk slowly stood from the wooden chair he had occupied for the past few pre-dawn hours.

Though his aching body longed for relief from the intense concentration his task was demanding, he could not risk wasting the precious time he would have alone in the Tower of the Winds.

He sauntered around the cramped, dimly lit room, as much to divert his attention from the devastating document behind him as to impose disciplined calm on an overworked mind. A musty stillness hung in the room, and the constricting tightness in his chest added to his need for fresh air.

Lifting the bolt and pulling back the tarnished metal hasp, the monk opened the heavy door and walked out into the empty Meridian Room, with its colorful fresco of a storm on the Lake of Galilee adorning the south wall. A shaft of brilliant morning sunlight streamed in through the open mouth of the Triton dominating the scene, casting its beam on the black meridian line bisecting a white circle on the marble floor. Originally built in 1582 by Pope Gregory XIII as an observatory, it was in this room at the top of the *Torre dei Venti* that the Gregorian calendar was conceived, forever changing the means by which the civilized world would record its history. But history would be reshaped even further if the information in the document the monk had just read was ever revealed.

Breathing deeply, the weary friar shuffled across the hall in his leather sandals and out onto the rooftop terrace of the Tower. From here, one could enjoy Rome's most breathtaking panorama, its beloved Pantheon eclipsing the skyline as dawn bathed the timeless city. The sharp contours of the buildings, their ocher tiled roofs and gilded steeples seemingly joined as one across the broad horizon, obscured the muddy flow of the Tiber River as Rome itself portrayed one of the ancient frescoes gracing the walls inside the room.

But there were no thoughts of enjoyment for Brother Calvino Mendoza this early morning. For him, the skyline beyond the Vatican walls took on a menacing oppression as he reflected on the explosive discovery he had just made.

CHAPTER

THREE

A few hours later that morning, two Swiss Guards, bearing the corps' less formal daily uniform of blue and black, smartly saluted as the Jeep Wrangler approached Saint Anne's Gate, the main entrance into Vatican City used by employees, visitors and tradesmen. Recognizing the vehicle's three occupants, the lead guard on duty raised the boom barrier and waved them through, smiling at Sergeant of the Guard Karl Dengler as he drove his SUV onto Via di Belvedere.

Parking across from the Vatican Bank next to the post office, Dengler, Dominic and Lukas unloaded their caving gear. "Thanks for a great time, guys," Dominic said wearily, spent from the long road trip. "I'm not sure I'd do it again, but as first experiences go, this was definitely one of those."

Dengler looked at him quizzically, unsure if Dominic's statement was sincere or not. "We'll get you back in the caves yet, Michael, just you wait."

Tossing them a wave, Dominic trudged back to his

apartment in Domus Santa Maria, the Vatican's guesthouse, then dropped his gear on the floor and fell onto the bed.

THE ALARM WOKE him forty-five minutes later, just the quick doze he needed before heading into the office. His mornings usually began with a brisk run through Rome, before the tourists came out in droves and the shopkeepers began their morning rituals opening for business. But there was neither time nor inclination for running today.

After showering, Dominic threw a clean black cassock over his head, fastening all thirty-three buttons—one for each year of Christ's life on earth, for nothing lacks symbolism in religious protocols—up to the starched white Mandarin collar encircling his neck. Satisfied with what he found in the mirror, he left his apartment and made his way to the Secret Archives.

L'Archivio Segreto Vaticano, known to the world by the more intriguing name, Secret Archive of the Vatican, had for several hundred years served as the sole repository of the Church's seemingly infinite collection of official documents.

All manner of books and papers acquired since the eighth century—political and religious tracts, account ledgers, personal records and correspondence of the popes and the Curia, the Vatican's governing body for ecclesiastical and secular matters—are spread out over some fifty-three linear miles of shelving in the vast underground section known as the Gallery of the Metallic Shelves and elsewhere in the tight confines of the Vatican. Over time, the sheer volume of materials had branched out into adjoining hallways, aisles, and side rooms, like a river finding its own path, as more documents had been added to the collections.

As assistant prefect, or *scrittore*, of the Archives, Michael Dominic had, by age thirty, found fulfillment in his life's ambition long before he had expected to. Aided since childhood by the influence of his patron and mentor, now Vatican Secretary of State Cardinal Enrico Petrini, Dominic fully realized the weight of privilege extended to him by his assignment to the Vatican so early in his religious career. His mother, Grace, had been rectory housekeeper to then-Father Petrini in the diocese of Brooklyn, New York, when Dominic was born. As he grew up, all his mother would tell him about his father was that he left shortly after his birth, and that's where the matter ended. That vacuum was solemnly filled by Enrico Petrini, who stepped in to foster Michael's development as a young man, ultimately leading him to college, seminary, and graduate schooling in courses of classical medievalism, paleography and computer sciences: three areas of study making him uniquely qualified for a life of service in one of the world's most historically important library institutions.

PASSING THE GOVERNMENT PALACE, Dominic walked through the papal gardens, plucking and savoring a ripe autumn apple from the trees lining the *Stradone dei Giardini* on his way to the Apostolic Library building. A fresh rain had come overnight, brightening the vivid colors of the trees, bushes and flowers, exuding a sweet petrichor over the many acres of Vatican landscaping that had served the contemplative meditations of popes for centuries.

Bounding up the steps of the Archives building,

Dominic came face to face with his superior, Brother Calvino Mendoza, prefect of the Secret Archives.

"*Buongiorno*, Cal!" Dominic said cheerfully.

Wearing the distinctive brown garb of his Franciscan Order of Friars, a simple white corded cincture surrounding his ample waist, Brother Mendoza greeted his assistant with a forced smile, his normally buoyant personality oddly subdued.

"I see you're back from exploring the caves of France, Miguel," he muttered. Mendoza favored giving affectionate nicknames to those close to him, reflecting the Portuguese equivalent of their name as an homage to his native home in Brazil. "Does that make you an official spelunker now?"

"Hardly," Dominic said with a smirk, trying to lighten his friend's dour mood. "And the appropriate term is caving. '*Spelunk*' is the sound an incompetent caver makes when he slips and falls in a puddle of water."

Mendoza managed a smile, then turned sullen again. "Well, don't write it off entirely, for '*the cave you fear to enter holds the treasure you seek.*'" The monk was also known for pithy quotes appropriate to the occasion.

"Speaking of treasures, what have you got lined up for us today?" Dominic asked.

"Ah, yes. Today you'll be working with the new technology team. Peter has set up our segment of the project down in the digitizing lab. Will you check with him on what he needs from us?"

"Sure, Cal. But what new technology? Sounds intriguing."

"Oh, Miguel," Mendoza sighed, rolling his eyes. "You know technology bores me to tears. Just ask Peter or Toshi for details."

Dominic headed down to the subterranean digitizing lab, where for the past year he had been assisting Peter Townsend and Toshi Kwan, the two scientists in charge of the team preparing digital versions of historical manuscripts from the Vatican Secret Archives, making them accessible to scholars worldwide. Due to the lack of space and support staff, the Archives' reading rooms can only accommodate around a hundred scholars per month. With an online digital database available to students and scholars, millions of previously inaccessible manuscripts can now be researched by anyone with a computer and authorized access.

Entering the lab, Dominic made his way through the maze of digital cameras, scanners, light boxes, and tables lined with ancient manuscripts, until he found the man he was looking for.

"Hey, Toshi, what have you got here?" Dominic asked the young computer scientist. Toshi Kwan was at the heart of the lab's work, a brilliant cryptanalyst with specialized expertise in steganography, the art of hiding information within information. Many historical manuscripts—popes' letters to their lovers written in code, for example, or secret communiqués to other world leaders—were peppered with hidden meanings crafted by medieval cryptographers in order to avoid potentially damaging disclosure to the popes' enemies.

"Hey, Michael, good to see you!" Kwan replied. "You're going to love this new project we've taken on, *In Codice Ratio*, or ICR. It's a first-of-its-kind undertaking in automatically transcribing the Vatican's ancient, handwritten manuscripts into computer-readable text using advanced optical character recognition, or OCR. It's totally unprecedented."

Kwan went on to explain that the ICR team had initially enlisted the help of over a hundred students in two dozen Italian high schools to manually identify a specialized dataset of characters based on a sample of thousands of medieval handwritten parchments from the thirteenth century. He pointed out that it's much easier for the human eye to distinguish characters and symbols from the wide variety of strokes that resemble patterns of handwriting than it is for computer-automated programs to do the same task. As a result, the high-rate of accuracy provided by the curated dataset now made it much less of a challenge for computers to "read" handwritten manuscripts using the newly trained OCR, making them more accessible to scholars searching on specific words and phrases.

His exuberance was contagious, and Dominic's own interest grew as Kwan continued. "We're talking about important documents here, Michael: letters to and from kings, queens and other world and religious leaders, official Curial correspondence, ecclesiastical and secular legal opinions, and a rich array of other historical communications which had never been transcribed previously, much less seen in modern times. Making such profound sources of knowledge from past civilizations and cultures transcribable was paramount to expanded scholarship, one of the main purposes served by the Secret Archives."

"This is a remarkable project," Dominic exclaimed. "But also, a bit alarming. How soon before I'm out of a job?!"

Kwan laughed. "I think you're good for a few lifetimes, Michael. There's still much to be done by us mere mortals before the Singularity occurs."

Dominic was impressed, knowing well the difficulty of transcribing arcane manuscripts in Ancient Greek, Latin, Aramaic, and other languages common to every place and era since the first century. His own work involved such often-formidable translations, as *scrittori* in the Secret Archives strived to interpret and index the millions of documents in its care. And that process alone would require multiple lifetimes by an army of specialists.

The Archives only had a full-time staff of some eighteen *scrittori* and assistants, the team responsible for transcribing, indexing and filing the Archives' vast collection of documents: more than thirty million manuscripts and growing at a million per year. To put things in perspective, one section of the Archives, known as the Miscellanea, contains fifteen enormous poplar cabinets called *armadi*. Each *armadio* contains an average of ten thousand packages of documents that have never been explored. To inventory just one package would require the full-time effort of two specialists over a week's time. To record all ten thousand packages in one cabinet alone, then, would take nearly two hundred years. That was the main obstacle faced by the small team of dedicated personnel serving the Archives, and it was by no means an insignificant one.

It was just last summer when Dominic, purely by chance, stumbled onto a letter that began a series of events that ultimately led him to discover an original handwritten manuscript by Mary Magdalene—a document that, had it been publicly revealed, would have forever changed the course of religious belief throughout history. At the pope's direction, however, that document had been sealed away in the enigmatic Riserva, a secured room where the

Vatican's most sensitive documents were kept under lock and key.

Dominic had personally hidden the manuscript deep inside one of the *armadi*, the great poplar Borghese cabinets, where he was confident no one might come across it.

God help anyone who did. And God help the Church if they revealed it.

CHAPTER

FOUR

T he conference center at the Rome Cavalieri
Waldorf Astoria was a bustle of activity as the
biannual Global Investigative Journalism
Conference got underway.

As a luncheon of linguine with lobster sauce was being
served in the *Terrazza degli Aranci* room, Hana Sinclair,
representing Paris's *Le Monde* newspaper, glanced around
the spacious banquet hall. One entire wall of floor-to-
ceiling windows looked out over a broad panoramic view
of Rome, with an ocean of ocher-colored roof tiles as far as
the eye could see. The room was so bright—its white-
clothed tables and chairs casting a radiant glow to the
room—that many attendees were wearing sunglasses.
Each table had ten place cards identifying who sat where
and which organization they represented.

As she noted walking around it, Hana's table hosted an
eclectic group of colleagues, including high-profile
investigative reporters from *The New York Times*, the
Financial Times of London, *The Guardian*, *The Wall Street*

Journal, The Intercept—and one name card she found curiously out-of-place: Signor Massimo Colombo, director-general of the *Agenzia Informazioni e Sicurezza Interna*, or AISI, Italy's internal security intelligence agency. Intrigued —and before anyone had yet taken a seat—Hana moved Colombo's name card next to hers.

As each guest took his seat, introductions were made around the table. "Tell me, Signor Colombo," Hana asked, after introducing herself. "How is it you come to be here? Considering a new career?"

Colombo leaned forward and laughed, which stretched the heavy bags under his dark eyes as he did so. "No, Miss Sinclair, I very much like the job I have now, thank you. I am here as a guest of the conference chairman, an old friend. The AISI is quite interested in how investigative journalists such as yourself acquire information, and the latest tools you use in the process. On at least that score, we work toward the same goals.

"I am especially interested in this afternoon's workshop on the Criminal Services Industry," he continued. "Organized crime—indeed, all criminal enterprises—rely on a vast range of support services they get from a cottage industry of accountants, lawyers, bankers and legitimate businesses acting as money launderers—anyone who can offer even a thin veneer of respectability."

"Such as?" Hana queried.

"Well, did you know that ATMs alone account for untold millions of dollars each month in cross-border cash transfers by drug lords?"

"ATMs?" Hana asked, her eyebrows raised with interest. "How are they involved in money laundering?"

"Well, for example, you have a team of street dealers in, say, New York. Once their drug sales are made, in cash obviously, they'll make small deposits in different banks in Manhattan, usually less than two thousand dollars each, which go into multiple accounts owned by people in, say, Argentina.

"So," Colombo went on, "their associates in Buenos Aires use their ATM cards to withdraw the money from these accounts in pesos, going from machine to machine in various places, withdrawing the same small amounts. It's a huge business now and avoids the risks of having to move large amounts of cash across many international borders."

Hana was impressed, not having given the concept any thought before. "And I suppose the banks get their little taste of the action too," she said.

"Oh yes," Colombo replied, "whether they are aware of it or not, banks are complicit in this illegal activity. But many of these ATMs are owned by well-funded private companies: fronts for drug cartels, set up for this purpose alone, the laundering of illicit street gains."

"I can see why today's workshop on the Criminal Services Industry would be of interest," Hana said. Then a thought struck her. "As it happens, I don't have anything scheduled for that time. May I join you?"

"Of course," Colombo said. "It would be a pleasure to escort such a beautiful woman. I will be the envy of everyone there."

Hana blushed at the compliment. *This man is Italian to the core,* she thought.

Finished with lunch, they exchanged business cards and agreed to meet later in the *Sala San Pietro* room for the forum.

WHILE SEARCHING for a particular folio in the Miscellanea section for a patron waiting in the reading rooms, Michael Dominic's iPhone buzzed in his pocket. He withdrew the phone and tapped the green button.

"Hey Michael, it's Hana!"

Dominic's heart leapt as he heard his friend's voice. Her image instantly appeared in his mind, and he smiled at the mere thought of her.

"Hana! Where *are* you? Tell me you're in town!"

"As a matter of fact, I am," she said, coifing her hair absentmindedly as if he were able to see her. "I flew in late last night for a week-long conference here at the Rome Cavalieri. I thought if you're free we could have dinner this evening."

"I'd love to. What time?"

"How about eight?"

"Eight it is. Where?"

"La Pergola, here in the hotel. My treat."

"It would *have* to be at La Pergola! A priest's salary wouldn't cover an appetizer there."

Hana laughed. "I'll meet you in the lounge, Michael. See you then."

Although they had stayed in touch by phone and email, it had been many months since Dominic had last seen his friend, and he looked forward to the reunion. Their adventures of the previous summer—the discovery of the Magdalene papyrus, Hana's abduction and rescue, and the recovery of millions of dollars in Nazi gold—had created in them a special bond unlike any other Dominic had known.

Putting aside those warm, reflective thoughts, he returned to his task. The recent release of Pope Pius XII's confidential papers had resulted in a barrage of requests by scholars to study his role in the Church's complicity with the Nazis during World War II. Though Pius XII was on the long and complex path to sainthood, that process had been slowed significantly by the release of millions of documents relating to his papacy. Claiming it has nothing to hide from history, Vatican leadership chose to wait until scholars had a chance to better understand Pius's decisions during a tense and tumultuous period for the Church.

And one noted scholar in particular was waiting for a cache of those very papers in the Secret Archives' Pio XI Reading Room.

CHAPTER
FIVE

"Ah, Michael, so good to see you! What have you got for me here, eh?"

Dr. Simon Ginzberg, professor emeritus for Rome's Jewish Teller University and Scholar-in-Residence at the Vatican, sat at the black leather-covered table, waiting for Dominic to drop several hefty folders of documents he had brought from the Archives' stacks for Ginzberg's research.

"Good morning, Simon!" said the young priest. "This should keep you busy for a while." He laid the pile of folders on the table, then sat down. "How's your project coming along?"

Ginzberg, a survivor of the Dachau concentration camp as a child during the Holocaust, had for the past year been researching Pope Pius XII's activities with regard to many of Adolph Hitler's top field marshals, and the pope's alleged complicity in standing idle while millions of Jews were sent to various concentration camps. It was a hot debate not just in the historical scholarly community, but within the Vatican itself, as staunch defenders of Pius battled with those who sought to reconcile with the Jewish community—indeed, with all the world—by admitting at least some form of collaboration with the Third Reich. Without further light being shone on the actual documents from that period, the battles raged on.

And that's where Ginzberg's work came in. He had been one of the few leading scholars in this sector of research since being given limited advance access to Pius's archives the previous year, his goal being not so much to castigate the Church's role in history as to clarify it.

"It is a slog through a complex and politically sensitive history, Michael," the old man said, his bony hand stroking the neatly trimmed Van Dyke framing his face. "I hope I'm still alive to witness the end of it, but there is just so much here…" He looked down on the table, spreading his arms across two thick folders packed with Pius XII's personal correspondence and official papers, a mere fraction of what was now available.

"By the way, Hana is in town for a conference this week. I'm having dinner with her tonight," Dominic said. "It'll be great to see her again."

"Ah, the delightful Miss Sinclair," Ginzberg said, smiling reflexively. "Please do give her my regards. What is she working on these days?"

"I will, thanks. She didn't say, but I'm sure I'll get an earful when we meet up."

"Oh, Michael…I nearly forgot. You'll recall my interest in the Crusades, yes? Would you be so kind as to find for me what you have on Guillaume de Sonnac, eighteenth Grand Master of the Knights Templar around 1250? He was a diligent historian of the Crusades, and of Templar chronicles in particular, and I'm keen to review what personal archives he might have left, looking for any particular relationships he might have had with the Counts of Toulouse. There's no rush, just round up what you might have when you can, yes? You know where to find me."

RETURNING TO HIS OFFICE, Dominic found Calvino Mendoza slumped in his desk chair, a look of distress on his face. The normally cherubic monk was clearly unsettled.

"Anything I can help with, Cal?" Dominic asked. "You really seem out of sorts today."

Mendoza looked up at him, despondent.

"Miguel, I don't know where to begin," he said. "I have come across something in the Riserva that has me deeply disturbed. I had never seen this manuscript before, and I... I don't quite know what to think about it."

Before he had even finished, Dominic had filled with dread, suspecting he knew what the monk was referring to: a singularly unique papyrus Dominic had hidden there the previous summer.

His hand shaking, Mendoza passed the manuscript across the desk to Dominic. "I found this folio on the top shelf of the *armadio*, along with a translation someone had already provided. It is apparently in Saint Mary Magdalene's own hand, Miguel, and speaks of such sacrilegious things...my faith is shaken to its core."

Dominic considered how best to handle this development. He had not informed his superior about his earlier discovery of this important document nor the actions surrounding its revelations.

"Cal, there's something I need to tell you…" Dominic began gently.

He went on to describe his having initially found a letter by a priest in the French parish of Rennes-le-Château, which led him to further research and the discovery of the papal legate's report about this priest having blackmailed the Church over the document's explosive content. Dominic described how he and Hana Sinclair had found the Magdalene papyrus in the attic of a niece of the priest's assistant and how he had transcribed the document. He told him of the later terrible events at the warehouse in Tor Bella Monaca, and ultimately of Cardinal Dante's being demoted for his collaboration with the Novi Ustasha, an underground group related to the Nazis in principles and practices.

"His Holiness himself made the decision to secretly archive the manuscript, Cal, with explicit instructions not to tell anyone else about its discovery. I'm truly sorry I was unable to share this with you at the time."

Mendoza was speechless, his face drawn, light tears streaming down his plump cheeks.

"I don't blame *you*, Miguel," he sniffed, "especially given the pope's personal directive. But apart from the manuscript's obvious historical importance, the fact is that its content speaks to every Christian on earth. How can this evidence be withheld from the world? How is one to move forward in abiding faith, given Magdalene's assertion that Christ's bodily resurrection hadn't occurred?"

Dominic had faced that crisis of spirit himself upon finding the manuscript. Throughout his life, he had accepted Church dogma and, later, his role as a priest as a necessary road to fulfill his compulsion to delve into history and gain knowledge. His lifelong faith had been more of an accepted assumption rather than an unquestioning premise as his intellect had searched for truth, not realizing the two might collide. When he found that manuscript, his belief in the goodness inherent in religion hadn't faltered in the face of this falsehood but been strengthened in learning more. Yet for those of unquestioning faith such as Cal...Dominic sighed. It was the reason he had complied with the pope's directive without looking back. Now, he had no answer for his friend.

"I think this is something that would be deeply intimate to every individual, Cal," he offered. "Christianity is more than any one miracle, and many would grasp that, and welcome the truth, as I did. But it would be deeply disturbing to others. The pope had his reasons for concealing such a volatile document."

"Yes," the monk said soberly, "it's clear the Church would have strong objections to its release for other reasons as well, given the obvious consequences for the institution's future. I just find it all so sad and conspiratorial. Like everything I had believed in all my life has simply evaporated." Mendoza looked utterly defeated.

Dominic stood to embrace his friend as the monk wept. This was not the way he'd wanted Mendoza to learn about the Magdalene manuscript. What this devout brother might do with this knowledge, though, was the real concern.

CHAPTER
SIX

The Special Representative of Interpol to the
European Union, Conrad Spiegler, was the
keynote speaker for the Criminal Services
Industry forum at the Global Investigative Journalism
Conference.

After lunch, Hana Sinclair and Massimo Colombo had
taken back row seats in the *Sala San Pietro* room of the
Rome Cavalieri, keen to learn about money laundering
and tax evasion for their respective organizations. The
room was packed with journalists and other interested
parties to hear Spiegler's take on how corporate crime was
costing eastern European governments alone over €220
billion each year in lost taxes from wealthy individuals
and drug cartels who hid their money in offshore accounts.

"Every major country in the world has a robust
industry that provides offshore tax evasion services to
corporations and individuals," Spiegler noted.
"Accountants, lawyers, company formation agents, and a
host of other specialists devise convoluted, barely legal

schemes for masking the true ownership of corporations and their assets. And business-friendly laws in these offshore havens then bind the hands of law enforcement in nearly every country, since most of these locations also have strict secrecy laws, much like Switzerland, Lichtenstein, and the Cayman Islands do."

As Spiegler went on, Hana made notes on her slim reporter's steno pad, while Colombo sat patiently, listening to much of what he already knew as director of Italy's internal security agency. He turned to Hana.

"Are you working on any particular project now that deals with this topic, Miss Sinclair?" he whispered.

"Please, call me Hana," she said softly in response. "Actually, for several months now I've been working on an investigative piece about the resurgence of a little-known group called the Novi Ustasha, whose odious roots in Croatia go back to World War II."

"Oh, we are very familiar with this organization," Colombo confirmed. "It has caused us no end of problems, in small but important ways. We must talk about this later, yes? Perhaps share what each of us knows—well, as much as I am able to, of course, given the obvious restrictions of national security. And please, call me Max."

Hana looked at the man with new appraisal. Providence had provided her with an impeccable source of material. "Yes, I would like that very much, Max," she said. "Perhaps we might have a drink after the forum?"

∼

THE TIEPOLO LOUNGE & Terrace at the Rome Cavalieri is a handsome, well-appointed room featuring tasteful Venetian art and sculptures, Renaissance oil paintings, and curved wood-paneled ceilings suspended over a dark wood-paneled floor. As Hana and Colombo walked into the lounge, Jaffa, the resident pianist, was performing a popular jazz piece on a polished ebony Petrof grand piano, the centerpiece of the room.

Though the lounge was filling quickly following the end of the day's conference activities, Colombo spotted an intimate sitting area for two in the back corner that would serve their need for discreet conversation. Each of them sat in plush, hunter-green leather chairs and, feeling indulgent after their long day of gathering information, ordered one of the house specialties, the Chestnut Cocktail, a frothy mix of pear-flavored vodka, white cacao and chestnut whipped cream.

"This drink means another thirty minutes on the treadmill for me," Hana said, flashing a lively smile.

"Make that an hour—we might have two!" said Colombo, laughing.

"So, Hana," he asked, "how did you first come upon the Novi Ustasha?"

Hana looked up toward the ceiling, recalling her first encounter with the sinister organization.

"Last summer I was on special assignment, covering the flow of Nazi gold and other stolen Jewish assets through the Swiss and French banking systems. I made a connection with an Interpol agent named Petrov Gović, whose father, Miroslav, was one of the organizers and leaders of the original Ustasha under the Independent State of Croatia in the mid-1940s—which, as you may know, was closely aligned with the Nazi party, serving as the interim government for Croatia at the time.

"Gović and I had arranged a meeting for an interview one evening at a warehouse outside Rome, in a sketchy area called Tor Bella Monaca, and like a fool, I went there alone."

At the mention of Tor Bella Monaca, Colombo's eyebrows furrowed in surprise, knowing of TBM's reputation as the drug capital of Rome.

Hana took a long draw on her cocktail. "When I got there," she continued, wiping the froth from her lips with a napkin, "I was shocked to find that he was the man who had been following my colleague and me over the previous week—in Rome, Paris, even on the train to Rennes-le-Château, a small village in southern France. At first, I assumed he had me under surveillance for something Interpol-related, but as it turned out, his plan was to hold me hostage in exchange for an irreplaceable ancient manuscript in the possession of the Vatican.

"Their goal was apparently to use the knowledge of that manuscript to blackmail the Church for a vast amount of gold held in the vaults of the Vatican Bank."

Colombo was now wide-eyed with interest. "That must have been some manuscript. What kind of information did it contain?"

Hana's face turned solemn. "I'm afraid I can't go into further detail on that, Max. I've given my word to treat it as confidential," she said.

"So, how did you manage to escape from captivity?" he asked, taking another tack.

"I was rescued by my cousin and two other capable Swiss Guards, as well as my research colleague, Father Michael Dominic."

"You were very fortunate. We know of this Petrov Gović fellow," Colombo said darkly, looking past Hana as he spoke. "We were aware that he was the Croatian liaison to Interpol, of course, but AISI had no knowledge of his affiliation with the Ustasha network until after this event you speak of. I do remember it making news at the time. Gović and his henchman were killed, attributed in the press to a drug deal gone bad. But the Italian police approached it as an Interpol rogue operation: Interpol theorized Gović had played his hand poorly in some Ustasha scheme."

As she took another sip of her drink, Colombo stared into Hana's eyes, a look of recognition gradually forming in his own. "Wait…aren't you the daughter of Baron Armand de Saint-Clair? Yes, now I know where I recognized your name."

"Guilty as charged, Agent Colombo," Hana said with a wry smile. "Though I tried to avoid publicity about that terrible experience, the Italian press was very persistent.

"So, if I might inquire in kind," she asked, "what is your interest in the Ustasha?"

Colombo paused, considering what he was able to discuss. "Well … apart from the obvious—a terrorist organization recruiting agents throughout principal European countries—we're looking into their money-laundering operations. Much like Al-Queda or ISIS in the Middle East, this group is largely itinerant, with no clear-cut base of operations, nothing like the Ustasha had during World War II, where it formed its puppet government in Zagreb. The Novi Ustasha of today is composed of regional cells in or near all major capitals—Rome, Paris, Berlin, Kiev, Madrid…Its tentacles grow far and wide, and its fast-growing membership is fiercely ultra-nationalistic. Wherever you see neo-Nazi protests these days, you can be sure the Ustasha is either close by or is directly responsible for the demonstrations. Most likely the latter."

"Frankly, I'd never heard of them before last summer's

incident," Hana said. "I had no idea of how widespread it is. It certainly keeps a low profile."

"The funding of this group is what concerns us most at the moment," Colombo added. "Apart from what assets it retains from its original days—gold, currency, properties, stolen artworks, and, as you say, former Nazi loot that has found its way to South America and other havens—we are aware of legitimate, well-funded corporations and institutions having conservative, even far-right agendas, who give the Novi Ustasha significant contributions through tax-exempt shell companies.

"We even have reason to believe that some components of the Church may be in collusion with these people, but I would ask that you not share that bit of information, especially not for publication."

"Of course, Max, I'll take that as off the record," Hana said, already aware of the fact. "But might you have any specific names of current Ustasha members you're able to reveal? I won't publish them, necessarily, but I might try to reach out for interviews, if at all possible."

Again, Colombo's face contorted as he considered what he was able to divulge, and how doing so might be either useful or detrimental to his agency.

"Let me think on that, Hana, and I will get back to you," he said. "In the meantime, there *is* one individual we are aware of who you might already be familiar with since you've met his father: a young man named Ivan Gović. He is believed to be a cell leader in Argentina, but he has ties to many Ustasha collaborators here in Italy and in France. Our sister agency, the AISE—which handles criminal intelligence outside of Italy—has agents in Buenos Aires who have informed us that the younger Gović was devastated by his father's death and may likely pose a threat to those involved with the TBM warehouse incident. Just be aware of that, Hana, as you start opening doors into that organization. Your name may never have been connected to it publicly, but they could become suspicious if you begin to poke around, or already suspect your involvement if they realize the true nature of what Gović was attempting."

"I will, Max, and thank you for mentioning it," she said, her face revealing a measure of concern. Caution like that, especially from someone who regularly grapples with organized crime, was not to be taken lightly.

As the waiter approached their table, Colombo asked him for the check. "I think that one drink will have to do it for me tonight," he said, smiling at Hana. "Please, allow me to pick this up."

"*Molto grazie*, Max. It was so good meeting you today, and I'm grateful for our conversation. If there's anything I can help you with, at any time, please do call on me."

They stood and shook hands. "It was my pleasure, Hana. And yes, I expect our paths will cross again. Do let me know of your progress, yes? And be mindful of your safety in the meantime."

CHAPTER
SEVEN

T he underground repository of the Vatican Secret Archives is a vast storage facility built beneath the broad expanse of the sun-drenched *Cortile della Pigna*, the Pinecone Courtyard north of the Tower of the Winds. Given its relatively sporadic use by staff, the entire space—including the Gallery of the Metallic Shelves, the Miscellanea, and other storage areas—is illuminated by amber lighting activated only when movement is detected by strategically positioned sensors, and which turns off when movement ceases. There are no windows or fluorescent lighting so as to prevent the damaging ultraviolet spectrum from harming sensitive ancient parchments and papers.

As Dominic walked through the Gallery, amber pools of light flooded his path through the long, dark aisles as he made his way to one of the subterranean index terminals. The experience reminded him of his time in the Lombrives cave that past weekend, where everything in the distance was pitch black and all he could see was what his helmet light illuminated. He shuddered at the memory. At least here, he reminded himself, he did not have to crawl.

From the index terminal, he could determine the general area where most anything could be found—at least those documents which had been catalogued—among them Guillaume de Sonnac's papers as requested by Simon Ginzberg. It was a challenging task, made more so by the random nature in which previous archivists, going back centuries, had chosen which documents were to be indexed, and which apparently had not merited cataloguing at the time.

Dominic found an entire section dedicated to the Knights Templar, which made sense, he thought, since the Templar's history extended over some two hundred years, and to index it by any criteria other than era would have made continuity incomprehensible at best. So, he started there, making his way back through the Gallery with the aid of the flickering amber lighting to guide his path.

This was the part of his work Dominic loved most: digging into hidden files that might not have been seen by anyone for centuries, possibly since they were first written by the ancient scribes themselves. The Vatican's historical holdings were nothing short of a boundless treasure hunt in time. No one alive really knew what was stored here, unexplored as the vast majority of it was, sparking Dominic's intrigue like nothing else ever had.

Peering into the deep shelves, he noted the Templar folios here had been sorted by century. Ginzberg mentioned that Guillaume de Sonnac lived around the year 1250, so he pulled out two folios: large, boxlike volumes bound by stiff boards on either side and wrapped in hemp twine, identified in Latin *"Tertius Decimus Saeculum"*—thirteenth century. He took them to the nearest reading table and, lest he be plunged into darkness with no movement in the aisles, switched on the table's reading lamp. Then he slipped on the white cotton gloves he carried in a pocket.

The adventure begins, he mused. Opening the first box, he pulled out a stack of papers of varying size and thickness—correspondence, petitions, indulgences limiting the punishment of sins, account ledgers, bills of sale—all manner of period documentation lay before him, written mostly in Latin and French, two of the several languages in which Dominic was proficient.

It took him some time to pore over the papers of the first box, finding nothing by or even mentioning Guillaume de Sonnac. Setting that box aside, he opened the second volume.

Here he found the usual abundance of documents as before, but this box also contained a large, sturdy stack of bound pages, obviously a journal of some sort, on the front of which had been hand-printed in French *Histoire des Templiers*—History of the Templars. Below that was printed the name Guillaume de Sonnac. *Eureka!* Dominic thought. *Exactly what Simon is looking for. He did say de Sonnac was the Templars' historian…*

Excited by the discovery, he set the journal aside and sifted through the many remaining papers in the box for anything else that Simon might find of interest. There was a fascinating set of military orders dated from 1244 to 1250, which put them from the end of the Albigensian Crusade through to the Seventh Crusade and the battles of Damietta and Al Mansurah in Egypt. Dominic was ecstatic.

Removing more papers from the box, at the bottom he finally came upon a strangely shaped document of sorts:

what appeared to be nine panels of parchment bound by some kind of flexible material attached to the edges of each panel. The artifact was maybe twelve inches square, but once unfolded from the box, two of the panels stood upright in one of the corners, while one corner panel space was missing entirely. Dominic had never seen anything like it and pondered what its purpose might be. At first glance, it looked to be some kind of art piece, abstractly mottled in black and caramel-colored parchment. There was a tiny signature on one edge of a panel reading *Pietro Vesconte.*

He decided to take it up to Simon to get his thoughts on this unique device, or whatever it was.

CHAPTER
EIGHT

"I believe I've found what you were looking for, Simon."

Dominic set the Templar journal down on the table in front of Ginzberg. The old man's rheumy eyes glistened as he read the cover, a look of entrancement coming over him. "*My God*, Michael, you are a wonder. You've found Guillaume's own journal?! Who had any idea this even existed before this moment? Can you imagine how valuable this will be to scholarly work on the Crusades?"

Ginzberg was overcome with gratification, and it pleased Dominic to see the joy on his friend's face. "There are many other documents down there if you feel you need more, but as you know, you can only work with three items at a time." They both looked at the table, strewn with Ginzberg's work on two other document parcels he had ordered from the assistance desk.

"Yes, yes, I know the rules," the old man mumbled. "I think this journal will keep me occupied for some time,

Michael, and I am immensely grateful to you for taking the time to find it. Just so I know, though, what else might there be of interest in the archives you found for him?"

"Well, now that you ask…" Dominic began, then laid out the strangely shaped document he found buried among de Sonnac's materials. "I have no clue what this could be. Have you ever seen anything like it?"

Ginzberg set aside the other documents in front of him and pulled the object closer. He examined it carefully, lifting it, gently folding the three-inch panels back and forth, peering at each panel's content. "This is strange, indeed," he said, deep in thought. "At first glance, it appears to be some sort of quaint puzzle. The drawings on each of these sections or panels do not line up with other panels adjacent to one another. And they all seem to be connected with some fibrous material." He pulled it up to his eyes, adjusting his reading glasses for closer inspection. "This tough, stringlike material looks to be catgut, Michael. The use of catgut—mainly derived from sheep intestines, though most any herbivorous animal could have been used—goes as far back as the ancient Egyptians and Babylonians. It's a flexible, durable cord that was typically used in archery bows and musical instruments."

"I noticed there's a signature on one of the panels here," Dominic said, pointing to one of the sections.

"Ah, yes. *Pietro Vesconte*. Well, Vesconte was one of the more prominent Italian cartographers of the late-thirteenth and early-fourteenth centuries, though I've never seen anything of his resembling this curious object. Many of his original maps can be found today in libraries and museums all over the world, notably the Bibliothèque nationale de France in Paris and the Museo Correr in Venice—and now, it would appear, here in the Vatican as well. What a fantastic find, Michael. Congratulations!"

"It is intriguing, isn't it? I'll have to spend some time with this in what spare moments I can find, maybe see if I can decipher its meaning."

"You do that," Ginzberg said, winking. "Meanwhile, I'll spend time with my new friend here, Guillaume de Sonnac. I'm still trembling with excitement at your discovery of his actual journal."

"As far as anything else in the Archives, Simon, there are also what appear to be military orders from the Albigensian Crusade involving a few of the battles de Sonnac fought in. You may want to keep those in mind for your next pull of materials. Just let me know."

"Thank you, Michael, you're too kind."

As he walked away, Dominic knew exactly what he would do with his newfound puzzle.

CHAPTER

NINE

L a Pergola, the only Michelin three-star restaurant in all of Rome, sits atop a grand hill overlooking the Eternal City, with the brightly lit dome of Saint Peter's Basilica dominating the breathtaking nighttime landscape below.

Inside it seemed less a restaurant than a well-appointed museum, with antique tapestries featuring scenes from ancient Rome hanging on the tall walls, and rich mahogany columns supporting an exquisitely inlaid suspended ceiling, offering its guests exquisite cuisine in a grand setting.

Just outside the doors to La Pergola, Hana sat in the Cavalieri's posh Tiepolo Lounge, busying herself with a Monument Valley geometric puzzle on her iPhone as she waited for Michael to arrive. Puzzles had fascinated her since her youthful years at St. Stephen's international boarding school in Rome, where she excelled in math, logic and critical thinking.

Having grown up in privilege in Switzerland, Hana

was largely unimpressed with lavish displays of affluence, part of the reason she had anglicized her surname from Saint-Clair to Sinclair when she struck out on her own as a reporter for *Le Monde*. It was far more gratifying to be recognized for her own achievements than for being the scion of a prominent Swiss banking family. Had her grandfather not held a residential suite at the Cavalieri, she likely would have stayed at a more modest hotel. But since her conference for the week was being held here, it was a more than convenient venue.

"Here you are!" Dominic said as he approached her in the lounge, a backpack slung over a shoulder of his dark blue blazer. "Jeez, it is *so* good to see you again!" Looking up, Hana smiled broadly, then stood as they both fell into a long embrace.

"I can't tell you how much I needed a hug today," she said, her pale green eyes glistening as she looked into Dominic's. "And not from just anyone, mind you—and you're still as handsome as ever. For some reason, you're much more attractive when you're not wearing that priest's frock!"

"The feeling's mutual—except for the 'frock' thing," he replied laughing. "But as it happens, I do carry my cassock and collar wherever I go." At this he lifted his backpack, making the point that his change of clothes was always with him. "One never knows when someone might need a priest in uniform.

"So, what have you got there?"

Hana looked down at the puzzle app on her phone. "Ah, just something to take my mind off investigative journalists. It's one thing being one, but it's quite another being told *how* to be one by any number of authorities at a conference like this. Just when you think you know it all, someone comes along and tells you something new."

Dominic laughed. "Hah! Good axiom. So, do we have time for a drink first?"

"Of course, I made our dinner reservation for eight thirty with just that in mind."

Waving down the cocktail waitress, Hana asked for a vodka martini, while Dominic ordered a Birra Moretti.

"You know," he said, "I had forgotten your interest in puzzles, and as it happens, I stumbled onto a big one today, more than metaphorically."

He told Hana of having searched the Archives earlier for Simon Ginzberg's interest in a particular Templar knight, and of his discovery of Pietro Vesconte's unusual paneled object, which Simon believed might be a puzzle of some sort.

"I'd love to see it, Michael," she said. "If it caught Simon's interest, it would certainly catch mine." She had met Simon through Dominic during last summer's events and admired his devotion to his pursuit of knowledge of Jewish history.

"Well, you're in luck," he said, reaching into his backpack. "I realize I shouldn't have removed it from the Vatican, but I intended to try to figure it out myself, ever the curious cat." Unfolding the object, he laid it out on the small table. "Since it's durable parchment, we don't really need gloves. Just take care not to spill anything on it." They both slid their drinks away from the artifact.

Dominic showed her how the panels appeared to swap places when turned and folded, changing the visual connections of each adjacent panel. "It's got what Simon thinks are catgut filaments strung along the borders of each panel, and as you can see, they appear to magically connect and disconnect the more you fold each panel. It's really got me intrigued, though I haven't spent much time with it yet. But Simon and I did notice it was signed by Vesconte." He showed her the tiny signature on one of the panels.

Hana picked it up, peering closely at each of the panels on both sides. "There's more writing down here. It's quite small ..." she said, pointing to another panel. "It reads 'Grotte Trou la Caune.' Grotte is French for 'cave.'"

"Wait, I went caving last weekend with Karl and Lukas. And though I didn't see it, Karl referred to a cave map that guided us through the caverns. Maybe he'll have some idea of what this represents."

"You went caving?!" Hana almost choked on her martini, moving the glass back away from the map as she mimicked struggling for breath.

Dominic looked chagrined. "I know, it surprised even me. But yeah, it was kind of fun and great exercise. Just a little intimidating when you consider how deep underground you are. And don't think the thought of an earthquake didn't cross my mind. I can see the headline now: 'Priest Buried Alive, Abandoned by God'." They both laughed at the image.

As he spoke, Hana fiddled with the panels, folding them over each other, then unfolding them in perpendicular directions, until the shape of the object was completely transformed. "This is a very clever puzzle of some sort, Michael. It reminds me of a mechanical folk toy called Jacob's Ladder. Something like this was even found in King Tut's tomb in 1922, so the general construct goes back to at least ancient Egypt. May I keep this for a few days, have a go at it myself?"

"Sure. This is more your expertise than mine anyway.

Just be sure your hands have no lotion or anything on them when touching it and keep it in the safe in the meantime. While I don't think we have to worry about someone trying to steal it now," Dominic noted, thinking back to their last adventure, "I did remove it from the Archives without permission. I'll need to go to confession when I get back…"

Hana looked up at him and chuckled just as the restaurant host approached them. "Your table is ready now, Signorina. You may leave your drinks; they will be brought to you."

Standing up, Dominic quickly grabbed his iPhone and took a photo of the puzzle to share with Karl later. Hana gently folded it and slid it into her bag as they headed into La Pergola for dinner.

"I'LL START with the Liquorice Consommé, then the Fillet of Sea Bass with Roman Mint Aroma," Hana said adeptly to the waiter. "Michael?"

"Hmm. I think I'll pass on the Pigeon today… How about the Turbot with Asparagus and Codium?"

"A very good choice, signore," the waiter said. "That comes with black salsify and *cardoncello* mushrooms in hay."

"Well, who could pass up a good side order of hay?"

"You have a great sense of humor, Michael," Hana noted, laughing. "Was your mother the same way?"

"She was, yes," he replied, "but we Jesuits are a funny lot anyway. It runs in the order, given our astute observations of the flawed human condition."

"And so very humble, too," Hana countered.

"I wish I had known my father, though," Michael said

wistfully, "and what traits he might have passed on to me. My mother did her best, of course, and Rico was always there as a masculine figure. But there's always been this strange void that couldn't be filled by anyone else. Mostly it was the toll I'd seen it take on my mother, not having a companion to care for her and share the load of raising me —and that wasn't easy. I guess I'll never understand why he left in the first place after I was born. A kid kind of takes that personally, you know? Like, what did I do wrong to make him leave?"

Hana reached across the table, gently placing her hand upon his. "That's not your fault nor your responsibility to find reasons, Michael. Who knows what motives he had? None of us have all the answers to what drives us. I'm certain it had nothing at all to do with you. Who couldn't love a baby boy? There had to be mitigating factors for him to disappear as he did.

"Tell me about your mother. What was she like?"

"She was a wonderful mom," Dominic said, his eyes getting moist. "Her name was Grace—which fit her perfectly. She was completely selfless, worked hard, and did everything she could for me. She was *very* Catholic, though, even puritanical in some ways. She had this odd little habit of clipping pictures of naked people out of illustrated bibles! I often wonder if that isn't why I had intimacy issues, and maybe even part of why I became a priest." His gaze was far off now, looking beyond Hana out over the terracotta-tiled roofs of the city.

Hana's eyes stayed fixed on Michael, as she removed her hand from the now-distant man sitting beside her, with her own thoughts in turmoil. Any maternal instincts Hana possessed rose in her fiercely as a lump settled in her throat, choking her with emotion. At this moment she couldn't love a man more deeply than she did Michael Dominic, wanting to relieve his burdens, to soothe that lost boy of long ago. But she held back, knowing this was an impassable road. She must respect his calling, an existence that could never include her in any form beyond friendship. The longing, the aching, was overpowering.

CHAPTER
TEN

Vatican Secretary of State Cardinal Enrico Petrini sat at his desk in the Government Palace, telephone receiver in hand, waiting impatiently on hold for the Archbishop of Buenos Aires to come to the phone.

"This is Cardinal Dante," the haughty voice eventually answered.

"Good afternoon, Fabrizio, it's Enrico," Petrini said. "I'm calling to make sure you'll be attending the consistory next week. The *camerlengo* tells me you have yet to confirm your attendance, and I wanted you to know, from me personally, that I am looking forward to your presence here."

Dante's voice was frigid as he responded. "Of course, I'll be there, Your Eminence. I apologize for my secretary's lapse in informing the *camerlengo*. I will rectify that and see you when I arrive in Rome on Monday." He paused. "Is there anything else?"

"No, that will be all." Petrini abruptly hung up the

phone. The two men suffered through an abrasive relationship, bolstered by the fact that several months earlier the pope had replaced Dante with Petrini as secretary of state. Dante's demotion and banishment to the capital of Argentina came as a shock to the aristocratic cardinal, who saw the loss of his vast power in the Vatican diminish to virtually nothing more than having a few well-placed spies in the institution's sprawling bureaucracy. He was not at all content to be in South America, far away from the pinnacle of influence he once enjoyed.

He placed much of the blame for his current predicament on that prying bastard Father Michael Dominic, whose collaboration with the Sinclair woman had brought down his carefully laid plans for the Magdalene manuscript. Had they not interfered in his legitimate claim to authority, things would be much different now. But here he was, exiled to some backwater archbishopric which held little interest for him.

He was reminded of a saying: *Sooner or later everyone sits down to a banquet of consequences.* Dante had been biding his time up to now, but next week's consistory in Rome may provide opportunity for recrimination.

∾

STILL WEARING black mourning clothes months after her husband was mysteriously killed in an Interpol-related incident in Rome, Ludmila Gović sat in her kitchen in La Plata, a Croatian settlement on the southern outskirts of Buenos Aires, drinking pomegranate tea with her son. The room was cold and still. Gray daylight filtered in from a small square window next to the table at which they sat.

"We have waited long enough, Ivan," she said sternly, a

shadow of cruelty in her tone. "It is your duty to avenge the murder of your father. The *gadovi* who did this must be punished."

"Yes, *majka*, I know this," her son replied tersely. "But there is a time and a place for such things. My colleagues are waiting for me to give the signal, as soon as I hear more from our friend in Buenos Aires."

Ivan Gović, the twenty-eight-year-old son of former Interpol Croatian liaison Petrov Gović, had taken over his father's covert role as *voða ćelija*, cell leader of the Novi Ustasha, a modern-day revival of the fascist World War II terrorist organization and Nazi-aligned government of the Independent State of Croatia. While the original fiercely Roman Catholic Ustasha's goal was nothing less than actively persecuting hundreds of thousands of Jews, Serbs and Roma gypsies to ensure a more racially pure Croatia, the present-day Novi Ustasha's ambitions were not far removed from its predecessor's, though on a much broader scale and with the use of greater political influence. Aided secretly by far-right confederates within the Church's hierarchy, the current organization's objectives were focused on ultranationalism, strong opposition to immigration, racial supremacy and active resistance to liberal democracies everywhere.

Discreet Novi Ustasha cells were especially active in France, Germany, Italy, the United Kingdom and the United States—indeed, anywhere non-indigenous ethnic minorities and disproportionate numbers of asylum seekers were prevalent. Governments and law enforcement agencies were only vaguely aware to what extent the organization had infiltrated their respective countries and jurisdictions. The Church's role, circumspect by nature, was led by ultraconservative bishops and cardinals whose prominent identities and spheres of influence were a carefully guarded secret among the Ustasha's leadership.

As the new cell leader for Buenos Aires, Ivan Gović was anxious to prove himself, motivated not only by the core ideology of the Ustasha, but by a burning desire to exact retribution for his father's death. And there was one person of influence to whom he could turn for help in both aspirations.

"HIS EMINENCE WILL SEE you now, Señor Gović," said Cardinal Dante's secretary, as she escorted the young man into the archbishop's opulent suite in the Metropolitan Cathedral's administrative office on the western edge of Buenos Aires.

ELEVEN

S ergeant of the Guard Karl Dengler had just gotten off his day shift, where he had been assisting the pope's advance team with last-minute security issues for next month's papal visit to South America. Though Dengler himself would not be going on the trip, he had coordinated protection protocols with the eight plain-clothes Swiss Guard agents who would accompany the pope, along with some thirty other officials, visiting São Paulo, Lima, Bogotá and Buenos Aires. As was customary, local law enforcement would provide the bulk of security.

As he was returning to his barracks, Dengler's phone chimed an incoming text message from Michael Dominic: **Are you free for dinner?** it read. Dengler texted back that he was, suggesting they meet in an hour at their usual place, Ristorante dei Musei, just north of the Vatican wall.

THE RESTAURANT WAS PACKED with chattering patrons when Dominic arrived, and the smells pouring out of the kitchen made his mouth water as he walked through the door. Aromas of simmering tomato sauce, richly infused with chunks of garlic and leaves of fresh basil, brought to mind his favorite neighborhood trattorias back home in Queens.

Dengler was sitting at a table near the window, a bottle of Lambrusco already opened and partially empty as he looked around the room, people-watching. A handsome young man sitting at the bar kept glancing in his direction.

"A penny for your thoughts," Dominic said as he sat down.

Dengler laughed. "Only a penny? Some guy at the bar is flirting with me. I'll bet his thoughts are worth a lot more. I'm doing my best to ignore him. If Lukas were here, we might have to leave, given the scene he'd likely start. He's a bit overprotective, you know."

After looking at menus, they both ordered the *Speciale del Giorno*, Rigatoni al Pomodoro, with sides of grilled zucchini and antipasti.

Dominic poured himself a glass of the red wine, then told Dengler about his unusual day, explaining how he had come across a curious puzzle while searching for material on the Crusades for Dr. Ginzberg, and finally Hana's offer to try to decode it.

"So, what do you think this might be, Karl? Ever seen anything like it before?" Dominic asked, showing Dengler the photos of the puzzle on his phone. "Hana said it mentions the French word for '*cave*.'" He pointed out the markings on a rear panel.

"Well," Dengler said, "Grotte Trou la Caune is definitely a cave, somewhere in southern France. I haven't explored it myself, but I've read about it in caving forums online. Apparently, it's supposed to have some connection to Saint Mary Magdalene, like that entire region does."

Mary Magdalene? Again? Dominic thought reflectively.

"And looking at the diagram itself," Dengler continued, "despite the panel edges not meeting up properly in what I assume is the puzzle's unsolved state, this sure looks to me like it could be a cave map. It's a lot more primitive than today's cave surveys, but I suppose that's to be expected if it's as old as you say it is. Hey! We should explore Grotte Trou la Caune on our next trip!"

Dominic grimaced. "Not so fast, caveman. Let's give Hana time to figure it out, if she can, then we'll talk about next steps. The thought of getting stuck again in one of those godforsaken crevices doesn't exactly fill me with inspiration."

Dengler laughed. "Michael, you have to know you're in good hands with Lukas and me. Where does this fear come from, anyway?"

Dominic looked at his friend with a brittle calm, recalling a paralyzing moment from his childhood. "When I was about ten, Uncle Rico—you know him as Cardinal Petrini, but he was just a parish priest then—took me fly-fishing on the Ausable River in upstate New York. Though we normally fished in shallow waters, one day we found ourselves near the base of a sizable waterfall, with heavy currents coming off the plunge pool. I'd slipped on a mossy rock, lost my footing, and got caught in an eddy line—kind of a whirlpool—which pulled me under the water and tossed me back and forth like a washing machine. It was terrifying, and ever since then, I've had periodic episodes of what's called 'bathophobia'—a fear of depths. I guess that now also includes caves."

Dengler was genuinely sympathetic. "We would never let you fall into harm's way, Michael. There's nothing else that compares to exploring the underground world. You'll get a feel for it in no time; just know I'll always have your back. And who knows where this map might lead us? There could be a great lost treasure buried there!

"Come to think of it," he added, "why would someone go to the effort of making such a map in the first place, *and* in the form of a puzzle—then hide it in the Vatican Secret Archives? Surely it must have some significance."

"Good point," replied Dominic, thinking back to the puzzle's location along with thirteenth-century Knights Templar documents. "Maybe I should talk to Simon again, see if Guillaume de Sonnac mentioned anything about this in his journal."

Dengler refilled their glasses with Lambrusco as the waiter set down their food. "By the way, the pope is leaving for South America next month, so the rest of the Vatican will be playing hooky, as usual, with lighter duty for everyone. Maybe that's a good time to visit your cave."

Dominic rolled his eyes. "Again, there's no point in making plans unless we know where we're heading, right?"

At that moment Dominic's iPhone vibrated in his pocket. Taking it out, he found a text message from Hana: **I solved the puzzle! When can we meet?**

Stunned, he looked up at Dengler. "Your cousin is remarkable—she solved the puzzle already! Want to come see her with me after dinner?"

Dengler smiled. "You bet I do! Let's go!"

Dominic texted her back: **Karl and I will be there within the hour**.

CHAPTER
TWELVE

"Your Eminence," said Ivan Gović as he entered the lavish office of the Archbishop of Buenos Aires. "It's good to see you again." In a plebeian gesture of respect, he took the bishop's outstretched hand and kissed his ring.

"And you, Ivan," Cardinal Dante said with the barest of smiles. "How is your mother getting along?"

"To be honest, Eminence, she is not well. My father's death has left her scarred and bitter, even these many months after the tragedy. That is what I came to see you about."

Dante had had a long and lucrative business relationship with Ivan's father, Petrov Gović, the former Croatian liaison to Interpol who, as discreetly known to the cardinal, was also a cell leader based in Lyon, France, for the ultra-Catholic Novi Ustasha. Petrov had provided Dante with a number of clandestine services over the years: background investigations, questionable wiretaps, profiling other cardinals and potential Vatican employees

—even the occasional need for intimidation of Dante's enemies as the situation required. As compensation for such services, Dante had drawn upon massive Nazi gold reserves secretly buried in the vaults of the Vatican Bank—gold that Gović needed to fund the Ustasha's expansion plans throughout western Europe.

In Gović's last mission for then-Secretary of State Cardinal Dante, the Ustasha agent kidnapped Hana Sinclair to exchange her life for an original manuscript thought to be written by Mary Magdalene, at the time in the possession of Father Michael Dominic. A risky but profitable goal was foiled when Dominic, with the assistance of three Swiss Guards—one of them Hana's cousin—laid siege to the warehouse where Hana was held hostage, killing Petrov Gović and his henchman in the fallout.

The hidden gold promised to the Ustasha was then quietly distributed to the heirs of the rightful owners, Jews killed decades earlier. Unfortunately for Dante, his hand in the secreted Nazi gold and the plot were discovered and the pope removed him from his lofty position, promoting Enrico Petrini to his office as secretary of state.

So, Dante, unrepentant and unforgiving, had scores to settle as well.

"How can I be of service, Ivan?" the cardinal asked.

"Eminence," Gović began, "I would like to know more about those responsible for my father's death. The last time we met you advised me to wait until you could gather more facts about the matter. Have you those facts now?"

Dante thought carefully about what the consequences might be for disclosing what he knew about the affair to this troubled young man. What was there to gain? Was there an opportunity for Dante to redress the grievances he himself had been subjected to? Possibly. While it may not be wise to take direct vengeance on Cardinal Petrini just yet, he could have a hand in exposing his ward, Father Dominic, as the lead player in all this. As for Dominic's associates: well, Gović could manage that bit of business on his own.

"Didn't you once tell me," Dante asked, "that you have a source inside the Swiss Guard?"

Ivan Gović grinned smugly. "Yes, Eminence. We have a capable member of our organization inside the *Cohors Helvetica*. Why do you ask?"

From his desk drawer, Dante pulled out a blank piece of stationery, then picked up his pen. He made note of two names—Father Michael Dominic and *Le Monde* journalist Hana Sinclair—then handed the paper to Gović.

"I am told these two had a hand in that warehouse operation, Ivan. Whether they had anything to do with your father's death, I must leave that for you to determine. You might, however, inquire with your friend in the Swiss Guard…" Dante looked knowingly into Gović's dark Slavic eyes, leaving it at that.

"I understand, Eminence. Thank you for your time, and for your candor in this matter. My mother will be grateful for your generosity."

"I would prefer this remain between us, Ivan," Dante responded, a cautious tone to his voice. "My own sources in Rome rely on anonymity as well.

"Oh, and there's one more thing. If you're free for a few days I would like you to accompany me at next week's consistory in Rome, as part of my entourage. Given your unique skills, there are one or two tasks I would like you to do for me there, services much like your courageous father provided for me over the years. And it may give you an opportunity to learn more about his death. My secretary will arrange your travel and accommodations, of course, but I would consider it a personal favor if you'll accept my offer."

"Your Eminence, I don't know what to say," Gović said eagerly, his eyes wide with interest. "I would be honored to assist you, however I can."

"Good. Now, do give your mother my regards. And tell her your family will enjoy VIP seating for the pope's visit next month. Until then, Ivan, I bid you good night."

∽

A HARD RAIN beat against the tall Queen Anne-style windows of the Madison Avenue mansion of Cardinal Jorge Bell, archbishop of New York, as a fierce storm passed over the darkened city.

Sitting in one of the leather club chairs in the library of his 15,000-square foot manor house, a mound of aromatic hickory logs blazing in its cavernous fireplace, the cardinal stared into the fire as he sipped a fine Montmartre Napoleon Brandy from a crystal snifter. A Victorian grandfather clock in the corner had just struck six.

The phone rang. Bell had been expecting the call, but the harsh ringing disrupted the serenity of the room nonetheless. Despite the peaceful atmosphere, the tension in the man's neck and shoulders tightened as he picked up the receiver.

"Cardinal Bell speaking," he answered cautiously.

"Good evening, Jorge. Dante here."

"Hello, Fabrizio," Bell responded, a touch of dread in his voice. "What is it I can do for you?"

"I have need of some information from your archdiocesan files," Dante said flatly. "It shouldn't be too hard to find, I imagine, but I would like you to treat this as urgent and confidential."

"And just what kind of information is it you need, Eminence?"

"First, you must give me your personal assurance that this matter remains between us. No one else is to know of it."

"You have my word, of course."

"Alright, then. When Cardinal Petrini was a parish priest in your archdiocese—in the borough of Queens, I believe—he had a longtime housekeeper named Grace Dominic, who I understand had a child out of wedlock while she was living in Petrini's rectory. Unusual, I realize, but times were different then. That was some thirty years ago now.

"I want you to find the birth certificate and baptismal records for this child, who goes by the name of Michael Dominic. I understand he grew up under the close patronage of then-Father Petrini. Anything else you might find could be helpful as well."

"Helpful to what end, Fabrizio? We *are* talking about the Vatican secretary of state now. I wouldn't want to be caught in his crosshairs."

"Then don't get caught," Dante spat. "And it doesn't matter what I want the information for, Jorge, just find it. Kindly email it to me once you've got it.

"By the way, how are your current legal problems faring? Do you need any special assistance?" Dante referred to the New York archdiocese's unfolding sexual abuse scandal involving more than a hundred members of the clergy under Bell's stewardship.

"These are challenging times for us all, Fabrizio. But we are handling the situation as well as can be expected. It would be much more tolerable if it weren't for the damned media hounding us. The publicity is making my life a dreadful nightmare, to be perfectly frank."

"We all have our burdens, Jorge," Dante said, bored with his colleague's complaints. "Can I depend on you to get that information to me? You'll join me for dinner in Rome next week. The guest list may surprise you."

"I'll see what I can do, Eminence, and as always, I do look forward to your dinner party. Until then, good night." Bell hung up the phone. He got up to pour himself a touch more brandy, then sat back down and continued staring into the fire.

What is that bastard up to? he wondered.

CHAPTER

THIRTEEN

After dinner, Dominic and Dengler took the Jeep Wrangler across town to the Rome Cavalieri. It was still early, around ten o'clock, and given that the curfew for Swiss Guards is 2:00 a.m., there was plenty of time for an after-dinner drink and discussion of Vesconte's puzzle.

The valet took the car when they arrived, and they made their way up the elevator to the seventh floor, heading for the corner Palermo Suite at the end of the hall. They rang the doorbell and Hana opened the door, a look of pride on her face.

"Of all the puzzles I've done in my life, this was one of the toughest," she said, hugging them both and welcoming them inside. "And you won't believe how it turned out."

Escorting them into the stylish five-thousand-square-foot apartment, Hana poured three glasses of Prosecco as they took seats in the sitting room. The puzzle had been laid out in its original form on the coffee table, still in its unsolved state.

"I'll have you know," she said, tossing back her chestnut brown hair, "that I missed two conference workshops today, I was so engrossed in solving this. But I couldn't figure out where to begin. The clever way the catgut filaments are strung along each of the panels' edges allowed for virtually any formation. For a while, I kept thinking along linear lines, like maybe the goal was to make it flat. But these two upright corner panels made that impossible.

"Then I searched the internet looking for unusual three-dimensional puzzles and found a brilliant puzzle maker in Greece named 'Pantazis the Megistian.' His website had a similarly complex puzzle, several in fact, that he designed himself. I sent him a photo of ours and he got pretty excited.

"He indicated this was done in the manner of what's called a 'folding plate' puzzle, explaining that Pietro Vesconte had cut the map into nine square panels, apparently rearranged them out of order to heighten the complexity, then affixed slender threads of flexible sheep's intestine in a cleverly repositionable design attached to the adjoining edges of each panel. To make it especially challenging, instead of laying all nine panels flat, Vesconte placed two panels upright in one corner creating a partial hemicube—an abstract polyhedron showing only two faces of a six-faced cube—while leaving the ninth slot vacant.

"So I started folding and refolding, thinking three-dimensionally..." Hana began folding one panel after another, turning some panels on their sides, flipping others over onto one another as allowed by the internally-strung catgut.

Dominic and Dengler watched in fascination as the once flattish map took on a new shape, that of a square cylindrical tower.

"... and *Voila!*" She said proudly, "I ended up with this!"

The reconstructed puzzle showed six panels facing the viewer, with one panel on top and two panels behind the upper rear section, with the whole map essentially standing on just two panel edges.

"You can see that all the contiguous paths now line up across the corners," Hana said, pointing them out. "It really is an intelligent design. All that remains is to figure out what it actually *means*, what its purpose is. Where does the path lead, and what's at the end? For that matter, where *is* the end?"

Dominic's face was a mask of wonderment, his jaw slack with admiration. "How in God's name did you ever manage to figure this out?!" he asked rhetorically. "This is really impressive work, Hana."

"And it's definitely a cave map, I'm certain of it now," Dengler said enthusiastically as he closely examined the object, then took a photograph of the rearranged panels. "While Michael and I were having dinner earlier I googled *Grotte Trou la Caune*. It's a fairly well-known cave not far from Périllos in southern France, a two-hour drive from Rennes-le-Château where you found the Magdalene manuscript last summer. In fact, it's rumored that Mary Magdalene visited Périllos, or even stayed in this very cave at one time."

"Tomorrow I'll ask Simon if he found any reference to it in Guillaume de Sonnac's journal," Dominic said. "That would help a lot."

Dengler looked at Dominic knowingly, his eyebrows hiked, a look of anticipation in his eyes.

"Yes, Karl, *I know*..." Dominic said with a sigh. "It's a complete map now. But we have to learn more before just diving into it, don't you think?"

Dengler smiled, cocked his head and held up his hands in surrender.

Taking hold of the finished map, Dominic turned it around, examining it more closely for any obvious entry and exit points, expecting to find an "X *marks the spot*" somewhere. But there was nothing obvious beyond the apparent jagged path through the dark cave, presuming that's what the drawing represented.

He carefully tucked the assembled map into his backpack. "Thanks so much for your time and effort on this, Hana. If it leads to anything, you'll be the first to know."

"Maybe Hana would like to come with us when we explore the cave!" Dengler offered.

"Now *that's* something I'd find intriguing," she said. "I have too much invested now to say *no!* Set it up and just tell me when, Karl. I'm in town for another week or so but could extend my stay as needed. If Father Dominic here can do it, well…" Hana grinned, letting the remark hang in the air.

Dominic glanced at his watch. "Oh, goodness, look at the time…"

They all laughed as Hana led them to the door.

"Seriously, that could be fun," she said. "Text me tomorrow with anything Simon might have to report, alright?"

"You bet," Dominic replied. "If Simon does have anything relevant to add about the map, next week might be a good time to head for France, right after the consistory."

Dengler pumped his fist silently in victory, a broad smile creasing his face.

Dominic pulled Hana into a warm embrace as they

parted, as did Dengler in turn. Calling for their car from the valet, they left the hotel and returned to the Vatican.

~

THE NEXT MORNING Karl Dengler and Lukas Bischoff were in the Guard's barracks changing room, getting outfitted for their day's uniform, when Dengler brought up the previous night's activity at his cousin's apartment.

"You should have seen her, Lukas. Hana figured out that puzzle in no time, and the map that appeared when it was assembled revealed a specific route inside the *Trou la Caune* cave in France, near Périllos—one that might lead to something important belonging to Mary Magdalene!

"Michael is meeting with Dr. Ginzberg today to see if he's learned more, but it looks like we'll all be heading up there late next week to check it out." Dengler, always excited about caving expeditions, went on to discuss the needed gear for the trip and other accommodations. Lukas listened intently.

But he wasn't the only one paying attention. The changing room was fairly quiet at that time of day, but on the opposite side of the lockers Sergeant Dieter Koehl was donning his own uniform. As he dressed, Koehl had been absently listening to his fellow Guards chat from beyond the wall of lockers.

When he heard mention of a map and a cave, then Mary Magdalene—as well as the planned caving expedition in France—his ears perked up. He listened further.

CHAPTER

FOURTEEN

L ater that morning, Simon Ginzberg sat in his office
in the Caprioli Palace at Teller University in
Zagarolo when Michael Dominic called his cell
phone.

"Hey, Simon," Dominic said when Ginzberg answered.
"Will you be in the Vatican today?"

"I'm just leaving now, Michael. Was there something in
particular you needed?"

"Yes. Have you had any time yet to review Guillaume
de Sonnac's journal?"

"Actually, I have, yes," the old man said eagerly. "And I
think there's something you'll want to see … a serious
discussion about your puzzle—and it is indeed a map, a
map leading to an extraordinary object. I would prefer not
to discuss it on the phone, though. Can you meet me in the
Pio Reading Room in an hour?"

"You bet, that's actually why I was calling. I'll see you
then." Dominic ended the call.

• • •

SIMON GINZBERG WAS deep in thought as he sat at his usual table in the Secret Archives' reading room, Guillaume de Sonnac's open journal the focus of his concentration. The multilingual scholar had no trouble translating the journal, written entirely in Occitan French, as he read. He had inserted small strips of acid-free paper at various page breaks to mark places he wanted to show Dominic, and his notepad was full of penciled scribblings from his research.

Dominic greeted the older man, then took a seat opposite him. "What have you found, Simon?" he asked, his eyes wide with anticipation.

"Well," Ginzberg began, "first I must give you the backstory preceding Guillaume, and how he later came onto the scene. You are, of course, familiar with the Counts of Toulouse, the great hereditary family of rulers of the city of Toulouse and its vast county lands in southern France, yes?" Dominic nodded.

"The central figure we're most concerned with here," Ginzberg continued, "is Count Raymond VII, an erstwhile leader of the Albigensian Crusade until he was excommunicated for failing to suppress the Cathar movement and allowing Jews the same liberties as his other constituents. In 1242 he unsuccessfully rebelled against King Louis VIII of France, and consequently was forced to accept French authority over Toulouse and all his lands."

As he spoke, Ginzberg paged through Guillaume's journal, referring to various handwritten entries on the marked pages.

"As it happened," he went on, "Raymond was in possession of a great secret, reputed to be the fabled lost treasure of the Cathars. As their numbers diminished in unsuccessful battles, certain Cathar leaders close to

Raymond, grateful for his sympathetic support of their movement, entrusted to the count a sacred reliquary that once belonged to Mary Magdalene. We're talking here, Michael, about the same reliquary the Magdalene mentions in her own manuscript you discovered a while back—the reliquary containing the bones of Christ himself! You'll recall her wishes were to have it buried with her, but apparently, that never came to pass.

"The sacred reliquary had since been handed down through generations of Magdalene devotees, until Godfroi de Bouillon, the first ruler of the Kingdom of Jerusalem, acquired it in France. After him, it was safeguarded by other notables in history—Raymond-Roger Trancavel, the Viscount of Carcassonne, then his lord of the realm Count Raymond VI of Toulouse, who then bequeathed it to his son, Raymond VII. As the son later feared that the French king would take possession of it—since he had already acquired all the lands throughout Toulouse—Raymond ultimately returned it to the remaining Cathar leaders at Montségur, whose secretly-escaped *parfaits* had hidden it in a cave somewhere in Languedoc during the siege of Montségur."

Ginzberg was thoroughly engaged now, his eyes wild with fire, paraphrasing from the historical record as Guillaume de Sonnac had written it in his own hand in the ancient journal spread out on the table.

"The ongoing sieges of Montségur didn't bode well for the surviving community of Cathars, and after ten months of battle, word got back to Raymond VII as to where the reliquary had been secretly buried. The count was adamant that history must record where the sacred treasure was hidden—in the Grotte Trou la Caune near Périllos—so he engaged the services of Pietro Vesconte, the famed Italian mapmaker, to chart the path through the cave in the form of an inscrutable puzzle. And as he himself was nearing death, Raymond gave the map over to his friend, Guillaume de Sonnac, the Grand Master of the Knights Templar, for safekeeping.

"I can only assume the rest," Ginzberg said, "that the Church ultimately acquired the history of the Templars in their exhaustive efforts to acquire all papers relating to Church affairs. Thus, it had been unknowingly tucked away here in the Secret Archives for hundreds of years—until you discovered it."

Ginzberg smiled, satisfied he had conveyed Guillaume's written history of the reliquary and the map sufficient for Dominic's understanding. And as always, whenever Ginzberg revealed the depths of his knowledge in such lucid storytelling, Dominic looked at his friend with fresh wonderment.

"This is nothing short of breathtaking, Simon," he gushed, shaking his head. He then removed the solved puzzle map from his backpack to show Ginzberg.

"*My God*, Michael, this is extraordinary," he said, marveling at its construction, "and such genius for its period in history. So, this solution is the work of our young Hana, is it?"

"Yes, she spent quite a while on it, even reaching out to a puzzle master in Greece who helped her understand its complex solution.

"But," Dominic continued, "does Guillaume mention where the entrance to the cave might be? And where exactly the reliquary is buried? The map itself doesn't point out these crucial elements."

Ginzberg's face lit up with a wide smile. "In fact, he does!"

The old man gleefully turned the pages of the journal to a particular marked section, using his finger as a guide to locate the passage.

Ginzberg translated the instructions. *"'With the finished apparatus turned at an angle toward he who holds it, the entrance to the cave will be found at the front base corner. The reliquary is buried in the topmost of two dead-end passages on the top plate, like fingers on a hand. Four stones form the reservatory.'"*

Holding the map as instructed, Dominic traced the path with his finger as Ginzberg read the words, until he reached the topmost panel. "I see it, here. But what about that *'Four stones form the reservatory'*?" he asked. "What's a reservatory?"

"'Reservatory' is simply an archaic word for a box. But in this case, inside a cave, I imagine it's some form of protective crevice, perhaps a covered hole or stone receptacle of a sort," Ginzberg said, anticipation in his voice. "I suppose we won't know until someone explores that cave."

He looked Dominic in the eye, a glint of anticipation in his own. "So, tell me, Michael, do *you* plan to visit this sacred cave?"

"I do now," he said with tepid eagerness, his fear of confining spaces nibbling at the back of his mind. "And I have the perfect team to help me: friends in the Swiss Guard who are expert cavers. Hana even wants to join in the hunt."

"This is all very exciting," Ginzberg said. "If I were able, I would most certainly go with you, but I'm afraid my days for such adventures are behind me."

Dominic looked kindly at the old man. "I'll let you know when we head out, Simon, and you'll be the first to see whatever it is we might find there. Keep your fingers crossed."

Ginzberg's expression turned reflective. "Michael, are you prepared for what you might find there? For the consequences of what it is you might discover? If you *do* find a reliquary purportedly containing the bones of Christ, what will that actually mean for you? And for the world?"

Dominic mirrored his friend's solemn manner. "I can't really say, Simon. I suppose we'll have to wait until I'm actually holding the object, if it's still there. Theoretically, though, such a discovery would surely have sweeping implications—and that would be an understatement. Let's see how our expedition turns out. Then we can ponder philosophical consequences."

CHAPTER

FIFTEEN

T he Pontifical Swiss Guard barracks form a
connected set of ancient three- and four-story
buildings constructed in the fifteenth century on
the orders of Pope Sixtus IV, who foresaw the need for
recruiting dependable Swiss mercenaries for the protection
of Vatican City and the pope himself. The 110 ten Guards
who live there, many with their wives and children who
all have free roam of the Vatican grounds, enjoy the same
modest comforts and conditions they had in Switzerland,
before earning their commission as soldiers in the
pontifical security force.

Managing the large kitchen on the first floor of the
barracks is a French chef who, along with five Albertine
nuns from Poland, provide three meals daily to the Guards
and their families, a culinary menu comprising recipes
from Italy as well as Germany and Switzerland, to help
make the troops feel more at home.

Sergeant Dieter Koehl, who had been a Swiss Guard
going on ten years now, was sitting alone at a small table

in the canteen savoring a traditional Swiss *Älplermagronen* —a hearty gratin of potatoes, cheese, macaroni, cream and onions, with the essential side course of stewed apples— when one of the Albertine nuns approached his table.

"Excuse me, Sergeant Koehl," she said in German, "but you have a telephone call at the front desk. Shall I take a message for you?"

"No, sister, I'll take the call. *Danke schön*," said Koehl. He got up from the table and made his way to the canteen reception desk.

Picking up the phone, he answered, "Sergeant Koehl here."

"Hello, Dieter. This is Ivan Gović. *Za dom–spremni*."

"*Za dom–spremni*, Ivan," Koehl whispered discreetly, responding with the traditional Ustasha salute, *For the homeland–ready*. Then, in a normal voice, "It's been a long time. I was sorry to hear about your father."

"Yes, thank you, that's what I'm calling about, actually. I'm wondering…do you know the people who were involved in that warehouse incident in Tor Bella Monaca? The one involving my father?"

"I remember the incident, yes, a kidnapping rescue for the daughter of one of the pope's closest friends, a very important man…a Swiss banker, I think."

"Well, you've been given the wrong information, Dieter," Gović said abruptly, masking the truth himself. "That was a sanctioned Interpol operation, a protective custody affair in which my father was killed, supposedly by accident. Regardless, I just want to know more details… my mother needs them for the life insurance forms. By any chance, do you know the Guards who were there on the scene?"

"Yes, of course. There were three, and they all received

commendations for their brave efforts."

Govič gritted his teeth at hearing this but maintained his composure.

"And...their names?" he asked tentatively.

"Let's see," Koehl began, "Sergeant Karl Dengler was there, along with Corporals Lukas Bischoff and Finn Bachman. And one of the *scrittori* from the Secret Archives was involved, a Father Michael Dominic. I'm sure they'll be able to help you learn more. They are all great guys, though rumor has it Dengler and Bischoff are *warme Brüder*, which isn't something I approve of myself. But in the end, we are all brothers in the Guard, so to each his own. As for Father Dominic, I don't know him all that well."

Govič made note of all the names. "Thank you, Dieter, I really appreciate this. Is there anything else you can tell me about them?"

"Well, just yesterday I overheard them talking in the barracks about a caving expedition they're planning in France. Something about finding a map that might lead them to an object related to Saint Mary Magdalene. I didn't believe it myself, of course, but they're all heading out next week on some kind of folly."

Govič was intrigued. "Did they mention where this cave was? And who did they mean by 'all'?"

"Near Périllos, not far from Carcassonne, as I recall. I don't remember the name of the cave, though I suppose I could find out."

"Would you? I'm just curious."

"Sure, I don't see why not. As for who is going, from what I could tell it will be Lukas and Karl, Father Dominic, and Karl's cousin Hana."

Govič was silently inspired by this new knowledge. But

he needed to keep Koehl close to him as he considered what had to be done. "By the way, Dieter, I'll be in Rome next week. Cardinal Dante has invited me to a dinner party at his palazzo. There will be many important people there. Would you like to come as my guest?"

Koehl was taken aback by the invitation, having never been in such esteemed company before, and in the home of such a prominent cardinal, yet. "Of course, Ivan, I would be honored!"

"I'll text you details when I arrive, then. What is your mobile number?" The two exchanged contact details and ended the call.

After finishing his meal, Sergeant Koehl returned to his apartment in the barracks to spend time with his wife and daughter before resuming patrol duties at Saint Anne's Gate.

Life is good, he thought, as he watched his young daughter play with her friends in the barracks courtyard. The Vatican was an infinitely better post than back in Afghanistan as the Swiss Army's top explosives ordnance specialist. If he never had to deal with disposing of another bomb, that would be just fine with him.

Koehl thought about the Novi Ustasha, how he balanced his affiliation with the group's ultra-Catholic ideology and his own strongly conservative views while being true to the Guard's motto, *"Acriter et Fideliter"* —*Fiercely and Faithfully*, in the protection of the Holy Father and the Vatican. He knew memberships in such external groups were largely disallowed, but his family had a long line of Ustasha loyalists before him, so it was more of a male ancestral tradition since the war. After all, he reasoned, it was important to protect one's faith at all costs. As for the Ustasha's darker wartime exploits, well, that was another time, long ago. Their goals were different now. He would bet his life on it.

CHAPTER
SIXTEEN

W aves of black and scarlet could be spotted throughout airports and train stations as some 200 cardinals from around the world descended on Rome in the days preceding the Secret Consistory called by the pope.

Generally held annually, the "secret consistory" was named not for its furtive nature, but for its audience being restricted to the pope and his cardinals, excluding lesser-ranked Church officials and laymen who might otherwise be invited to public consistories.

Deliberations planned for the coming gathering in Saint Peter's Basilica included an address by His Holiness reviewing the condition of the Church in general and its constituent parishes worldwide—whether deserving praise or condemnation—along with the naming of several new cardinals.

Restaurants and shops surrounding the Vatican enjoy brisk business during consistories since each cardinal and cardinal-elect is often accompanied by an entourage from

his home diocese. Rental properties are of particular
interest to visiting cardinals, since such gatherings afford
Church princes the opportunity of learning the latest
gossip firsthand—who is on the way up or out, as each
man jockeys for more power or influential position; and
which scandal, old or new, merits further distance from it
—so securing the finest rental properties for intimate
dinner parties is foremost on everyone's mind.

THE PALAZZO CARAVAGGIO in the Via Condotti quarter of
Rome is among the most resplendent palaces in the most
fashionable district of the Eternal City. For a man of
Cardinal Fabrizio Dante's noble birth and ancestral wealth,
its lease at 2,000 euros per night was hardly an issue, and
he only planned on staying a week or so anyway. Besides,
it wasn't as if it came out of his own pocket. The Vatican
paid handsomely for cardinals' housing, travel and official
entertainment, as befits a prince of the Church. Among the
Curia, a cardinal's residence is that most precious of status
symbols, attesting to how much he counts in the scheme of
things.

After his privately chartered jet landed in Rome, Dante
and his entourage—comprised of security personnel,
secretaries and assistants, and a few other people of His
Eminence's choosing—were met by chauffeured
limousines at the exclusive Signature terminal of Leonardo
da Vinci Airport, where Customs was a simple red carpet
affair for the privileged class: no baggage inspections, and
only a cursory glance at the passports of those arriving. A
waiter bearing a tray of crystal flutes of Prosecco greeted
each passenger in the sumptuous lounge while porters
attended to transferring the luggage to waiting cars.

. . .

CARDINAL DANTE HAD RESERVED the Palazzo Caravaggio specifically for its luxurious dining room, its Red Verona marble table the centerpiece of the intimate room, surrounded by original sixteenth-century oil paintings by the Baroque master Michelangelo Caravaggio. There were important impressions to be made at the opulent dinner party the cardinal had planned, and every detail mattered.

Dante's table had for years been admired for its stimulating variety of guests, and the first of tonight's soiree began to arrive shortly after eight o'clock. Cardinal Baltazar Antić, Archbishop of Zagreb, and Bishop Klaus Wolaschka, the president of the Vatican Bank, arrived together in one limousine, followed by Cardinal Jorge Bell, Archbishop of New York, in another. Father Bruno Vannucci, Dante's former private assistant when he was secretary of state—whose discreet services as an embedded mole in the Vatican were still valuable—came alone by taxi.

The next guests to arrive were the young Argentinian Croat Ivan Govič and his colleague, Sergeant Dieter Koehl of the Vatican Swiss Guard. While not high-caliber luminaries, these men would be particularly useful for Dante's plans while in Rome, and he needed their cooperation. Nothing would impress them more than the cardinal's guest of honor for the evening: the Pope Emeritus, the recently retired pope, who arrived with his personal security detail of two Vatican *gendarmeries*.

With the possible exception of His Holiness, all those assembled were known members of the Novi Ustasha. The Pope Emeritus was simply invited for added star power. Though there were rumors—not least of which was the heavy hand he dealt in the affairs of Opus Dei—his own affiliations were a well-guarded secret, so even though Dante did not know for certain, it was still prudent not to discuss Ustasha business at tonight's gathering, as he had quietly cautioned those attending beforehand.

While the kitchen staff was busy preparing the appetizer—duck foie gras with apple and chestnuts—the men gathered in the great room of the palazzo with sundry cocktails passed out to loosen tongues. They lounged on the red damask sofa and chairs as they shared gossip of the day and the latest rumors floating around the Vatican. Papal consistories brought together all cardinals from around the globe, and scandalmongering was best done face-to-face.

The waiters had set small silver plates of foie gras on the table and filled crystal aperitif glasses with a Chateau d'Yquem Sauternes. "Gentlemen, Your Holiness, shall we take our seats?" Dante asked, his arms gesturing toward the table. Golden place cards indicated who sat where, with the Pope Emeritus at the foot of the table opposite Dante at its head.

His Holiness offered to say grace, after which the gossip in vogue continued apace as the assembled party savored their appetizers and chattered well into the first course, pumpkin risotto with veal sweetbreads.

As Dante looked around the table, he considered how each man here could best be used to achieve his goals—chief among them the reestablishment of his power in the Vatican hierarchy. Once the second-most important figure in the Church, behind the pope, Dante sought to regain his office at the Secretariat of State however possible, which meant the removal of Cardinal Enrico Petrini by any means. The guests at his table, who were clearly enjoying themselves, were all ultraconservatives, while Petrini's liberalism foreshadowed not only a slackening of Christian values but stricter controls on the cardinalate, who, Petrini believed, enjoyed too many luxuries while in service to Christ's mission of tending to the poor. That this was also the pope's mission hardly deterred a man with Dante's cunning and Machiavellian ambitions.

As the main course—leg of lamb with goat cheese and caper leaves—was being served, Dante steered the conversation toward Church finances. He rued no longer having direct control over the Vatican Bank's gold reserves, specifically those that were largely off the books —vast holdings still attributed to former Nazi officials and leaders of the original Ustasha from the Independent State of Croatia. As World War II had been winding down, an avalanche of assets was offered to the Vatican for safekeeping on behalf of its more prominent supporters, including former Nazi officials who escaped through ratlines operated by Franciscan monks. And much of those reserves had been sitting in the bank's secret vaults ever since, even though some of it last summer had been, apparently, returned to heirs of the Jews who had been led to believe their gold would save them from the gas chamber.

Dante's more well-heeled and influential benefactors in Buenos Aires included the families of hundreds of former members of the Third Reich, Nazi leaders who decades earlier had found safe haven in South American countries, notably Argentina and Brazil. Restitution of those assets now weighed heavily on Dante's mind, as certain high-value constituents of his Metropolitan Cathedral had been discreetly demanding since he had taken over as archbishop of Argentina's largest city. They knew they had

Dante's sympathy, and certainly a far better receptiveness than his predecessor, who was now the current pope.

"My friends," Dante began, "as most of you are aware, the Vatican Bank has for decades now been holding special reserves of gold aside for longtime friends of the Church. Surely I am not alone among us in thinking that these reserves must be restored to their rightful owners." He turned to Bishop Wolaschka. "Klaus, how much of those special reserves remain now?"

Dabbing his napkin at the corner of his mouth, Wolaschka was prepared for the question. "I would estimate, Eminence, that remaining reserves—after last summer's 'withdrawal'—now account for around one hundred million U.S. dollars."

A few gasps were heard around the table. "Yes," Dante continued matter-of-factly, anticipating the reaction. "That is a significant amount."

Cardinal Beneventi of Sicily posed a question lingering in the minds of others present. "If I may ask, Klaus, to what does 'last summer's withdrawal' refer?"

Wolaschka was about to respond when Dante interrupted. "During my tenure as secretary of state, I authorized the transfer of some portion of that gold— which, I remind you, is not among the assets of the Church —to Petrov Gović, young Ivan's father..." Dante gestured toward Ivan, "who was an Interpol official at the time. Unfortunately, there were complications in Agent Gović's operation, and the gold was stolen after its delivery and has since disappeared. The Vatican, naturally, was no longer involved, but Signor Gović here is just one of many who seek further recompense for what belonged to his family, and the beneficial organizations they represent."

As Dante spoke, the waiters cleared away the dinner

plates, and set down a selection of premier Italian cheeses and chilled silver bowls of Risotto Cream with Marzipan for each guest. Fresh aperitif glasses were filled with Delamain Vesper XO Cognac, and the lights were dimmed. "Please, my friends, enjoy this extraordinary dessert. It was handmade for me by the *pâtissier* at La Pergola."

The men continued to talk over dessert, after which Cardinal Antić of Croatia lit a Montecristo cigar, then lifted his glass of cognac in a toast. "Gentlemen, to our host, Cardinal Dante, with blessings on him for this sumptuous repast." The others lifted their glasses in unison as Dante basked in the praise.

"Fabrizio," Antić said, his face now showing concern, "with due respect to Cardinal Petrini, you are the one who should be running Vatican City again. How can we help make this possible? Is it something you even desire?"

Dante feigned humility. "Ah, Baltazar, thank you. I appreciate your vote of confidence. I serve at the pleasure of His Holiness the Pope, of course, but truth be told, I do miss my old job. While Buenos Aires is a fine archdiocese, my Italian is much better than my Spanish." Everyone laughed, as the fragrant wooden box of Montecristos was passed around the table. "And my home, *il mio cuore*, is here in Rome. If His Holiness wishes me to return, I would consider it an honor."

Cardinal Antić turned to the Pope Emeritus and simply arched an eyebrow in an unspoken gesture of encouragement to offer a hand in the matter. The others at the table noticed the subtle exchange but said nothing. Father Vannucci, however, ever the sycophant, raised his own glass and exclaimed, "Here, here!" The others followed jubilantly, the liquors of the evening having served their purpose.

"As always, gentlemen, the Church must continue to remain humble in regard to these matters," Dante said, taking a sip of the fine cognac. "But we must find ways to encourage Cardinal Petrini's hand in the matter of restitution. I am open to suggestions as you give this further thought. Not tonight, of course; we can discuss matters further during the consistory. For now, just enjoy your cigars and aperitifs."

Ivan Gović caught the cardinal's attention. "Your Eminence?" he asked quietly, "Would you mind if Sergeant Koehl and I stepped out onto the balcony for a few moments?"

While others at the table chattered among themselves, Dante simply waved a hand excusing the two men, nodding his head in consent.

Their glasses of cognac in hand, Gović led Koehl through the great room and out onto the wide terrace overlooking the city, framed in bougainvillea surrounding the balcony. Smells of roasted chestnuts drifted in the evening air from vendors down on the nearby Piazza del Popolo.

Gović began. "Dieter, there is something I must ask you to do for me, a great personal favor."

"Name it, Ivan, anything." Koehl lifted his glass and took a sip of his cognac. He had clearly been enjoying himself among these extraordinary gentlemen—a gathering he was completely unaccustomed to—and was in a most agreeable mood.

"While visiting Rome with Cardinal Dante I am staying with my cousin on the outskirts of the city. He has a small farm there, and while I'm here he's asked me to help him with a few chores, one of which involves demolishing a massive boulder in the middle of his cropland. No heavy equipment is up to the task, and we thought using explosives would be the best way to remove it.

"I know you have a background in ordnance and was hoping you could put something together for us. Though I've never actually built a bomb myself, I do have experience placing explosives properly—from my time in the Croatian army—so I would just need you to acquire something suitable to the task. Is that something you could handle for us?"

"What kind of device are you looking for?" Koehl asked, a little surprised by the request.

"I'd say a small Semtex charge should be sufficient. Something pliable but stable in transit. I'll be placing the charge myself, so I just need to round up the explosive." Gović said this matter-of-factly, as if he were asking Koehl to provide him with something as ordinary as a bag of fertilizer.

"That is a rather big ask, Ivan," he said. "Is there no other way to remove the rock?"

"As I said, we've tried other means, but nothing has worked so far. My cousin really needs the land free of obstructions so crop tilling is easier. I would be grateful for your help, Dieter."

Koehl was well aware the Swiss Guard armory had a secure supply of various explosives on hand if it was ever needed in defense of the Vatican, but getting his hands on it would not be easy. On the other hand, owing to his wartime experience, as supervising guardsman in charge of the armory it wouldn't be impossible.

"Let me think about this, Ivan," he said. "There may be a way, though I can't promise anything."

"Since I'll be going back to Argentina next week we'll need it soon, say a day or two?"

GARY MCAVOY

Concern creasing his face, Koehl simply nodded, then downed the last of his cognac. "Shall we rejoin the others?"

Gović smiled and slapped Koehl on the back. "Let's top off that glass of yours," he said, as they turned to go back inside.

THE EVENING'S affair having wound down by midnight, Fabrizio Dante had seen his guests to the door and bade each of them good night. Everyone, that is, except Cardinal Bell, whom Dante had asked to stay behind.

As was his custom when at home, the New York archbishop had refilled his cognac glass and taken a seat by the fire, transfixed by the gas flames licking the faux logs, his mind focused on the incendiary information he was about to impart.

Dante took a seat across from Bell and got right to the point. "So, Jorge, what have you learned about Cardinal Petrini and our young Father Dominic?"

Clearly uncomfortable discussing the topic, Bell shifted nervously in his seat. "Fabrizio, the material I've uncovered is utterly provocative and could bring great harm to Petrini. If proven—and should it ever get out—it will surely unseat him as secretary of state, and undoubtedly remove him from the *papabile*, those cardinals standing for consideration as the next pope."

"Get to the point, man!" Dante shouted, his eyes blazing with expectation. The lively activity of the waitstaff cleaning up in the kitchen suddenly subdued, whether out of respect for the cardinal's conversation or to better hear it.

Bell reached into a valise he had set on the floor next to

his chair and withdrew a sturdy kraft folder thick with various documents. He spoke in nearly a whisper.

"We found a verified copy of the Certificate of Live Birth for Michael Patrick Dominic in church records, showing Grace Anne Dominic as the mother. But, as you can see, there is no acknowledgment of paternity shown on the form itself." He handed the document to Dante for inspection.

"My investigators learned that Petrini was present at the birth and cared for Grace and her son in his Queens rectory until Michael left for college. Even after becoming bishop, then cardinal, Petrini discreetly paid for all needed expenses, including Michael's education throughout his life. You might already know that Petrini has family wealth, so no church funds were ever used.

"However," Bell continued, "my associates *did* find something of particular interest in Petrini's parish archives, something even he likely never knew about: a private diary that Grace Dominic had kept over the years, discovered in a storage box of old church records. She used the same type of composition notebook for her diary as she did for church registers, so it was probably just tossed in with the rest of them after she died. My team was thorough in going through everything."

Dante perked up on hearing this, the trace of a wicked smile forming at the corners of his mouth. "And what did she have to say in this diary?"

Fidgeting in his seat, straining with unease, Bell leaned forward, proffering another document. "Well … it contains a rather compelling admission of an intimate relationship she had with then-Father Petrini around the time Michael was conceived."

"*I knew it!*" Dante erupted, clapping his hands together

loudly. He took the document from Bell's outstretched hand and scanned it. "This is excellent news, Jorge. You have done well." He stood up and began slowly pacing the room.

"Now, I just need conclusive proof of paternity to make my case," he said to himself, staring out the window into the dark night. "And I have just the man to carry out such a task."

SEVENTEEN

T he undistinguished seven-story building at 127 Via Giovanni Lanza seemed a fitting home to Italy's intelligence security headquarters, Hana considered, as she walked toward the entrance of the terracotta-hued structure.

Invited for lunch by the AISI's director-general, Massimo Colombo, Hana suspected this was more than a social call. Colombo's voice had an urgency to it, unusual for someone she initially perceived as being more assured and self-restrained.

While the receptionist called the director's office, Hana took a seat in the waiting area, checked email on her iPhone, then busied herself with a puzzle app. After fifteen minutes she checked her watch. She disliked being kept waiting.

A few moments later a petite young woman in a black Armani jersey suit approached her. "Miss Sinclair?" Hana looked up and nodded. "The director will see you now."

They must pay well here, Hana thought as she stood and followed her escort. *That suit cost at least a thousand euros.*

The elevator ascended to the second floor, which opened directly into the suite of the director-general's offices. The young woman led Hana to a set of sleek rosewood doors, knocked twice, then swung both doors open, gesturing for Hana to enter.

Massimo Colombo sat behind his desk signing papers as Hana approached him.

"Miss Sinclair—I'm sorry, Hana—it's so good to see you again," he said, holding out his hand. "Please, have a seat."

"Hello, Max." Hana took his hand in a firm grip, pumped it briefly, then sat down in front of his blue tempered glass and stainless-steel desk. Looking around, she noticed a proper white-clothed luncheon table had been set up next to one of two arched windows overlooking the city, a pair of silver serving domes covering the food, with a bottle of S.Pellegrino sparkling water placed next to a small vase of white roses. The room itself smelled vaguely of lavender. She found the atmosphere quite pleasant and relaxing.

"How is it your office smells so wonderful, Max? This building doesn't seem all that new."

Colombo beamed proudly. "We have it discreetly infused through the building's air conditioning system. Our work here is quite enervating and can often impose an intensive, stressful environment. So, I brought in a fragrance consultant to evaluate the most appropriate atmospheric scents for the kind of work we do here. She recommended a gentle blend of sandalwood and lavender, and it has done wonders for staff stress levels, not to mention its effect on the number of sick days. Many organizations are doing it now."

Hana smiled self-assuredly. "It's really quite soothing, without being overbearing. My compliments to your fine sense of ambience."

"Thank you, Hana. Shall we have lunch while we talk?" They both rose and headed for the window. Ever the Italian gentleman, Colombo pulled back Hana's chair to seat her at the table, after which he took his own seat and poured sparkling water into two glasses. Removing the silver domes revealed a pair of lightly dressed Langostino Cobb salads with asparagus spears.

"We have our own chef here who does magical things with fresh seafood. Please, enjoy your salad."

"It smells marvelous, Max, thank you for arranging such a fine meal."

"You are most welcome, Hana. Unfortunately, there is some not-so-good news I must impart as we eat." Colombo reached for a folder he had placed on the table and opened it.

"An Interpol alert arrived yesterday informing us that Ivan Gović has come to Rome from Buenos Aires with none other than Cardinal Fabrizio Dante, apparently as part of his entourage for the pope's consistory this week."

Hana's expression quickly turned dour at the mention of Dante's name. She brought her hand up to sweep back her hair, then rested her fingers on her forehead, angling her head slightly downward. She thought back to last summer's exasperating encounter with the man, not someone she'd ever like to cross paths with again.

But to hear Gović's name alongside Dante's added more discomfort, especially given Colombo's earlier caution about her safety.

She looked up into Colombo's eyes, searching for meaning. "Have you any idea why these two might be working together? It seems an odd pairing, to say the least. I know Dante had been collaborating with Ivan's father in some nefarious Ustasha scheme involving Nazi gold from the vaults of the Vatican Bank, but…" Trailing off, she looked out the window, trying to fathom this new information.

"There's more," Colombo added gravely. "Young Gović seems to be rallying his supporters in Rome and southern France for some kind of operation, the details of which are still unclear to us. But we also know they have a collaborator inside the Vatican Swiss Guard, and given the security implications for the pope, this concerns us a great deal. I have people watching the Vatican closely now, as well as an observation team in Lyon, where Gović's father, Petrov, led a major Novi Ustasha cell. They have a great many loyalists in both areas."

"While I don't feel so much a personal fear given this information," Hana said, "I am concerned that a known Ustasha leader may be collaborating with a prominent Church figure, one whose ethics have already been compromised in dealings with that organization. I'm surprised he's still so highly placed, to be honest."

"Vatican politics often rival those of Rome's own corrupt institutions, my dear," Colombo offered. "Even with the sexual abuse scandals of the past two decades, Vatican authorities often move priests and bishops around like chess pieces…if one pawn finds itself in jeopardy, it's simply moved to another location, out of harm's way. But it still stays on the board and in the game."

Though Hana had by now mostly lost her appetite, she took a half-hearted bite of langostino and set down her fork. She dabbed a napkin at the corners of her mouth, then returned it to her lap. Another thought came to her.

"I wonder how someone in the Swiss Guard could ever be involved with such a lunatic fringe like the Novi Ustasha. Aren't they carefully vetted for their duties in protecting the pope and the Vatican?"

"Well, yes, they do go through extensive background checks and rigorous training. But every organization, despite its best efforts, often discovers, as the Americans like to say, the occasional bad apple.

"In fact," Colombo continued, "the Swiss Guard has suffered a few unbecoming blemishes in recent years. In 1978 they were implicated in a mysterious cabal involving the death of Pope John Paul I, in a case known as Operation Pigeon. That, too, involved the Vatican Bank, which has its own shady history. Then there was the 1998 murder-suicide purportedly carried out by a Swiss guardsman named Cédric Tornay against Commander of the Guard Alois Estermann and his wife. That case carries its own strange narrative, but many still believe Tornay to have been framed for the murders, and that he himself was then killed by the perpetrators.

"So, as you can see, it's not inconceivable that a Swiss Guard might have been compromised by outside forces. What we really need to know—and I intend to find out—is what they are up to now, and mainly that there is no conspiracy aimed at the Holy Father personally. That would not only be an unforgivable embarrassment to the Swiss Guard but a black mark on the competence of this agency as well. Fortunately, we have a mole inside Gović's organization, someone close to him. We should be receiving more information soon."

"That's a lot to take in, Max," Hana said, poking at her salad. "I assume there's a reason you're telling me this?"

"Though it's always nice to enjoy a meal with a new friend, Hana, there are few things I do without purpose. So, yes, apart from my continued caution to watch your back, I'm hoping that—in your research of the Novi Ustasha for your current assignment—you consider sharing anything of interest that you might uncover. Even the smallest of details could help us in ways you may not yet understand. As long as you're in Italy, we want to help keep you safe as well."

"I appreciate that, Max, thank you." Hana reached into her purse and brought out a small canister of pepper spray, displaying it for Colombo. "As you see, I travel prepared."

Colombo chuckled. "Well, that's better than not having any protection at all, I suppose. Pity the man who gets on the wrong side of you."

"I also have a bit of martial arts training, thanks to the soldiers I embedded with in Afghanistan," Hana added, "but yes, should I come across anything unusual, you'll be the first to know."

ACROSS THE STREET from the AISI building, at 129 Via Giovanni Lanza, sits a three-story Palladian residential villa with a construction crane adjacent to it. Workmen were remodeling the top floor, so all residents had been temporarily relocated during construction. As it was time for *pranzo*, all the workmen were gone for their two-hour lunch break.

The top apartment in the far-right corner, though also vacant, had not been scheduled for remodeling, yet two men, having bribed the foreman for an hour of undisturbed time in the room, had situated themselves at an open window behind partially closed wooden louver blinds.

A Nikon D6 camera was fastened onto a tripod facing the window, fitted with a powerful Nikkor 500mm lens, which was aimed across the street at the second-floor office of director-general Massimo Colombo.

"Sinclair doesn't seem to be enjoying her salad," the man sitting at the camera said to his companion. "But Colombo has a folder next to him with a picture of Ivan sitting on top." He took several more shots of the scene while his companion worked with a highly sensitive parabolic microphone, also aimed at the window across the street.

"As expected, the AISI must have an audio jammer in place," the second man said. "I'm unable to pick up much of anything useful."

"Looks like they're finishing up anyway. Let's break this down and get back to Gović."

∼

AFTER HER MEETING with the director-general, Hana had a desperate need to see Michael Dominic. To share with him what Colombo had told her. To ease her mind and feel safer. For a woman of such ready confidence, feeling uneasy was not something Hana Sinclair was accustomed to.

Taking her phone out of her purse, she texted him: **Are you available around five? It's somewhat urgent.**

A few moments later Dominic's response appeared: **Sure, let's meet in the Terrace Lounge at the Paolo VI Hotel, across from St Peter's Square. See you at 5.**

. . .

HANA HAD ARRIVED at the Paolo VI Terrace early. The *ponentino*, a cool wind blowing off the Tyrrhenian Sea, washed over Rome as it did almost every late afternoon. In the sweltering summer heat that can be a blessing, but in the fall it was utterly chilling as the temperature plummeted toward day's end.

The staff had closed the tall, sliding glass walls to the outside terrace for the evening, and while guests still had a splendid view of the Basilica and the Apostolic Palace down the street, the room was now toasty and inviting.

As she took a sip of her pinot grigio, Hana looked out toward the Vatican and saw Michael Dominic walking across Saint Peter's Square toward the hotel. He had changed out of his cassock and was wearing light blue jeans and a black t-shirt, with a leather bomber jacket over that. *That is one gorgeous man*, she mused, taking measure of his assertive stride as his long black hair tossed in the wind. *If only....*

Exiting the elevator, Dominic walked into the lounge and looked around. Several heads turned to see the new arrival who earned admiring glances from both men and women. Seeing Hana near the window, he made for her table.

She stood to embrace him, a wide smile on her face. "Oh, Michael. I'm so glad you could make it."

"Your text made it pretty clear not coming wasn't an option!" He laughed easily, waving for the waitress to join them.

"I'll have a Birra Moretti, please." The waitress set down a paper coaster in front of Dominic, making sure he saw her commendable breasts. As the waitress left, Hana, mid-sip with her wine, nearly choked with laughter at the obvious calculation.

Dominic blushed, then smiled as he cocked his head. "If only she knew how misguided her attentions were!"

"Come on," Hana urged, "you know you have that effect on everyone. This entire room stopped talking when you walked in."

"So," he coaxed, changing the subject, "what's so urgent?"

"You'll need that beer first."

"That bad, eh?"

"Well ... I had lunch today with Massimo Colombo, director-general of Italy's intelligence service. I met him earlier this week at the investigative journalist's conference I'm here for, and he shared with me some intel he'd gotten from Interpol. Apparently Cardinal Dante is back in the picture. He's here in Rome for the pope's Secret Consistory this week and he's brought along a new friend: a young man named Ivan Gović."

The amply blessed waitress returned and set down Dominic's beer, but he didn't even look up. He took a long draw from the frothy glass as he considered this new information.

Hana continued. "I hadn't mentioned this to you yet since it didn't seem relevant until now. But Ivan is the son of Petrov Gović, the mastermind of my kidnapping last year. He and Dante flew in together from Buenos Aires, and Max—that's Colombo—told me Gović may want to bring harm to me, as some form of revenge for his father's death. And since you were also involved in that Tor Bella Monaca incident, you might be in his sights as well. Max didn't have much more to say on the matter, but when the director of the AISI tells you to watch your back, you listen."

"Well, if this Govic character has done his homework, he'll also know about Karl and Lukas, and Finn too. Maybe I should mention this to them."

"Oh, Max also said they have reason to believe that whatever they're planning—and he seems to think they *are* planning some kind of operation—that Govic has already infiltrated the Swiss Guard ... which would make it doubly important that at least Karl know. We should meet with him together, I think. And soon."

Dominic looked out the window back at the Vatican, eyebrows furrowing as his face took on a look of dark concern. Hana studied him as she took a sip of wine, the taste of it suddenly seeming bitter. The lounge had grown packed with mostly young patrons drinking and laughing, in stark contrast to the oppressive weight now settling over both her and Dominic.

"Karl and I are going for a run in the morning," he said. "We'll have coffee afterward and I'll talk with him then. He needs to know what's going on. I don't trust either Dante or this new Govic guy. I think we have to assume malevolence runs in the family."

Hana took a deep breath and sighed. "I agree, Karl must know. He should also keep an eye on his fellow Guards to see if anyone is acting suspiciously. Given what we went through last year, I'm really concerned, Michael."

"I doubt there's reason for worry, Hana. Let's let things play out and deal with them as they come along."

CHAPTER

EIGHTEEN

A quarter moon hung over the darkened city as a taxi turned onto the historic Via del Corso, slowly making its way up the two-lane avenue. As the vehicle passed the church of Santa Maria dei Miracoli, the pealing of its seventeenth-century bells announced the nine o'clock hour. Local residents strolled along the narrow sidewalks lining the Corso as they took in their *passeggiata*, the nightly ritual promenade for Italians to see and be seen in fine attire—*fare la bella figura*—after their evening meal.

The taxi pulled up in front of the Palazzo Caravaggio. Golden shafts of strategically placed up-lights hidden in the lush garden illuminated the gilded Baroque architecture of the villa, making it all the more imposing. The rear door of the taxi opened and out stepped Ivan Gović. Walking up the steps to the palazzo's grand entrance he pulled his jacket in closer as a cold autumn breeze swept over him. He rang the bell.

After a few moments, the door opened a crack and a young nun appeared. Gović recognized her as one of the sisters from the cardinal's household in Buenos Aires. "*Sí?*" she asked timidly.

"*Buenas noches, hermana,*" Gović said, continuing in Spanish, "I have an appointment with Cardinal Dante. My name is Gović."

"Yes, please come in, *señor,*" the nun said as she opened the door wider. "His Eminence will see you in the study. Please follow me."

The nun led him through the elegant marble foyer to a richly appointed room lined with well-laden bookshelves and several fine oil paintings. A fire blazed in a spacious baronial fireplace adjacent to tall windows overlooking Rome, and in one of two burgundy leather wingback chairs facing the fire sat Cardinal Dante, a snifter of amber cognac in hand.

"Ah, Ivan, thank you for coming," Dante said, remaining seated. As Gović approached him, Dante held out his hand for the younger man to kiss his ring.

"Would you like a cognac? Help yourself, there on the credenza."

"Yes, very much so, thank you. It's quite cold tonight." Gović removed his jacket and hung it on a coat rack in the corner, then poured a four-count of cognac into a tumbler and took the chair next to Dante.

Abhorring small talk, Dante lit a Chiaravalle cigarette and got right to the point.

"Ivan," he said, exhaling a plume of blue smoke, "I have a special task for you, much like your courageous father did for me over the years. One that will require special finesse and absolute secrecy."

"Anything you wish, Eminence. I am at your service."

"Yes, I appreciate that. There is a priest from whom I need something…well, rather unusual. Do you recall the names I gave you of those who were present at that incident involving your father? Father Michael Dominic, in particular?"

Govíc's face turned steely at the mention of Dominic's name. "That is not a name I will forget, Eminence. In fact, I have a plan to—"

"—I would rather not..." Dante suddenly interrupted him, raising a hand, "be apprised of any plans you might have, Ivan. But now that you know of whom I speak, I need you to find a way into his apartment in Domus Santa Marta to obtain a sample of his hair. I'm sure you'll find strands of it in a brush or perhaps in the shower. I'll leave the details to you. But I am told—and this is most important—that we must have hair samples with the roots attached, not just the shaft alone."

Knowing it was probably best not to inquire as to the reasons for such an odd request, Govíc simply nodded his assent. "Yes, this is something I am sure we can obtain."

"Can you have it to me within forty-eight hours?"

Govíc considered a moment. "I will do my best, Eminence."

"Good. Our business for the evening is concluded, then. Where are you staying while in Rome?"

Govíc swallowed the rest of his cognac. "I have taken a room at a small hotel in the Trastevere. It's not much but it serves my purposes while I'm here. When do we return to Buenos Aires?"

"The consistory should be over by the weekend, so we'll likely head back on Monday—one reason I need that sample soon."

"And you shall have it, Eminence. I'll see myself out. Good night."

As he walked down the steps of the palazzo, Govíc

reached for his phone. Opening the messaging app, he texted Dieter Koehl: **Meet me at Pergamino Caffè tomorrow 0730.**

After a brief pause, a Thumbs Up emoji appeared on Govič's screen.

CHAPTER
NINETEEN

Having raced each other up the 138 Spanish Steps, Michael Dominic and Karl Dengler were both gasping for breath when they reached the upper Piazza Trinita dei Monti, their chests heaving in the cool morning air. This was their favorite route, for conquering the 300-year-old steps gave them an aerobic workout like none other. From the piazza, it was just an easy fifteen-minute jog back across Ponte Cavour to Pergamino Caffè next to the Vatican, where they could chat quietly.

"I THINK we should leave for France this weekend, Michael," Dengler said, nursing a steaming espresso and biscotti on the sidewalk table they had taken at Pergamino. It was just past seven o'clock and the morning sun had been up about half an hour, giving the city that bright ocher glow for which it's known.

"The consistory will be over by then," he continued,

"Hana will still be here, and a few of us from the Guard can take some much-deserved time off after tending to all the cardinals' needs this week. They treat us like servants, you know, especially those who don't visit Rome often. It's unbefitting our official duties to the Holy Father. We are not their subjects!" Dengler grumbled a bit more, then bit off another chunk of biscotti.

"I expect most cardinals understand and respect the Swiss Guards' role here, Karl. I also know a few who do take advantage of their rank to get what they want, and they're not likely to change, no matter what. Maybe bring it up to your commander?"

"It's not worth kicking the hornet's nest, Michael. The commander answers directly to the pope, and this is not something he is likely to complain about to the Holy Father."

Dominic turned the conversation back to a subject he knew Dengler would appreciate.

"As for a visit to Grotte Trou la Caune, I think the weekend is a fine idea. Perhaps even Friday." Dengler's face lit up at hearing this, it having been his goal for some time now.

Dominic continued, "You'll need to give me a refresher on equipment, of course, and this will be Hana's first time caving, so be prepared to handle two novices."

"As I mentioned, *Trou la Caune* is an easy cave with mostly horizontal passages, not so many verticals. We'll have a great time!"

"As for finding that Magdalene reliquary, Karl, I wouldn't get my hopes up. According to Guillaume de Sonnac, it was placed there nearly 800 years ago, and surely someone has discovered it by now if there's even anything left of it." Though he wouldn't admit it, Dominic himself had high hopes of finding the sacred artifact, especially if it was indeed an ossuary containing the bones of Christ—in which case, he would deal with the weighty issues of divinity later.

"But there's something else I need to talk to you about," Dominic began.

The sun was rising higher now, warming the sidewalk on which they sat. As he listened, Dengler raised his head to meet the sun's rays, soaking in the warmth, when he noticed a fellow Swiss Guard walking across the street toward the Pergamino. It was Dieter Koehl, guardsman in charge of the Armory, and he had someone with him. Dominic noticed the object of Dengler's attention and also watched as the men came closer.

"Dieter!" Dengler called out. "It's good to see you up so early. Father Dominic and I just finished a long run through the city. Will you join us?"

As the two men approached the table, Koehl introduced his companion to Karl Dengler.

On hearing both Dengler and Dominic's names, Koehl's friend suddenly stiffened. But it was too late to turn back, as Dengler had already started to make introductions.

"Dieter, I'd like you to meet Father Michael Dominic." Smiling, Koehl shook hands with the priest, then made his own introductions.

"Father Dominic, Karl, this is an old friend from Buenos Aires visiting Rome for the week: Ivan Gović."

At the mention of Gović's name, Dominic sat up and froze. *It can't be!* He and the Croatian locked eyes for several awkward moments, each man clearly aware of the tension filling the gap between them.

"I'm afraid we can't join you just now," Gović said

quickly. "We have some urgent business to discuss and wouldn't want to impose that on you."

Dengler, noticing Dominic's peculiar reaction, didn't press the issue. "Well, some other time, then. Good to meet you, Ivan."

"You as well, Karl … Father," said Govíc tersely, not taking his eyes off Dominic. Koehl and Govíc went into the café and took a table inside.

"Are you okay, Michael?" Dengler asked. "That guy seemed familiar to me, but I can't place it."

"I can," Dominic said darkly. "I killed his father last year."

Dengler looked at his friend and just blinked, shocked at hearing the words he had just spoken. "*Mein Gott!* In that warehouse operation where we rescued Hana? How do you know that's the guy?"

"It's sort of a long story, but that's what I was about to tell you. Hana just filled me in last night. And she was informed by the director of Italy's intelligence agency that Ivan Govíc may be seeking retribution for his father's death. From that look in his eyes, I'm pretty sure he already knows who we are."

"But why would he be with *Dieter*? This makes no sense!" Dengler was confused by the quickly unfolding facts.

"Listen, Karl," Dominic cautioned. "We need to watch our backs with this guy. No telling what he has in store. I know he came here as part of Cardinal Dante's entourage, so somehow they're connected. And as we know, Dante is usually up to no good.

"The AISI director also told Hana that Govíc and his cronies might be trying to infiltrate the Swiss Guard for some kind of operation, which could account for your friend Dieter's relationship. But he did say Gović was 'an old friend'… In any event, if they did need a confederate in the Swiss Guard, it looks like they have one now."

"Should I warn my commander? Do you think the Holy Father might be in danger?"

"I just don't know, Karl. We should probably tell Hana about this development so she can pass it along to the AISI. It may be helpful to them."

Dominic looked at his watch. "Let's get back to the Vatican. I need to be at work soon."

DIETER KOEHL WAS JUST as curious about the brief and obviously strained encounter with Dengler and Dominic.

"Is it just me or was there some tension in the air when I introduced you to those guys?" he asked Gović.

"No, it wasn't just you, my friend," said Gović matter-of-factly, taking a careful sip of the hot coffee they had ordered. He set the cup down and looked directly into Koehl's eyes. "It was Father Dominic who murdered my father."

Stunned at hearing this, Koehl simply looked at Gović disbelievingly.

"How can you possibly know this to be true?!" he asked.

"I have it on credible authority. That's all I can say now."

Koehl looked around the small room to see if anyone nearby might have overheard their conversation. He turned back to Gović.

"What are you really here in Rome for, Ivan?" he whispered.

"I was coming to that, and you must believe me when I

say that what I'm about to ask of you has nothing to do with any feelings I might have toward Father Dominic. It is just coincidental that Cardinal Dante has asked me to obtain something from the priest—but I will need your help to do this."

Koehl took a sip of his coffee. "And what's that?" he asked cautiously.

"First, I need to know that your loyalty to our cause is still strong and absolute. As you know, the Novi Ustasha has certain expectations of its members. Your family has a long association with our organization, Dieter, as does Cardinal Dante. He speaks admiringly of you, by the way."

"I didn't realize he even knew who I was, apart from our dinner the other night." Koehl grinned appreciatively, that such a powerful cardinal as Fabrizio Dante would even concern himself with a humble soldier of Christ.

"Oh, yes. He has been watching your career, as I have, for some time now. And he has a special request that might very well land you a promotion, or possibly even the Benemerenti Medal, when the time comes."

At the mention of the elite Corps' most prestigious decoration, Gović now had Koehl's full attention. "Then what is it I can do for His Eminence, Ivan?"

Gović explained what Dante required from Dominic's apartment in Domus Santa Marta. "For what purpose, Dante did not elaborate, nor did I expect him to. His reasons are his own."

Koehl's expression was a mix of apprehension and bewilderment. He shifted nervously in his seat, looking down as he swirled the coffee in his cup.

Gović pressed his point more vigorously, aware of Koehl's uncertainty. "I would have no hesitation doing this myself, Dieter, but obviously I do not have the access you do inside the Vatican walls. Would you prefer it if Cardinal Dante asks you himself? Or should I tell him you're not up to the task?"

The thought of imposing on or even disappointing the esteemed cardinal made Koehl feel sheepish. "No, don't bother His Eminence. I will do it. When do you need these items?"

"Within forty-eight hours, preferably sooner," Govic replied. "Like most joggers, Dominic probably takes a run every morning. You can do it then, while he's away. Or even while he's at work. Didn't you mention he works in the Secret Archives?"

"Yes."

"You'll have plenty of opportunity then, and it will only take a few minutes. Cardinal Dante will be very grateful. I'd rather not let him down if we fail such a simple task."

We? Koehl thought. *This is all on me now!* He thought of his wife and daughter, and what might happen to his career if he were caught. Though he had been inside Domus Santa Marta many times on official business and would be allowed to pass by the guards—keeping in mind this was also the pope's residence—a deep sense of dread made his stomach tighten. But he *could* do it. The sooner he got this over with, the better.

Resigned to his mission, Dieter Koehl got up to leave the café.

But Govic had one final question, which he spoke in nearly a whisper as he rose and leaned into Koehl's ear. "There's one more thing, Dieter. My cousin still needs to remove that large boulder on his farm. Were you able to acquire that item we spoke of?"

Koehl suddenly felt nauseous, a man torn between the two vocations he loved most—being a noble Swiss Guard and carrying on his family's tradition as his generation's member of the Novi Ustasha. But something just felt *wrong*.

"Yes, of course. I'll have that for you tomorrow, Ivan."

The two men left the café and parted company on the street.

CHAPTER
TWENTY

O wing to a late night spent reading Pierre Chevalier's classic book, *Subterranean Climbers*, in preparation for their next trip, Dominic had slept in for the morning, foregoing his usual run.

Dragging himself out of bed, he showered and trimmed his five o'clock scruff—or 'permashadow' as Hana had often teased him—brushed his teeth and, finding his cassock from yesterday had a few wrinkles, pulled out the ironing board to give it a once-over. Unlike cardinals, lowly Vatican priests didn't have nuns attending to their every whim.

While the iron heated up, he decided to call Hana and report the previous day's event. Putting her on speaker while he pressed the garment, Dominic related meeting Gović with Dieter Koehl, the conspicuous tension between himself and the Croatian, and his discussion afterward with her cousin Karl Dengler.

He suggested that she inform Massimo Colombo as soon as possible since he'd want to know of the Swiss

Guard's relationship to a known subject of interest. She agreed to do so, urging Dominic to be careful.

He ended the call, finished the ironing chore, dressed for work, brushed his hair, checked himself in the mirror—then left the apartment to start his day in the Secret Archives.

It was ten o'clock when Sergeant Dieter Koehl approached the two guards on either side of the entrance to Domus Santa Marta. He knew both of them well and stopped to chat about the extra rigors placed on their brethren during the consistory when visiting cardinals often treated them as errand boys. Some even complained, privately of course, about the occasional unwanted sexual advance a few of the cardinals were known to solicit. This was a common problem for Swiss Guard soldiers—young and fit and desirable to older men of special rank and privilege in a closed culture. The complaints often went unheeded, and those who did lodge protests were often simply reassigned. But very little could change the conduct of the offending cardinals, and they suffered no punishment at all for their unwelcomed behavior.

Their conversation concluded, Koehl entered the building, checked the directory in the lobby for Dominic's room, then headed straight for the priest's apartment on the third floor. The building had few people in it this time of the morning, and since it was guarded day and night for the pope's security, virtually no one had need to lock their doors. Including Father Dominic.

Seeing no one around, Koehl knocked on the door. If the priest were there and had answered, Koehl was prepared to invite him to go running sometime, now that they had been introduced by Dengler. But he was in luck. His knocking went unanswered.

Trying the handle, he found it was open, so he slipped inside, closing the door behind him.

"Father Dominic?" he called out. No answer.

Koehl looked around the small apartment, noting that Dominic was a tidy man. Everything was clean and orderly. He headed to the bathroom, where he found the items he was looking for. Since Swiss Guard uniforms have no pockets, he placed the items inside the shoulder pack most guardsmen carried, then returned to the door and left the apartment.

CHAPTER

TWENTY-ONE

E nrico Petrini was not looking forward to his meeting with Cardinal Dante, but the archbishopric of Buenos Aires was an important post, and as secretary of state it was customary for Petrini to meet all members of the cardinalate visiting Rome during the consistory. So, the invitation was extended, and Dante would arrive shortly.

In the meantime, Petrini had been meaning to call his old wartime friend Pierre Valois, now the president of France, to discuss the possibility of an official state visit to his country by the pope. Ever since the reign of Charlemagne in the ninth century, Roman Catholicism had been France's state religion, and the Church the largest landowner in that country. But in recent years—with the rapid rise of atheism among French people of all ages—the Church's influence on its flock there had diminished significantly. This worried the pope, who was determined to reinvigorate the faithful where it mattered most. And France was an important province for the Church.

Petrini had just picked up the phone to call Valois when his secretary, Father Nicholas Bannon, knocked at the door.

"Yes, Nick?" Petrini asked, looking up when Bannon entered the room.

"Your Eminence, Cardinal Dante has arrived a bit early. Shall I ask him to wait, or would you like to see him now?"

Petrini sighed. "No, now is fine. I can make my call later. Please see him in." He set the telephone receiver back in its cradle, then glanced at his desk to make sure no important documents were lying about. He had good reason not to trust this man.

A few moments later Father Bannon opened the door and Cardinal Dante sauntered into the room. Dante's face was unfailingly stony, his countenance grim. Lacking any natural warmth, the smile he attempted on entering didn't do much to change that.

"Good afternoon, Eminence," Dante said as he approached the opposite side of the desk, not bothering to shake hands. He took a chair and sat down.

"Good day, Fabrizio," Petrini responded. "How is it being back in Rome after all these months?"

Dante looked around the grand office, with its spectacular view of Saint Peter's dome—the office he had occupied himself until Petrini replaced him as secretary of state the previous summer.

"It is always a privilege to be in Rome, Enrico. For one, the food is vastly superior to Argentina's. One can only eat so much barbecued Asado and fried empanadas." Another poor attempt at a smile.

The two men carried on with a more or less collegial conversation, discussing affairs of the Church in Dante's adopted country, the pope's upcoming visit to South America, and other relevant topics. Twenty minutes later, collegiality had run its course, and Petrini made it clear the meeting was winding down.

"When do you return to Buenos Aires, Fabrizio?" Petrini asked.

"We'll be leaving on Monday, Eminence, unless you have any reason I should remain here…?"

"No, that won't be necessary. I'm sure you'll be glad to get back home."

"*This is* my home, Enrico," Dante replied archly. Then he lightened his tone. "But I serve at the pleasure of His Holiness, wherever my services are most needed. Right now, that is Argentina."

"The Holy Father is pleased with your work there," Petrini said halfheartedly, standing to say goodbye.

Dante also stood, this time reaching out his hand. When Petrini took it, Dante squeezed Petrini's own hand firmly.

"*Oooow!*" Petrini yelped, swiftly jerking his hand back and inspecting a fresh wound. "*What the…?!*" Blood began oozing out of his middle finger.

"My goodness, I am *so* sorry, Enrico," Dante said with little emotion. "I've been meaning to get this ring repaired. One of the raised adornments has come loose. My apologies…are you alright?"

Petrini, still smarting from the puncture, waved off Dante's concern, reaching for a tissue to stanch the bleeding.

"I'm fine, Fabrizio. You should get that fixed."

Dante turned and made for the door. "Of course, Eminence. *Arrivederci.*"

Once outside the Government Palace, Dante looked around, ensuring that no one was nearby, then carefully removed his Ustasha Ehrenring—still bearing a drop of Enrico Petrini's blood—and placed it into a plastic zip-top bag he had withdrawn from his pocket.

His dry, pursed lips formed a sneer of a smile. *That was easier than I expected*, he thought.

~

HIS WORK in the Archives finished for the day, Michael Dominic returned to his apartment to change clothes and freshen up before he met with Karl and Hana for a beer.

He was still worried about Calvino Mendoza. The monk had been deeply dispirited since discovering the cataclysmic Magdalene manuscript hidden in the Riserva, and Dominic was concerned for his friend's now-wandering faith. He imagined how shattering it might be for a man who had dedicated his entire life, more than fifty years in the Franciscan order, to all that encompassed the divinity of Jesus and the Resurrection. He thought of how Christ bestowed on Saint Francis the wounds of his suffering, marking him with the stigmata; and how Mendoza must now be burdened by his own painful mark —an imprint of fraud on everything he had believed.

For Dominic, faith was more an abstract, a cognitive affair involving thought and experience, a sense of belonging to a more or less subtle order that embraced empirical theology. And there were many in the Church who were quite comfortable adopting that belief structure, though Dominic thought of himself more as a Christian agnostic, uncertain of anything beyond the basic principles of Catholic faith. And even those were often challenging to espouse.

But like most people of faith, Mendoza was all in, and for him, this was a moment of crisis. *There must be something I can do to ease his burden*, Dominic thought.

While pondering that dilemma, he stripped off his collar, cassock and undergarments, washed his face and dampened his hair to revive himself from dealing with musty old books and manuscripts all day. After drying himself off he reached for his hairbrush—but it wasn't where he'd left it earlier that morning. He looked in the drawers of the bathroom and on the dresser in his bedroom. Not there either. *Things don't just disappear....*

He recounted the steps of his morning routine. *Woke up late. Brushed my teeth. Ironed cassock. Spoke to Hana. Got dressed. Brushed my hair. Mirror check. Left apartment.*

Going back into the bathroom, he looked again. Now he noticed his toothbrush was also missing. The glass tumbler he kept it in was empty. *What's going on?!*

He stood there looking at himself in the mirror, thinking. *Someone has been here.* He did a search of the entire apartment to see if anything valuable—as if he had anything of particular worth anyway—was missing, but everything else seemed in order. *Strange.*

Checking his watch, he saw he would be late meeting Karl and Hana, so he let the mystery pass for now. He threw on a pair of jeans, his customary black t-shirt, and his favorite bomber jacket. *Thank God they didn't take that.* On leaving, he locked his apartment for the first time in months. He'd have to report this. Although, admittedly, it would be a rather strange report of a missing hairbrush and toothbrush, and he wondered at the skepticism he would encounter.

∾

THE CHATTER of passersby drifted in the evening air from the nearby Piazza del Popolo as Ivan Govi rang the doorbell of Palazzo Caravaggio. The same young nun as before opened the door.

"*Buenas tardes*, Señor Govi," she said, welcoming him inside with a meek smile. "His Eminence is expecting you."

She led him to the study, where Dante was sitting in his usual fireside wingback chair, a snifter of cognac in his hand.

"Ivan…thank you for coming," he said, setting the cognac on a side table. "Were you able to get those items I requested?"

Govi simply smiled and handed Dante a white paper bag. Peering inside, he found a hairbrush matted with dark hair, and a plastic bag, inside of which was a visibly used toothbrush.

"Very good," said the cardinal. "I hadn't even thought about getting the toothbrush, too, just in case. You have done well, Ivan."

"Eminence, my colleague who obtained these items— the one in the Swiss Guard—has become concerned that, as a good Catholic, he might be involved in something dishonorable. I tried to reassure him this was simply a small task, a test of loyalty of sorts, and that he would not suffer any harm from the handling of it. But I sense he feels he has done something wrong, and his conscience is weighing on him."

Dante's eyes darkened. "You must keep him in line, Ivan. I assumed when I gave you this task that you'd find someone who could keep his mouth shut. Let's hope he is worthy of the responsibility, or steps will be taken. Do we have an understanding?"

With a sly grin, Gović nodded, now clear on the freedom given him to handle the situation as he saw fit. "We do, Eminence."

CHAPTER

TWENTY-TWO

H ana, Karl, and Lukas were seated at a table near the window of the Ristorante dei Musei, nibbling from a large oval plate of fresh *antipasti* set between them, as they nursed their drinks while waiting for Dominic to show up. The aroma of assorted pizzas, the house specialty, and the ever-present scents of garlic and basil made their mouths water.

All heads turned upon hearing a double tap on the glass window. Dominic waved at them from the sidewalk as he headed toward the entrance. Dengler had just ordered a beer for him which was waiting on the table as Dominic seated himself next to Hana. After a quick exchange of greetings, he drank thirstily.

"Just two more days until we leave for Périllos and Grotte Trou la Caune!" Dengler said excitedly. He turned to his partner then leaned closer in, shoving him playfully. "Lukas and I will take care of all the gear we need. Maybe we'll even camp inside the cave for the night."

Wiping the froth from his lips, Dominic paled. "Do we *have* to sleep in the cave? Isn't there a hotel nearby?"

"Not to worry, Michael. I got some Xannies from the Vatican pharmacy to help manage your anxiety. You'll be fine."

The young priest looked at his friend skeptically. "I could have used one of those an hour ago. Someone entered my apartment and stole my hairbrush and toothbrush. Nothing else from what I can tell, just those two things. Don't you find that strange?"

Hana put a hand on his arm. "That's awful! How does that even happen in the Vatican? And what would anyone want with your brushes?"

"I haven't a clue," Dominic said. "It's just odd. Most rooms are never locked in Domus Santa Marta because security is so high since the pope has an apartment there too. I figure it was either an inside job or the guards let someone in who was known to them. Either way, I'm reporting it."

Dengler brightened. "Well, you won't need a hairbrush where we're going anyway." He withdrew a road map from his jacket pocket.

"So, we'll leave around 0500 on Friday, stopping for lunch in Genoa, then drive along the coast until we get to Perpignan where we'll have dinner, then a few miles later we'll arrive at Périllos, around seven. We can stay at a hotel there for the night, starting out early Saturday morning for the cave, then head back on Sunday. Sound good to everyone?"

"Sure," Dominic said. "That should give us plenty of time to search for the reliquary, if it's there at all."

"Be sure to bring the 'treasure' map, Michael," Dengler said, grinning at the thought of adventure.

"I've got it right here, Karl, just in case we needed it for planning." Dominic opened his pack to let the others get a glimpse of the object.

"Oh, hand it over," Dengler asked. "I want Lukas to see this." Then, turning to Lukas, "This is the map to the Magdalene artifact I told you about."

Taking hold of the object, Lukas marveled at the intricate design of the puzzle. The thought of following the map through the cave put a gleam in his eye.

While they had been talking, Hana's investigative reporter's instinct returned to the matter of Dominic's theft. It had her perplexed. Why would someone leave anything of value and just take such peculiar personal accessories?

Then a new thought struck her. *There's only one reason someone might want items of such an intimate nature!*

"Michael, can you think of any reason why someone might want or need your DNA?"

Startled at the notion, Dominic was taken aback. "No! Why would anyone want *my* DNA?"

"It's the only thing that makes sense," Hana replied. "It's the most logical reason someone might require your hair or saliva."

"Well, that doesn't give me much to worry about now, does it?"

TWO YOUNG MEN sitting at an adjacent table, drinking beers and leisurely nibbling on pizza, had been intently listening to the group's conversation since Dominic's arrival. At Ivan Gović's direction, they had staked out Saint Anne's Gate and followed the priest to the nearby restaurant.

The two had been enjoying their meal quietly, taking

mental notes of the dialogue at the next table. But at the mention of a *"Magdalene object"* and a *"treasure map,"* their eyes met purposefully. This was definitely something Gović would want to know about. One of them set down his slice of pizza and went to the restroom to make a phone call.

Returning to the table a few minutes later, the man called Victor whispered to his brother, Eric, that Gović had given them specific instructions. It would depend on what the priest did when they all left.

"LUKAS and I are heading back to the Vatican. I've got gate duty in a few minutes. You guys want a ride?"

Hana raised her hand. "If you're going by way of the Rome Cavalieri, I'm in, thanks!"

"It's a nice brisk evening," Dominic said. "I'll just walk the few blocks, thanks." He hugged Hana as they all stood to leave.

Outside the restaurant, Dengler, Lukas and Hana got into the Jeep Wrangler and made their way to Hana's hotel a few blocks away. Dominic headed west toward the northern Vatican wall, then crossed the wide Viale Vaticano, turning south along the wall toward Saint Anne's Gate. There were no streetlights in the parking lot flanking the Pigna Courtyard, which gave the two men following him the cover they needed.

Accelerating their pace, they silently ran up behind the priest and jumped him. One pinned his arms while the other punched his stomach in rapid succession. Shocked, Dominic kicked erratically. His feet flailed, missed his attacker. He struggled sideways, but muscular arms held him fast in a powerful grip.

Blow after blow knocked the air out of him, weakening him from pain with each punch. Suddenly, the grip released and his immobilized body crumpled to the ground. The two men grabbed his pack and ran off. Not a word had been spoken during the melee.

Stunned and injured, Dominic lay on his back for a few minutes, breathing heavily. Lifting himself up on one arm, he shook his aching head to take stock of himself, sending waves of pain through his skull, his gut aching.

Then he noticed his pack was gone. The map! *They've taken the map!*

CHAPTER

TWENTY-THREE

D ominic wobbled to his feet and took stock of his body. He touched the back of his head where it had hit the ground. No blood. His other arm instinctively still held tight against his aching gut. Given a little time, he would heal physically and be back in order.

But his pack had been stolen.

Given the unusual events of the past few days and the threats Hana had warned him about, he wondered if this were just some random robbery or if he might have been targeted. He decided on the latter, which gave him no measure of comfort at all.

Walking slowly back to the Vatican, he found Finn Bachman on duty at Saint Anne's Gate. Seeing Dominic slightly staggering as he approached him, the young guard rushed to the priest, putting an arm around him to support him.

"Father Michael, what happened?!" Bachman guided Dominic to a nearby bench.

Just then Dengler's Jeep approached the gate. Bachman

waved urgently to Dengler, who told Lukas to park the vehicle inside. He ran to where Dominic was sitting.

"Michael, what happened?!"

"I was just mugged back there, Karl, along the wall. They took the map!"

"What?!" Dengler cried out, then, "Let's take a look at you first." He checked Dominic's head for lacerations, then both of his arms. "Is it painful anywhere in particular?"

"Not really. They gut-punched me a bit, but my jacket absorbed most of it. They came out of nowhere, surprising me. I don't think this was some random incident either, Karl. Given everything that's going on, I'd say this has Govic's name all over it."

"You say they took the map?"

"Yeah, they got my whole backpack. There wasn't much else in it except for the map itself, plus my notes from Ginzberg and a few loose items. But that object is more than just a map, it's a historical artifact that belongs to the Vatican! We *must* get it back."

Dengler thought for a moment. "If this was a purposeful attempt to get the map, it can only mean that these people intend to use it. Our one chance to find them and retrieve the map for the Vatican is to catch up with them in Périllos. We can still use the photos I took that have the cave system mapped out, so at least we have that as a backup."

"Even if we don't catch up with them and retrieve the map, we can't allow them to find the reliquary if it is there," Dominic said firmly, massaging his neck as he spoke. "We have to get there before anyone else figures out the puzzle. We leave the day after tomorrow, as planned."

~

THE WEAPONRY USED by the Pontifical Swiss Guard is kept in an orderly row of upright wooden gun racks forming a wall between the shelves on which are stored the plumed helmets and body armor worn by the Corps while performing official duties. Hundreds of weapons are stored there for whatever military purposes the unit sees fit to use: submachine guns, assault rifles with bayonets, halberds, swords, vintage maces and truncheons, and highly efficient HK MP7 submachine guns used by the security servicemen closest to the pope when he appears in public. All Swiss Guards are equipped with standard-issue Sig Sauer P220 handguns which are worn at all times.

The man in charge of the modern armory, Sergeant Dieter Koehl, was now standing at a workbench inside a secure, heavily fortified magazine far from the Apostolic Palace, built along the wall at the northwest corner of Vatican City. Surrounding him were individual concrete bunker boxes, each separately stocked with hand grenades, TNT, sticks of dynamite, and the plastic explosives C-4 and Semtex—along with specialized chemicals and equipment for crafting specialized explosives. Dank odors hung in the air of the concrete arsenal, distinct smells of motor oil and shoe polish and almonds marking the signatures of the various compounds.

It was Koehl's responsibility to ensure a proper inventory of these items, and while they had not been used in many years—and were only infrequently refreshed as their shelf life expired—he was the only one who really knew the contents intimately. No one else had bothered to double-check his inventory in the ten years he had been there. Though it would be simple enough to confiscate just one block of a Semtex charge, as a devout Catholic the mere thought of theft bothered him.

Still, he hesitated. The alternative, of course, would be to fashion a bomb himself and keep the inventory in check. The prospect of that appealed to him more than stealing the pope's ready munitions.

Dieter Koehl had attended Zurich University of Applied Sciences, where he mastered in Physical Chemistry. His training expanded during his years as a combat engineer in the *Kommando Spezialkräfte*, the Swiss Army Special Forces Command. As part of the elite counter-terrorist unit known as Army Reconnaissance Detachment 10, Koehl specialized in explosive ordnance missions, and was rated as one of the army's top experts in building and defusing IEDs—improvised explosive devices—as well as demolition of field obstacles and enemy fortifications, all of which came into gainful use during his tour of duty with Operation Enduring Freedom in Afghanistan.

Academically inclined, Koehl had studied and admired those who had made major contributions in his fields of interest, chief among them the inventor and philanthropist Alfred Nobel. Long before his eponymous Nobel Prizes became the world's most coveted awards for scientific, academic and cultural advances, Alfred Nobel had invented dynamite and gelignite, or blasting gelatin, the latter of which Koehl had determined would be the best course for Gović's project. He donned a hazmat suit and respirator and began his work.

With a measured confidence grounded in years of training, he guardedly concocted a mixture composed of nitroglycerin, saltpeter, wood meal and collodion cotton. When carefully blended in certain ratios, the stable but potentially volatile compound resulted in a stiff, pliant substance known as *plastique*, which has a combined explosive power greater than either of its primary ingredients. One that could be shaped into most any form needed. Once the putty-like substance was prepared, the only remaining step was the insertion of a blasting cap and a fuse, something that could be done on-site at the last minute.

Covering the charge in olive-colored Mylar film wrap, Koehl reached for a fuse and blasting cap, placed all materials in his backpack, cleaned up his workbench, and left and secured the magazine.

TWENTY-FOUR

Not far from the muddy banks of Rome's flowing Tiber River sits the campus of Genomics Molecular Genetics Laboratory, one of Italy's premier DNA diagnostic and analysis centers, a modern state-of-the-art facility specializing in genetic testing, research and development.

The unusual package from the Vatican, marked *"Urgente e Confidenziale,"* had arrived by special courier, addressed to Dr. Gabriella Sanguino, head of the company's DNA extraction unit and a personal friend of Cardinal Fabrizio Dante since the two had met at a Science & Theology Conference several years prior.

Dr. Sanguino had been expecting the package since Dante's fervent telephone call the day before.

"Gabriella," he had said, "I have need of a special favor. Samples of hair and blood—from whom we'll call a person of interest—will be couriered to you tomorrow, and I would be most grateful if you could determine a paternity relationship between the two samples. The blood is from the presumptive father and the hair from someone whom I believe to be the son. This is a matter of the utmost personal importance, and time is of the essence. Are you able to do this within a day or so?"

"Of course, Eminence," Dr. Sanguino had responded graciously. "It shouldn't take long at all once we have the samples. I'll put our best technician on it immediately."

GENOMICS' DNA Extraction Room 2 was any scientist's dream lab, its seamless sky-blue resin floor reflecting the stream of natural sunlight pouring in through large windows overlooking the campus. The most modern diagnostic equipment imaginable filled the room, and as lead technician, young Enzo prided himself on order and precision. His lab was the model on which all labs should be based, he believed, with no room for error in his work.

Donning a white lab coat and snapping on a pair of purple nitrile gloves, Enzo opened the special package from Vatican City, its golden papal coat of arms resplendent on the return address. He had never had such an order from the Vatican before, and as a Catholic scientist, he was eager to take on such a distinguished project.

He withdrew the wooden hairbrush tangled with black hair, a toothbrush in a plastic bag, and another bag containing an unusual ring with a small red smear of dried blood at the end of a sharp adornment. Inspecting the ring more closely, he was surprised to find what appeared to be runic symbols surrounding a nearly imperceptible swastika. *That's strange*, he thought, extracting all items and arranging them in a neat row on the stainless steel lab table.

Using a clamp-mounted illuminated magnifier, Enzo found and extracted the most usable strand of hair he could find—one with a thick white bulb at its root—and set that on a sterile tray. Now that he had the fat-rooted hair follicle, the toothbrush analysis likely would not be needed, though it would offer a supportive confirmation.

The first step involved breaking open the cells in the hair to release the DNA molecules, a process known as lysing. Once the cells were dissolved in lysin enzymes, Enzo ground them down finely and added them to a positively charged salt solution, protecting them from the negatively charged phosphate groups found in the backbone of the DNA. He then added a detergent to remove lipids in the cell membrane, releasing the DNA itself.

The next step was to separate and degrade proteins found in the DNA to ensure a pristine sample, after which he added ice-cold ethanol to wash away the previously added salts. Following further cleaning and purification protocols, he suspended the DNA in an alkaline buffer, now making it ready for analysis.

Enzo then went through the same process with the blood sample and the toothbrush. Once both sets of DNA had been extracted, he amplified the amounts using a polymerase chain reaction, making them more workable by producing millions of DNA molecules attributed to each sample.

Using a method known as Short Tandem Repeat Analysis, Enzo evaluated a range of sixteen to twenty genetic markers from each sample to capture the relevant DNA information from each marker, then turned both amplified samples over to the lab's geneticist, Sofia Bartoli, for final analysis and determination.

Using an automatic sequencer with fluorescent technology, Sofia separated the amplified DNA fragments by size, resulting in two specialized barcode charts displaying Exclusions and Attributions. In the Exclusions barcode, if the child being investigated did not possess genetic characteristics found in the alleged father's profile, there would be no paternal match. On the other hand, if the Attributions barcode presented the genetic characteristics transmitted to the son, paternity would be firmly established.

Having completed her analysis on the computer, Sofia prepared the final workup report, signed it, then hand-carried it to Dr. Sanguino's office and personally handed it to her, along with a sealed packet containing Dominic's brushes and Dante's Ehrenring. The process for the entire analysis had taken no more than two hours.

Picking up the phone, Sanguino called Cardinal Dante's private cell number.

"*Buona sera*, Eminence," she said. "We have your results ready."

CHAPTER

TWENTY-FIVE

T he nondescript white panel van from the Vatican motor pool had traveled some twenty kilometers east of Rome to the *agriturismo* town of Corcolle when its driver, Dieter Koehl, turned onto a dirt road leading to the farm where Ivan Gović had instructed him to meet. The late afternoon sun cast long shadows across tall rows of ancient, twisted olive trees surrounding an old farmhouse, the woodsy licorice aroma from thousands of olive blossoms permeating the air.

The package rested securely on the floor at the back of the van, well behind the driver's seat, enclosed in a metal case covered and supported by rolled foam sheeting to prevent its contents from suffering undesirable shocks from potholes in the road. Though fairly stable in transit, Koehl took no chances with the explosive he had so carefully prepared.

Pulling the van up to the farmhouse, the Swiss Guard noted two other vehicles parked between the farmhouse and a Quonset hut some distance away. Turning off the engine and setting the brake, he got out of the van. As he did so four men sauntered out of the farmhouse, with Gović in the lead. All of them had the self-assured bearing of soldiers, suggesting military backgrounds.

"Dieter, so good of you to come," said the smiling Gović, a bottle of beer in one hand and a cigarette in the other. He embraced the new arrival and introduced the other men by first names only: Victor, Eric and Jean-Claude. "While part of our brotherhood, they are all also brothers themselves," Gović said admiringly.

"Well, I'm just a half-brother," said the one called Jean-Claude, seeming to press the point. "Same father, different mother." Koehl noticed that Victor and Eric looked at him uneasily. There was clearly some tension there.

"Eric, Jean-Claude," Gović asked, "would you wait for us inside?"

The two men looked at each other, shrugged their shoulders, and returned to the house.

When they were gone Gović turned to Koehl. "Have you got the package?" he asked.

"Yes, but I'd prefer you extinguish that cigarette before I bring it out."

"You have a point," Gović said, tossing the butt on the ground and crushing it with his boot.

"I'd be happy to set the charge on that boulder for you," Koehl said. "Where is it?"

"No—" Gović said quickly, holding up a hand, "that won't be necessary. We won't be doing that today anyway. We leave for France tonight for some business we must attend to."

Koehl gave Gović a long, hard look. Something wasn't right. The look on Victor's face seemed off, too. Suspicion hung in the air.

He opened the back doors of the van and gently removed the foam wrapping surrounding the case, then removed the plastique. Reaching for a packet containing a long fuse and the blasting cap, he gave Gović instructions on how to prepare it.

"When you've set the charge beneath the boulder, gently push the fuse into the hollow end of the blasting cap. Then crimp the hollow metal end around the fuse, and carefully insert it into the plastique. When the fuse burns down, the flash charge is ignited, detonating the base charge."

"Yes," said Gović with slight irritation. "As I told you, I've done this before."

Koehl wasn't convinced. He locked eyes with Gović. "Just make sure you're at least 300 meters away when the charge goes off, Ivan."

"Thank you, Dieter, you've been most helpful," said Gović, as he handed the case to Victor, who headed toward the Quonset hut to store the package there. "As for that other matter, Cardinal Dante was very pleased with your cooperation and success. I'm sure he'll be putting in a good word to your commander under some other pretense."

Despite the words of support, Koehl didn't believe he deserved a commendation for breaking and entering, not to mention bomb-making. Exchanging goodbyes, he got into the van, started the engine, and headed back to the Vatican.

~

HAVING RETURNED TO THE FARMHOUSE, Gović and his men gathered around a table with a large map of southern

France laid out on it.

"This operation has four targets and two objectives," he began. "The targets are those who were responsible for my father's death: Father Michael Dominic, a journalist named Hana Sinclair, and two Swiss Guards, Karl Dengler and Lukas Bischoff. We know they will all be inside the cave on Saturday afternoon."

Jean-Claude asked what the objectives were.

Gović pointed to the location of the cave on the map of France. "First, we get hold of this 'reliquary' they seek, some kind of object they say is connected to Mary Magdalene." He picked up the ancient Vesconte artifact, turning it appraisingly.

"There is obviously some value attached to this. The map and notes Victor and Eric found in Dominic's pack will lead us to the location of this reliquary, if it is still there. That's the first objective."

"And the second?" Jean-Claude asked.

Gović looked at each of the men around the table, then said coldly, "I'll tell you that when we get to the cave."

TWENTY-SIX

I t was nine in the morning when Dengler, Lukas, Dominic and Hana drove through greater Florence, north on Autostrada A1, stopping for gas on the outskirts of the city after four hours on the road. The ancient red bricks capping Brunelleschi's Duomo of the Cathedral of Santa Maria del Fiore stood out in the distance. As the tallest building in Florence, it was easy to spot.

The cargo bay of the Jeep Wrangler was packed with caving and camping equipment—coiled lines of rope, carabiners and anchors, flashlights, helmets, MREs, bottles of water—along with each of their small personal bags. They had stopped at her hotel to pick up Hana, who was determined to go back to sleep in the car when they left Rome. Dominic rested his head against the backseat window, looking out over the passing landscape as he thought about how to regain possession of Vesconte's map. He now felt foolish having brought it to the restaurant that night—not to mention guilty for having removed it from the Vatican's archives in the first place; if it were found out, his entire career could be jeopardized.

"It won't help agonizing over it, Michael," Hana said, watching him closely from the opposite seat. "What's done is done. Now we just have to find a way to get it back."

"*Just?*" he asked dejectedly. "Where would we even start? And we don't really know *who* took it. Maybe it wasn't Gović, and now some random thief has a valuable artifact he knows nothing about. It was irresponsible of me to remove it from the Vatican in the first place."

"Let's just focus on finding what we can in that cave," Hana said. "If the Magdalene reliquary does exist, I think Vatican authorities would be far more interested in that than in the map it took to find it."

"And if there's nothing there?"

"Well, nobody knows about the map except us and Dr. Ginzberg, right? Will anyone else be the wiser? You know the answer is *No*. It's just your conscience you're struggling with. And while that may be commendable, it's not useful to you or anyone else to beat yourself up over it."

Dominic turned back to watch the hilly Tuscan terrain speed by as the car now headed west on the Autostrada toward Genoa. Of course, Hana was right. No one else knew about the Vesconte map except Simon. That didn't make his ethical predicament any less discouraging. All he had to deal with now was the guilt plaguing him.

After stopping for lunch in a little seaside town near Genoa, Lukas now took the wheel, heading southwest on the A10 through the Italian and French Rivieras while Dengler settled in for a nap in the passenger's seat. Several hours later they reached Perpignan, had dinner, then, finished driving for the day, settled into a small boutique hotel for the night.

THE NEXT MORNING after a full breakfast they departed the hotel, with Dengler driving north on the scenic D5 Autoroute toward Périllos. "The cave is about two kilometers past and just north of the town, maybe another 10 kilometers in all now," said Dominic, reading from a map on his lap. "Once we get there we'll have to park and walk through the scrub to find the cave."

Dominic looked around at the vast and breathtaking Occitanie landscape as mental images of its history filled his head. Medieval castles, ancient villages, Romanesque abbeys: this was the heart of Cathar country, where 800 years ago a small sect of Protestants challenged the Church's ostentatious pomp and obscene reverence for worldly wealth and political dominion. The Cathars were a peaceful and highly principled people who espoused two opposing deities in eternal conflict: *Amor*, representing the Good God of the New Testament and creator of all things Spiritual, and *Roma*, the Evil God of the Old Testament who created the Physical World and all things Material.

As the Cathar movement grew, the Roman Catholic Church—whose dogma allowed for only one God— viewed Catharism as heretical, a movement that had to be destroyed, especially since Cathar theology was spreading throughout the Languedoc faster than Catholicism, threatening the Church's tight hold over its shepherding of an obedient flock. Dominic thrived on this era and its rich history, and his excitement grew the closer they got to their destination.

· · ·

PASSING the largely abandoned ancient town of Périllos on what was now a dirt road, Dengler spotted a wooden sign at the head of a trail reading "Grotte Trou la Caune," with an arrow pointing north along a footpath.

Having parked the car, the four got out. Their backpacks loaded, they trudged up the dirt path through the hilly scrub. After about 500 meters Dominic spotted a breach in the hillside, with trees and bushes nearly obscuring the entrance to a cave.

Looking at a photograph of the grotto that he'd found online, Dengler noted the similarities. "This is it. Ready for some adventure?!"

The tall domed entrance to the cave sat beneath an overhanging orange and white-streaked limestone cliff. Passing through the portal, Dominic and his team found themselves in a spacious chamber littered with loose rocks and huge boulders, with tall freestanding limestone columns and pillars that, while obviously natural, seemed surreal and otherworldly being underground. Shafts of daylight from open light wells in the high ceiling above them cast bluish beams across the multihued granite walls, and even the slightest whisper was amplified throughout the massive cavern.

Dengler took out his phone, tapped the Photos app, and opened the image of the Vesconte map he'd taken before it was stolen from Dominic. Orienting himself, he found the main passage that led far back into the cavern and, hopefully, the room where the reliquary was hidden.

"Looks like this is the way in," he said, pointing to the passage. "It shouldn't take more than a half hour to get to the dig in this last hall, depending on the topography."

· · ·

AT THAT SAME moment back in Rome, Dieter Koehl sat in the kitchen of his apartment, absently watching a spider outside the window as it waited patiently in the shadows for a fly to meet its web. But the soldier's mind was on another predator. Something wasn't right in his dealings with Ivan Gović. The Croatian said he needed the bomb quickly, yet now he's going to France? That drive alone is two days round trip, not counting whatever business they planned to do there. And he did mention they're returning to Buenos Aires on Monday. It's the timing that's off. *And why did they act so suspiciously when I delivered the explosive? What am I missing?*

It's France…What's the connection there?

Wait…I heard Dengler mention he and his friends are going to France—also this weekend…And what was it Gović had asked—'Who were those involved with my father's death?'… *No…It can't be! He couldn't possibly…*

But it all made sense now. Gović has got to be planning some sort of revenge for his father's killing! But what's the bomb for?

Dengler mentioned a cave…

My God! He's going to blow up the cave while the others are inside!

The awful pieces now fell into place. *How could I have been so foolish?! But I must do something…*

Koehl picked up his phone to call Dengler and warn him. But then he himself would be implicated! It must be anonymous.

First, he entered #31# to conceal his phone number, then placed a thick cloth around the phone, tapped in Dengler's number, and masked his voice.

"This is a friend. Gović is on his way to blow up the entrance

to the cave. You're all in danger. Don't go in! And if you are in, get out now!"

In the underground depths of the French cave, thick stones deadened incoming signals. Koehl's urgent message went straight to voicemail.

TWENTY-SEVEN

I van Gović and his three companions had left Rome just before midnight Friday, driving their Fiat Fullback pickup truck straight through to Périllos with only brief stops for gas and fast food, putting them in the area of the cave just before noon on Saturday.

While they had no proper caving gear, what Victor had found online about the cave's structure assured him they wouldn't need much. Flashlights, a spade, and bottles of water seemed sufficient. But Gović had handed each of them an item he believed they would find much more useful—fully loaded Glock 19 pistols.

"What do we need weapons for?" Jean-Claude asked hesitantly.

Gović turned in his seat, facing his questioner. "It should be obvious, don't you think?"

Parking the truck next to Dengler's Jeep, the four emerged from the vehicle, stretched their arms and legs from the long trip, and opened the trunk to get their backpacks. Loaded up, they headed along the dirt path toward the limestone cliff and the entrance to the cave.

"Sound travels easily in these caverns so be as quiet as possible," Gović said. "As planned, the job is to get hold of whatever object it is they're looking for. Then—we tie them up."

"Tie them up?! Why are we tying them up?" Jean-Claude asked, a trace of concern on his face.

"I have yet to mention our second objective," Gović said. "We're going to set an explosive at the cave entrance, sealing them in."

Jean-Claude's shocked reaction was mirrored by Eric's, neither of whom were privy to this part of Gović's plan. Victor, already aware, showed no reaction.

"How is the taking of four lives an appropriate measure, Ivan?" Jean-Claude asked, incredulous at the new development. "Isn't there a more honorable way you can get closure for your father's death? We are all Catholics here. Aren't we held to higher standards? Cold-blooded murder is just wrong!"

Gović's face reddened with anger. "This isn't the time for second thoughts, Jean-Claude. Are you with us, or should I make it five?" He rested his hand on the pistol tucked in his belt.

The two stood eye-to-eye for several seconds until Eric broke the tension.

"I'll be right back," he announced. "Nature calls."

Jean-Claude then nodded to Ivan, lowering his eyes. "Me, too," he said gruffly and sauntered off into the trees some distance away from Eric's location. Gović watched his back as he walked away, wondering if the man would return.

When they all reconvened a few minutes later, the

group entered the cave with Victor leading the way, following the path laid out on the map.

A FEW MINUTES earlier the satellite phone next to Massimo Colombo's seat in the AISI's Bombardier Challenger jet gave out a subdued ring in two short bursts. He picked it up immediately.

"Yes?" he answered anxiously. Listening intently to the caller, he then said, "We're on our way. We should be there within the hour. Our team will be prepared. *Grazie*."

He ended the call and turned to the others seated around him in the cabin. "That was Jean-Claude. Gović and his men are entering the cave now. His plan is to bomb the entrance, trapping Hana and her friends inside. We must act quickly. Is the French RAID team standing by?"

"Yes, two French Sûreté vehicles are meeting us, along with RAID's special weapons and tactics unit," his aide confirmed. "Périllos is normally a half hour's drive from the Perpignan–Rivesaltes airport, but they're giving us a police escort. We'll be ready."

CHAPTER
TWENTY-EIGHT

L eading the others through a narrow passage off the cavern's large entrance chamber, Karl Dengler was in his element. Like his colleague Dieter Koehl, both were alumni of Army Reconnaissance Detachment 10, the Swiss Army's elite counter-terrorism unit. Part of their training took place in the depths of the magnificent cave system at St. Beatus-Höhlen near Interlaken in the Alps, which fueled the passion Dengler now enjoyed as he explained the natural wonders to his friends who were new to the sport.

"The only rules to caving are 'Leave nothing but footprints, take nothing but pictures, kill nothing but time,'" Dengler recited. "But if we *do* find that reliquary, it's an exception to the rule. If it's not part of what Nature left there, it doesn't count."

Dengler had provided each of the others with helmets fitted with LED lamps. As they moved through the passages taking them deeper into the earth, shadows danced on the walls as light exposed hidden rifts and crevices, making the cavern seem alive with activity beyond their own movements. A slight breeze floated over them from time to time, suggesting open air pockets or light wells farther back in the cave.

"Though it's hard to tell from this photo," Dengler said, referring to the cave map image on his phone, "it looks like the way forward should be fairly clear. Apart from a few turns it's mostly a straight path until we get to the end. It's just deeper than I'd expected."

Dominic, already perspiring from anxiety in the tight confines, was less enthusiastic. "How long before we do reach the end, Karl?" he asked.

"Time for one of those Xannies, Michael?" Dengler asked lightheartedly while showing concern for his friend.

"No, not yet anyway, but thanks."

"Should be another fifteen or twenty minutes," Dengler responded. "It depends on what conditions we have yet to encounter. But as you can feel, we seem to be getting fresh air down here. And this cave is hardly the degree of difficulty as the Lombrives Cathedral we took you to a few weeks ago. You did great there, and you'll be fine here, I promise."

Hana turned around to glance at Dominic. Tiny beads of sweat on his forehead glinted in the light of her helmet, and his face was slightly contorted, more from apprehension than fatigue, she imagined, since he was in better shape than she was, and she was doing fine.

Just as they entered a wide part of the passage, Hana spoke up. "Can we stop here for a few minutes, guys? I need to get a drink and catch my breath."

"Sure," Dengler said. "That'll give me a few minutes to recheck our bearings."

Several large boulders lay about this section of the

cavern, and each of them took one as a seat. Hana noticed Dominic was having some respiratory distress, and grew concerned that he was trying to be braver than he really felt.

"You know," she whispered to him, leaning in closely from an adjacent rock, "I thought this was going to be much more challenging. But that breeze…do you feel it? It's good knowing we have access to fresh air, and it's really quite a lovely experience, don't you think, Michael?"

Dominic looked into her eyes, his tense expression softening. "I know what you're doing, Madame Freud. And I'm grateful for it, really. It's just that, when I was a kid, I nearly drowned in an eddy line beneath a waterfall, and ever since I've had trouble with confined spaces, especially in situations where I don't have control."

"But you *do* have control here, don't you see?" Hana said softly, comfortingly. "Karl and Lukas are taking good care of us and I trust them as much as you do. Why don't you take the Xanax Karl offered? Trust me, those things work."

"Alright," he said. "I'd rather do that than cause anyone else concern. I know it's all in my head, but that doesn't make it any less real."

Hana reached over to squeeze his hand, then got up and went over to Dengler. "I'll take one of those Xannies you've got, Karl."

Dengler, clearly aware it was for Dominic and not his cousin, reached into his pack and withdrew the prescription bottle, removed one blue pill, and handed it to her. She returned to where Dominic was sitting.

"It should kick in by the time we reach our destination," she said, handing him the pill with a bottle of water. He took it and washed it down.

"Okay, let's get back to it!" he said, mustering an eagerness he didn't quite feel. Standing up, the team grabbed their packs and headed farther back into the cave.

IT WASN'T long before Dengler stopped mid-stride, checking the map on his phone. "We should be close now. One big left turn coming up and then a loop to a dead-end passage that leads to the fork—and where, if Simon's notes are correct, we should find the reliquary.

"Hana, my phone is running low on battery. Let's transfer this to your phone so we have a backup."

Using the Bluetooth AirDrop utility, Dengler sent a copy of the map to Hana's iPhone. Checking her own battery, she saw it had plenty of life.

"That's odd," Dengler said, noting a red flag on the visual voicemail icon of his own iPhone. "I've got a message here from 'Unknown Caller.' Guess I didn't hear it come in."

"Could be it came in just as we were entering, you know, on the fringe of the signal," Lukas said. "What's it say?"

Dengler tapped the message so they could all hear it on speaker. The deep voice had an urgency to it, but the message was too scrambled to make out much of what the caller said.

"This is a friend…Gović…blow up…all in danger. Don't… out now!"

"Let's hear it again," Hana said. Dengler complied, tapping the Play button. They all leaned in closer to better hear the words.

"It's too choppy to understand," Dominic noted. "But why would anyone call *you* about Gović? '*Blow up*' leaves little room for interpretation—but blow up *what*? Does he mean *the cave?!*"

"Whatever he said, I don't like the tone of his voice," Hana cautioned. "I have a bad feeling about this. Let's be done soon and get out of here."

CHAPTER
TWENTY-NINE

T he walls of the cave were now getting narrower
the closer they got to their destination. With
Dengler still in the lead, they came upon a three-
way fork.

Using the image on Hana's phone now, Dengler
rechecked the map, deciding to take the middle passage,
the only one that would lead them to the turn-around
loop, and then on to the final dead-end hall.

But the middle fork had a squeeze that barely
accommodated the girth of a human body, with little room
to spare. It seemed unlikely this way would encourage any
previous visitors to the cave, and it was all Dominic could
do to maintain his resolve at managing the situation,
despite the anti-anxiety medication having kicked in a
short while earlier.

The first to go through, Dengler removed his
backpack, dropped it to his feet—an area that was barely
wider than where his chest was squeezing through—then
dragged it behind him by its strap. The others followed

suit, each one struggling to inch his way through opposing limestone walls that offered little more than a sixteen-inch gap. Hana and Lukas were next, and though they had their struggles, they made it through somewhat easily.

As the last of the team got through, it was now Dominic's turn to wedge himself into the narrow fissure. Looking through to the other end, all he saw were three headlamps facing his direction. *At least I have plenty of light,* he thought, conscious of his friends' concern.

"Come on, Michael," Dengler said encouragingly. "It's not as hard as it looks."

Dropping his pack to foot level as the others had done, he began inching his way through. Bits of limestone shavings from the scraping of his helmet against the walls fell onto his shoulders and arms as he slowly squeezed through the crevice.

Being fit and taller than the others, Dominic had a broad, muscular chest, which didn't serve him well in this situation. The constriction of the walls gave him trouble breathing in, a sensation that only added to the growing unease of his rib cage being clamped between two immovable slabs of rock.

"Michael, can you reach your arm out?" Lukas asked. "I'll pull you through."

Taking multiple quick mini-breaths, Dominic felt he was on the verge of passing out. *No...I know I can do this!*

"I'm okay, Lukas, thanks," he said, grimacing out the words. "*I'll make it...*"

Using his right leg as leverage, he pushed with all his strength to force his upper body through the narrow space. Making progress inch by infuriating inch, he finally got through, breaking free with a rush of release from the claustrophobic grip of the walls and landing in Lukas's waiting arms.

"See? That wasn't so bad, was it?" Dengler smiled as he moved in to hug his friend and give him encouragement.

His chest heaving between deep gulps of air, Dominic was euphoric. "Well, if that was the worst of it, I think I'll be okay. Now—on to the prize."

STRAPPING ON THEIR PACKS, the team proceeded toward, then around, the loop shown on the map, entering a large chamber with a natural open light well in the ceiling, some ten feet high and eight inches in diameter, sufficient to bathe the room in a stream of bright sunlight. Off the room there were two dead-end passages. Dengler read Ginzberg's translated instructions.

"'The reliquary is buried in the topmost of two dead-end passages...like fingers on a hand. Four stones form the reservatory.'"

"That would be this passage on the left, then," he said, pointing in its direction. They headed down the wide limestone hall.

"So, we're looking for something in the form of a receptacle, right?" Hana asked.

"Yeah," Dominic confirmed. "Simon said it was like a box, maybe a protective crevice or covered hole of some sort."

There were many rocks and boulders scattered about the wide passage, some seemingly stacked in piles, others naturally jutting out of the limestone walls. The sunlight from the adjacent room didn't quite reach back into the dead-end hall, so the team depended on their helmet LEDs for illumination.

GARY MCAVOY

"There's something over here!" Hana exclaimed. "But I'll need some help with it."

One of the apparently random stacks of rock, she observed, had a nearly hidden flat rock beneath several larger boulders. Dengler and Lukas began hoisting the topmost stones off the pile and setting them aside. Thinking of authentication and the historical record, Dominic took out his iPhone and began video recording the event. The anticipation in the room was palpable, with everyone taking an eager role in what could be one of history's greatest discoveries.

With the boulders now cleared from atop the flat stone, Lukas and Dengler each took a side of the heavy flat rock, sliding it off the other rocks on which it rested. It was now clear that this was indeed a receptacle, with three vertical flat slabs of stone forming a protective box.

Four heads bent over the opening, their lamps illuminating an ancient wooden box with iron ornamentation covering each of the eight corners, with an iron handle on each side. On its front panel, Dominic noted, was an archaic Egyptian ward lock.

The passageway fell silent as each of them looked into the faces of the others, all of them conscious of the moment, letting the discovery of whatever this was sink in. Dominic shivered as he considered what this could mean. That the puzzle map he had accidentally found in the Vatican Archives led them to this place—that this might be the legendary treasure of the Cathars as heralded in Guillaume de Sonnac's own journal—was now a formidable fact.

Hana broke the silence. "What do we do now?" she whispered.

"Why, you hand it over to us, of course," echoed a

voice with a Balkan accent from the opening of the passage.

Gasping, Hana and the others turned, looking back toward the entrance.

There, beneath the open light wells of the larger room at the end of the hall, stood Ivan Govič and three other men. Four pistols were pointed in their direction.

THIRTY

A light rain fell across Vatican City as Cardinal Dante, a small leather valise in hand, walked through the papal gardens on his way to the Government Palace and the office of the secretary of state. His aide, Father Bruno Vannucci, walked closely beside him holding an umbrella over the cardinal's head, nattering on about unimportant gossip.

The cardinal sighed. "Bruno, I couldn't care less about who's doing what to whom in the Curia right now," he said with irritation. "I'm about to negotiate the terms of Petrini's surrender and our return to the Secretariat of State. Get your head in the game, man."

Rebuked, Vannucci took a long nervous drag on the cigarette he was smoking with his other hand, then flicked the burning ember off as he pocketed the remaining filter. Littering the papal gardens with cigarette butts was forbidden, though even Dante himself did it when no one was looking.

As they entered the building, Vannucci furled the

umbrella, shook off the rain, then opened the door for His Eminence. Recognizing Dante, the stern nun at the reception desk waved a hand toward the elevator. "His Eminence is expecting you, Cardinal Dante," she said flatly in Italian. "You may go up."

"Forgive me if I don't offer you my hand, Fabrizio," Petrini said cautiously as Dante entered his office. "You left quite an impact on your last visit." Petrini looked down at his hand and the healing puncture mark. "What is it I can do for you today?"

"I bring an important matter of some personal sensitivity to you, Eminence," Dante began, feigning a sympathetic expression on his face, as if it pained him to be the bearer of bad news.

"I have come to understand," he continued, "that Father Dominic was born in your rectory when you were a parish priest in New York, and that he never learned who his real father was."

Now seated behind his desk, Petrini stiffened as Dante spoke the words, then flushed as his hands began trembling.

"And what has this to do with me?" he asked Dante in a near whisper.

"Well, Eminence, I have it on good authority that we do, in fact, know who the father was. Is there anything you have to say on the matter?"

"Stop with this cat-and-mouse nonsense, Fabrizio! What is your point?"

Dante opened his valise and withdrew the paternity report from the Genomics Molecular lab, laying the papers out in front of Petrini.

"Remarkable things can be done using DNA analysis these days, Enrico. If you will refer to the summary statement at the bottom of the page..." Dante reached over and pointed to the prescribed location on the report, "where it reads 'DNA Paternity Index 99.9998%. The conclusion confirms the subject is the biological father.'

"It may interest you to know that the 'subject' of this report is identified here as *you*, Eminence. *Your* DNA along with Father Dominic's showed an indisputable match. Michael is your son, Enrico."

Petrini paled, sitting back in his chair to absorb the impact of this stunning announcement, one he had been dreading might emerge for more than thirty years.

"You're mistaken, Dante," Petrini said, attempting a confidence he didn't quite feel. "Wherever you got your information, it's wrong."

"And yet," Dante responded, enjoying the moment, "one of Italy's preeminent DNA laboratories proves otherwise. Read more before making a fool of yourself."

Petrini scanned the documents Dante had handed him. He knew his secret was now no longer safe, especially in the hands of this psychopath.

He looked up to meet the cardinal's eyes. "You're an evil bastard, Dante. *Why* are you doing this? What good can come of it?"

Dante's return gaze hardened. "All these years you've been living a dark lie, *Cardinal* Petrini, and one of the worst kinds. The Holy Father will not look upon this matter lightly. No, not at all. In fact, he'll have no choice. You'll be 'asked' to leave the Church, and you'll lose your exalted position among the *papabile*, so you can kiss being pope goodbye."

Petrini was crushed by the allegation. By the truth of it.

His mind raced for a reaction, for something that made sense in the chaos of the moment. Again, he looked into Dante's face, a light of recognition appearing on his own.

"What kind of monster are you, Fabrizio? How dare you subject me to such intrusions! I suppose that finger-prick of a handshake last week was part of your vile plan, too? I can only imagine how creative you were to have gotten Michael's DNA as well. You *bastard!*"

"I'll admit to monstrous conduct if it makes you feel any better," Dante said. "Getting the required samples was fairly easy, actually. I went on a hunch, and it paid off— handsomely, I hope."

"You hope? What do you mean? What's in this for you?"

"Ah, now we're getting to the point of it all, I suppose," Dante said with a smug curl of his lip. "Actually, I have no intention of taking this matter to His Holiness, nor anyone else, for that matter. And young Michael need be none the wiser if you prefer it that way."

"Keep talking," Petrini demanded.

Dante leaned back in his chair, steepling his fingers as he looked out the window and up at Saint Peter's rain-glistened dome.

"I want my old job back, Enrico," he said matter-of-factly. "As secretary of state. Your job. Beyond that, I have no immediate needs."

"Meaning, I presume," Petrini began, "that you'll keep proof of this affair handy in case it's needed for future blackmail."

"I see we understand each other completely," Dante said. "You're welcome to take my place in Buenos Aires if you wish. While I do have some powerful friends there now, I would much prefer to be here where I can be more useful to Holy Mother Church. I was born for this office and all it represents."

"What if the Holy Father doesn't see it that way? It is his decision, not mine."

"I expect you to urge him to see the wisdom of such an important change, Eminence. It's not as if I'm unqualified for the position, having held it for many years before *you* stepped in. Tell him the Holy Spirit interceded, and you wish to return to your pastoral mission as archbishop of New York."

"This can be a messy affair, Fabrizio, and not one that can happen overnight."

"You should have thought of that thirty years ago, speaking of messy affairs," Dante spat. "I'm in no hurry, though I expect we should have things wrapped up in a month or so, right after the pope's South American visit, I think. Yes, that would be good timing for everyone."

Enrico Petrini stood and walked slowly to the window. Standing there, he saw in his reflection a defeated man, one who had been tested and failed. His seething anger toward Dante had given way to an unwilling acceptance of his predicament. His only concern now was to limit any backlash to him alone.

"I have one condition, Dante. And that is that Michael never finds out. I will do whatever it takes to prevent that. I will speak with His Holiness about this and recommend you as my replacement. Just leave Michael out of it."

"As you wish, Enrico," Dante said, retrieving the DNA reports from the desk. "Since we have an agreement, it need go no further. I shall make appropriate arrangements for returning to Rome in the next month.

"For now, I'll see myself out. *Buona sera*, Eminence."

CHAPTER

THIRTY-ONE

Hana shivered less from the cave's cold interior than from facing this new predicament. She turned to Dominic, whose jaw clenched with contempt for Gović and his thugs as their weapons made clear their intentions.

Gović and his men walked slowly into the hall, switching on their own helmet lights as they advanced toward the others.

"You saved us a great deal of work here, Father Dominic," the Croat said in the self-satisfied manner of someone who had just changed the dynamics of a situation. "And what is it you found, may I ask?"

Dominic stepped forward in front of the others, his arms instinctively raised in protection of his friends, as if herding them behind him.

"You have no business here, Gović," he asserted. "We are acting on behalf of the Church."

Gović's cold laughter echoed off the walls of the cavern. "So, you're saying the four of you were officially sanctioned by the Vatican to conduct an archeological dig in France seeking an object belonging to Mary Magdalene? If so, they do business quite oddly these days."

"What is it you want?" Dominic asked as Govié stopped right in front of him.

"For one thing, an eye for an eye." In a flash, Govié quickly raised his pistol and slammed the butt of it down hard on the side of Dominic's head. Dominic fell to the ground, his hand reaching for his neck as blinding pain incapacitated him.

"*Michael!*" Hana cried out, kneeling down to help him. Then looking up to Govié she said, "*Stop it!* There's no need for violence. Take what you want and leave us alone."

"Right on both counts," Govié replied. "We will take what we want, and we will leave you, as you say, alone. Tie them up."

As Govié's men circled the group, Dengler and Lukas acted instinctively.

With Victor closest, Dengler snatched the larger man's gun hand. He pushed Victor's arm up with all the force he could muster as his elbow chopped his opponent's windpipe. Momentarily stunned, Victor recovered almost instantly. Bigger and stronger than Dengler, he wrapped a powerful arm around the smaller man's neck, ensnaring him in a firm choke hold. Dengler struggled as his legs thrashed to free himself. Victor snarled at his captive for the seven seconds it took for unconsciousness to drop Karl to the ground in a heap.

During the same time, Lukas had tackled Eric, wrestling him to the ground. But as they fell Eric's gun fired. A deafening blast echoed in the cavern. The stray bullet hit Lukas's forearm; he howled in pain as he lay on the cave floor. Eric stood up, found his ground, then aimed the pistol at Lukas' head.

"NO! Stop!" Hana shouted. She rushed toward Lukas.

But Gović grabbed her, raising his pistol to her head. Dominic began to rise toward them.

"Stop, or I'll kill her now!" Gović shouted at Michael, who froze in place. Eric and Victor looked at Gović. Jean-Claude snapped his head from one quick assault to the next, pointing his gun at no one in particular, waiting to see who would emerge the victor.

As Dengler regained his senses he looked over at his partner, blood oozing from his left forearm. *"Lukas! No, no, no!!"*

Hana struggled free from Gović's hold and ran to Dengler and Lukas, kneeling next to them. "Karl, are you hurt?! Oh my God, *Lukas!*"

Tears streamed down Dengler's cheek as he held Lukas in his arms, checking the severity of the wound. "The bullet passed through your arm, thankfully."

Heedless to the guns still trained on them, Dengler snatched off his jacket, ripped the arm off and began applying pressure onto the wound. Lukas was still conscious but in obvious pain. He looked pleadingly into Karl's eyes.

"You fucking bastards!" Dengler shouted at Gović. "I swear to God you'll pay for this."

Gović and his men, now in full control, snatched all the knives from their captives—the only weapons they had—then, using plasticuffs, bound Dominic and Hana with their hands tied behind them. Then they cuffed Dengler and finally, despite his condition, Lukas.

"Why are you cuffing *him*?" Dengler shouted. "He'll do you no harm! He needs a hospital!"

Gović paid no attention as he and Victor surveyed the reliquary in its stone receptacle. "What have we here?" he asked. "Let's get this and move out. Our work here is done for the moment."

The reliquary was not heavy at all. Victor took hold of both handles on the chest, hoisting it out of its 800-year-old resting place, then set it on the cave floor.

Dominic looked at it, trying to make out as much as he could in the semi-darkness before it was taken away. It seemed smaller than a typical ossuary—some twenty inches long by twelve inches wide and fourteen inches high—but was not composed of traditional limestone, that much was clear. It was aged hardwood adorned with inlaid Byzantine ivory, by tradition suggesting its contents were deemed sacred. And it was indeed secured by an Egyptian ward lock, one that required a specific skeleton key to access it—though Dominic doubted that would stop Gović from opening it.

He then noticed a faint inscription on the front side of it, but since his helmet had fallen off in the scuffle, he couldn't aim his light at it.

"You could at least give me a better look at what it is we found here," he said to no one in particular. Gović frowned, then nodded to Jean-Claude, who obliged him by shining his own helmet lamp onto the reliquary. All Dominic really wanted was to make out that brief inscription, which he saw was in Aramaic script, and which could easily place it as far back as two thousand years. Staring at it in the cold, steady light of the lamp as he leaned in closer, he made out the block-like figures of the ancient alphabet, one by one.

Leaning back slowly, Dominic was stunned at what he had just read. His fluency in Aramaic was reliable, so there was no doubt in his mind. And if true, the enormity of what was in that reliquary could change everything.

He sat there, at once humiliated and humbled, and angry that this important discovery might end up in the hands of some private collector, or worse.

Watching his reaction closely, Govic knelt down in front of Dominic. "What is it you saw there? Something I might need to know?"

Dominic looked at him balefully. "Your guess is as good as mine."

Govic knew he wouldn't get more from the priest. "Let's get out of here," he said to the others. "Say goodbye to our new friends, comrades. *Za dom-spremni!*"

As Eric and Victor took hold of the reliquary, arguing over who should carry it, Jean-Claude said, "I'll make sure their hands are tightly bound." The others left the hall for the larger lit room, the two brothers holding the box between them, the discussion now on how to pass it through the narrow entry to this chamber.

Jean-Claude went around the room, checking each of them, but when he got to Dengler he placed one of the confiscated Swiss Army knives into his bound hands, whispering as he fidgeted with the plasticuff, "The AISI are on their way to rescue you, but stay away from the entrance. Govic is going to blow the cave and seal you in. I can't stop him alone, so you're on your own for now."

Startled by this revelation, Dengler just coughed to mask Jean-Claude's whispering.

"Let's go!" Govic shouted. "We still have work to do."

Govic and his men proceeded back through the cave to the entrance, sliding the reliquary along the floor through the narrow fissure. When they were far enough away,

Dengler snapped open the knife and worked on cutting off the plasticuffs binding his wrists.

As he did so, he whispered to the others. "Jean-Claude is with the AISI! He dropped a knife into my hands. And we now know what that voicemail meant—Govíc is going to blow up the entrance to the cave. He also said Colombo and his team are coming to rescue us. We must find a way out of here."

When his binds snapped off, he quickly cut through the plasticuffs tethering Michael and Hana, then ran to Lukas. "Are you okay for now? How bad is it?"

"It's really painful, Karl. I think I'll be fine, though I can't be of much help with this arm."

Dengler reached into his pack for the first aid kit, withdrew packs of gauze and surgical tape, and replaced the impromptu bandage with the proper pressure onto the wound. Then he kissed Lukas' forehead. "You stay strong, *mein Lieber*. I will get you out of here and we'll find proper care for this."

"What do we do now?" Dominic asked.

Dengler considered the possibilities. "Gather your things and follow me." Assisting Lukas, Dengler led them to the open room at the head of the hall and dropped his gear. He looked up at the ceiling, then down at Dominic and Hana, mentally calculating the situation. He then knelt and opened his backpack, pulling out a long coil of orange rope and a small pickaxe, then pocketed a few carabiners and anchors.

"If Govíc is using explosives to blast the cave entrance, then that way's not an option for us. We're going to try to open up this light well and get out that way.

"Michael, I'll need you to hoist me onto your shoulders and hold me there for a while until I can pick away at the opening to widen it. Thankfully it's not very high. Hana, stay out of the way from falling debris, but standby with this rope when I need it, okay?"

"Anything you say, Karl," she replied. "Thank God for the Swiss Army."

"These bastards have no idea what Swiss revenge is like," Dengler muttered. "But they're going to find out. Ready, Michael?"

"Come on up, Karl," Dominic said as he sturdied himself. He placed his hands behind his back, gripping them tightly. Dengler placed his foot into the cradled hands and boosted himself atop Dominic's shoulders, his legs around his neck, giving him just the height he needed to start picking away at the light well with the axe.

The hole itself was about eight inches in diameter and ten inches in depth, surrounded by a solid mixture of rock and packed soil, but the sharp pickaxe made good work of it. Chunks of stone and dirt fell onto Dominic's head, now gratefully protected by the helmet, as Dengler continued chopping away.

Twenty minutes later the hole was large enough to accommodate a man's girth, but not much more.

"Okay, Michael, now I'm going to stand on your shoulders and hoist myself up through the hole. How are you holding up?"

"I'm good, Karl, but it's a good thing you don't weigh much more. Let's get this done with. We have to get that reliquary back."

"Hana?" Dengler asked. "Can you toss me the rope?"

Hana grabbed the coiled line and handed it to her cousin, who placed it over his head and around his neck.

Strapping the pickaxe to his belt, Dengler carefully shifted his position on Dominic's shoulders as the latter

helped guide his legs to a bent-over standing position.
Reaching for the ceiling to help stabilize him, Dengler
reached through the hole and, positioning his arms on
either side outside the hole, heaved himself up and
through. He disappeared for a few moments, then stuck
his head back over the hole, smiling at his three friends
waiting below as he took a moment to catch his breath.

"Okay, I'm going to fasten a rope up here so we can get
you out. Don't go anywhere."

Dominic looked at Hana blankly. "As if we have a
choice," he said, chuckling. Hana was sitting next to
Lukas, making sure he was comfortable, rechecking the
wound and applying more pressure to the wrapped gauze
pack. The wound seemed stable for now.

Topside, Dengler had found a solid boulder around
which he had knotted a rock anchor. He pulled on it with
all his weight to make sure it was secure, then, measuring
assumed distances back down to the cave floor, fastened
several bowlines on a bight to act as footholds in the length
of rope, forming a makeshift ladder. Lastly, he attached a
carabiner below the bowline to lift their packs through.
Then he tossed the rope into the hole.

"Michael, first attach all the packs together top to
bottom and secure them to the carabiner at the base of the
rope. We'll bring those up first."

Dominic did as instructed and Dengler pulled the
packs out with little effort.

"Now let's bring Hana out, so she can help me bring
Lukas up."

Hana looked at Lukas, ruffled his hair, and said, "See
you up there in a few minutes."

Walking toward the ladder, she looked at Dominic.
"What have we gotten ourselves into this time?" He

reached out and pulled her into a strong embrace, which she gladly returned.

"Let's get you up there," he said, his hands readying both her shoulders.

Hana stepped into the first loop, then the second, and before long, her head was sticking through the hole of the light well. Dengler grabbed beneath her arms and hoisted her up onto the ground. Then he leaned back over the hole and looked into Dominic's face.

"Michael, be very careful with Lukas, okay?"

"Precious cargo, on its way," Dominic said cheerfully. He lifted Lukas up gently. "How are you feeling, buddy?"

"Humiliated," the soldier said simply. "It was stupid of me to try to grab that gun."

"You only did what you were trained to do. We were outnumbered by trained military goons with weapons. Don't blame yourself."

Dominic helped Lukas get a foothold, then guided him up, since the Swiss Guard only had one useful arm. But he was strong and determined and made it to the top. From there Dengler took one side of him as Hana took the other, and together they lifted him to the surface. Dengler hugged him fiercely, then helped him to a large rock he could sit on while they got Dominic out.

"Last man standing," Dengler said, looking down at his friend.

Dominic looked around the cave to make sure they'd gotten everything. He took one long last look at the hall where they had found the reliquary, sighed, then stepped into the knotted foothold.

Just as he did the entire cave shook violently as an explosion rumbled throughout the chambers. As seismic debris bombarded him, Dominic fell to the ground.

CHAPTER

THIRTY-TWO

A s the Fiat pulled away, Ivan Gović looked back at the high plume of smoke billowing out from where the cave entrance used to be, a satisfied grin on his face. He could now tell his mother that his father's death had been avenged, with the bonus of having captured what could be a vital religious artifact—an ancient reliquary which now lay hidden under a tarp in the truck's cargo bed. His smile faded as he heard the faint but increasing "whup-whup" blade slap of a helicopter.

A CHOPPER APPROACHING from the south began hovering over the blast site as three police vehicles converged on the town of Périllos in a symphony of blues and twos. A BRI sniper armed with an MK14 Enhanced Battle Rifle and Steiner binoculars sat in the open doorway of the chopper, surveying the area. Spotting a truck pulling away from the scene at high speed, he radioed his observation to ground forces in the Sûreté vehicles.

From his own SUV, AISI director-general Massimo Colombo instructed the chopper, along with the two other vehicles escorting him, to stay in pursuit of Govič's truck while he drove on to the cave site. He gritted his teeth as he watched the deadly smoke rise higher in the sky.

~

BURIED by fallen earth and rocks loosened by the explosion, Dominic saw nothing but blackness. In a terrifying moment of panic, he tried moving to get a feeling of how much debris he was entombed under, if escape was possible—or if this was how he would die.

His arm now free, he cleared the dirt from around his face. Then he saw light. He pushed back the fear.

Shrugging off the debris surrounding him, relieved that he'd been wearing his helmet, he pushed himself up. The hole of the light well had now opened even wider.

"Are you alright, Michael?" Dengler shouted down to him.

Dominic took a deep breath. "Yeah, I'm okay. Is that rope still secured up there?"

Dengler rechecked the fastness of his anchor. "Yes, still good here. Come on up before anything else collapses."

Dominic planted each foot carefully into the bowline loops as he made his way up the improvised ladder. Once he reached the top, Dengler grabbed his hand and pulled him up to safety. The two embraced in relief, then Dengler went back to attend to Lukas.

In the distance, Hana had heard the two-toned sirens of emergency vehicles, and based on what Jean-Claude had told Karl, she figured that must be Colombo and his team. She pulled her phone out of her backpack and called the director, hoping it was indeed he who had arrived. Colombo answered on the first ring.

"Hana! Are you and your friends safe? Are you still in the cave?"

"Max! It's so good to hear your voice. Yes, we made it out just in time," she said. "But we need an ambulance, or at least a fast way to a hospital. One of our friends was shot by Gović's men. He's stable but needs immediate medical attention."

"Where are you now?" he asked.

"I'm not really sure. But I heard your sirens so we're not far. Hold on a moment…" She turned to her cousin. "Karl, how far and in which direction would you say we are from the cave entrance?"

Dengler looked around the landscape and noticed the helicopter hover at some distance then head in the opposite direction.

"We're maybe a quarter of a kilometer east of the chopper's current position," he said.

Colombo had overheard Dengler's report to Hana.

"Stay where you are, Hana. I'll have the chopper come get all of you."

"Thanks, Max. I owe you one." She ended the call.

Colombo radioed the pilot to turn around and head east, watching for four people in the brush, then to pick them up and take them to Centre Hospitalier de Perpignan.

As they watched the helicopter turn around and head back in their direction, Dominic stripped off his shirt and began waving it so the pilot could better find them. Dengler found a fairly flat area nearby and led the group to it, supporting Lukas around his waist as they walked.

Spotting Dominic's shirt flag, the helo pilot made his

way to their location, then descended to the landing area Dengler was pointing at. On touching down, the soldier in the gunner's seat jumped out to help bring Lukas aboard. With everyone now strapped in, the chopper lifted off and made its way to the hospital in Perpignan.

As Dominic began putting his shirt back on, Lukas remarked, "No need to do that on my account, Michael."

"Nor mine," said Hana, smiling bashfully.

"Hey, what about me?!" Dengler added.

They all laughed as Dominic blushed.

"Good to see you're still frisky, Lukas," he said. "But the show's over. I'll just be glad to get far away from this cave and caving altogether."

~

THE BLACK FIAT FULLBACK had a long head start on any chasing police vehicles potentially dispatched by that chopper. As they sped northeast on D9—the opposite direction of where the helicopter was now heading—Gović was confident they'd lost their pursuers.

Still, to be safe, he instructed Victor to pull off at Port Fitou on the Mediterranean, where they could hide out for a while. They parked in front of an unremarkable seaside bistro where, while they took in a late lunch of fresh local prawns and beer, they could keep an eye on their cargo.

CHAPTER

THIRTY-THREE

While Lukas was being treated in the emergency room, Dengler paced the hospital's waiting area as Dominic and Hana sat talking with Agent Colombo.

"If it hadn't been for Jean-Claude, we could all be still stuck in that cave now," Hana said to the intelligence director after explaining the events of the previous hours.

"He is one of our best undercover agents," Colombo said, "and we've been working a long time on this Ustasha operation and Gović's actions.

"Fortunately, he was able to help save you, and even though we lost track of that truck, we still have our mole in Gović's organization, and we'll know whatever he plans to do with your artifact. But I'm a little more concerned about his relationship with this Vatican explosives expert in the Swiss Guard, Sergeant Koehl."

"Do you think Dieter had something to do with the bomb?" Hana asked.

"Actually," Dominic said, "someone left Karl a

186

voicemail message trying to warn us about Govič, but we didn't get it in time, and what we did get was too garbled to make out. Plus, the caller's number was concealed. Who would have known about Govič and the bomb? Think Karl should talk with Dieter about it?"

"You can be assured *we* will be speaking with Sergeant Koehl on the matter, Father Dominic," Colombo asserted. "This appears to be more than coincidental.

"By the way, may I ask what was in this reliquary you found? How important is it?"

With some eagerness, Hana began to explain. "We think it was—"

"Actually," Dominic interrupted, glancing at her, "we don't really know. We had only just discovered it based on some clues I found in the Vatican archives, though none of us understand what's really inside the box. But it's critical that we get it back from Govič—untampered with, if possible. It could be extremely important for the Church."

"Perhaps Jean-Claude can be of assistance there. When he makes contact again, I'll stress the gravity of the reliquary staying intact. As you can understand, the situation could be fluid, so it's difficult to know what he'll be able to do."

"We'd be very grateful, Max, thank you," Dominic said. Colombo left them as a physician came up to speak to Karl.

"LUKAS WAS INCREDIBLY LUCKY," Dengler told Dominic and Hana after speaking with the attending physician. "The bullet passed through the forearm muscle without hitting bone or tendons and he should heal up in a few weeks, though he'll be off duty for some time. Now I just have to explain all this to our commander. That won't be fun, especially now that the AISI is involved."

"Well," Dominic suggested, "just tell him we encountered some rough locals while caving and leave it at that. Colombo will handle his part of it discreetly, I'm sure, though your friend Dieter is likely to come under harsh light through his affiliation with Gović.

"By the way, I'd prefer that you not mention anything about the reliquary yet, at least until we get a better handle on things."

"Of course," Dengler replied. "But I do want to be there when we track down that sonofabitch."

"I know what you mean, Karl," Dominic said, "but we need to be smart about it. Gović probably assumes we didn't make it out of the cave, so that could work in our favor."

"Well, for now I'm going to stay overnight here with Lukas. Hospital staff are very accommodating and are arranging for me to sleep on a cot in his room. Are you and Hana heading back to Rome?"

"Not without you, we aren't! No, we'll find a hotel and camp out there for the night. We won't return until Lukas is able to be moved. I'll make the necessary calls to the Vatican. See you for breakfast in the morning."

~

HAVING FOUND a suitable hotel near the hospital in Perpignan, Dominic called Enrico Petrini, saying they had run into car trouble in France—and other events which he'd explain later—and asking him to clear Karl and Lukas's truancy with the commander of the Swiss Guard, as well as informing Brother Mendoza of his own absence. They would all return in another day or so.

For the first time since the helicopter picked them up, Dominic and Hana were alone, and starving. Neither had brought much in the way of a change of clothes, but they changed into what they had then headed to the hotel's bistro for a late dinner of sole meunière with lentil salad and a chilled bottle of Côte d'Or Chardonnay.

As the wine took its desired effect, both of them wound down from the extraordinary events of the day, when the conversation turned to the reliquary.

"Have any idea how we're going to get it back, Michael?" Hana asked.

"Not yet. But since you're the puzzle master, I'm sure you'll come up with some brilliant scheme sooner or later…

"I'm more concerned with what Govíc plans to do with it," Dominic continued, his brow knitted with concern. "He'll most likely try to fence it on the black market, and if that happens, we might never see it again. Antiquities smuggling is a huge trade in Italy, and that artifact will likely fetch an obscene price. The upside for us is that it will also bring notoriety, for objects of this rarity don't stay anonymous for long. We need to find someone connected to Rome's underworld who might hear of such an item being offered."

Hana poked at her salad, her thoughts turning back to their discovery of the 'reservatory' and the sacred object within, then of their capture by Govíc and his men.

"Jean-Claude's timely appearance was a nice surprise," she noted. "I hope he can somehow prevent Govíc from losing it to the black market.

"By the way, I've been meaning to ask—what was it

you saw inscribed on the side of the reliquary? Anything important?"

Dominic set down his fork, dabbed a napkin to his mouth, then feigned casualness as he looked her in the eyes. "Oh, that. Yes, I forgot to mention—it read, '*Sarah, daughter of Yeshua and Mariam.*'"

CHAPTER

THIRTY-FOUR

H ana's fork clattered onto the bone china plate as it fell, her mouth opening in slack-jawed astonishment.

"I can't believe you didn't bring this up earlier!" she whispered, as the few other dining patrons glanced in their direction. *"Sarah, daughter of Jesus and Mary?!"*

"There was no time until now!" Dominic whispered back defensively. "And it only makes the situation that much worse anyway. All this time we presumed it contained the bones of Christ! But if the inscription truly does reveal the contents as being that of *Sarah*, well, that puts an entirely different light on things—though either way it's a shattering notion."

"Jesus had a daughter?!" Hana exclaimed, still in shock. "How does Sarah fit into the picture?"

"While Scripture doesn't mention this, oral tradition—and I must stress, these are only legends—has it that Mary Magdalene was pregnant at the time Christ was crucified. Three months later she bore a female child named Sarah, the Hebrew name for 'princess,' which would certainly be appropriate for the King of the Jews. Legend further tells us that Sarah was born in Egypt, which is distinctly possible since Israeli Jews whose safety was in jeopardy often sought asylum in Alexandria.

"At the time, Israel was under Roman occupation, and it would have been extremely dangerous for Mary to have been known as the wife of Jesus, much less that he had offspring. That sacred knowledge would have been protected at all costs by Christ's followers.

"One day, many years after the Crucifixion, a group of Jews in Jerusalem cast Magdalene and her siblings—Martha and Lazarus, along with Joseph of Arimathea and others, *and* a 'young maid' to Mary named Sarah—adrift in the Mediterranean, in a rudderless boat without oars or sails, expecting them to perish at sea. But in what many consider a miracle, the boat eventually washed ashore at the tip of southern Gaul, just northwest of Marseilles in France."

Hana was transfixed by Dominic's elaborate rendering of a tale she knew nothing about. Her journalist's mind was buzzing with details, seeking to make sense of this new information. She was trained to seek substantiation, validation, and yet she felt out of her depths with all she had just heard.

"What about the Magdalene's own papyrus, the one we found last year?" she asked. "She specifically stated that she'd brought a reliquary with her to France, one carrying the remains of her husband, Jesus. So where is that now?

"Yes," Dominic agreed, "where *is* that now? There aren't many times in my life where I've felt truly helpless, but these last twenty-four hours have been a real awakening. I don't know where to turn at this point."

"What about Simon?" Hana suggested. "Is there anything he might help us with?"

"Well, I do intend to discuss all this with him, of course. That would be best done in his office, or anywhere outside the Vatican. I'll get in touch with him when we get back.

"Meanwhile, let's turn in for the night and see what Lukas's condition is in the morning. Hopefully, he's well enough to travel. We need to get back to Rome as soon as possible."

It was unseasonably warm in Perpignan the next morning as Dengler, Hana and Dominic leisured over a late breakfast on the terrace of their hotel overlooking the Têt River. The manicured lawns along the banks of the river extended for miles in both directions, testament to the pride of the town's citizens who cherished their heritage on the Roussillon plain.

"Lukas is being released at noon, so we can head back then," Dengler said, taking a sip of espresso in one hand as he clumsily juggled a fresh, buttered croissant with the other. "There will be some scarring, but thankfully no permanent damage."

It was clear to Hana her cousin had probably stayed up most of the night watching Lukas, caring for him in ways only a loving partner could.

"Let me be first to drive, Karl. It's a lovely day for a road trip and you could use the rest."

"Deal," he replied. "We should head back to the hospital now and get Lukas ready for transport. The first thing I want to do when we get back is to have a chat with Dieter Koehl. I'd like to know if he had a hand in our little adventure. I don't much like the idea of him being pals with Gović."

"I think you'll find the AISI has the same goal, Karl," Dominic said. "Max is quite keen on interviewing Dieter himself. I'll be curious to see where that leads."

WHILE HANA and Dominic fueled up the Jeep Wrangler for their return trip, Dengler checked Lukas out of the hospital, pushing his wheelchair to the waiting room windows.

"Really, Karl, you can stop fussing over me now. We're both tough commandos and have to work through these things, right? I'm fine, honestly. The bullet didn't hit bone or an artery, it was only a flesh wound."

"You'll be fine when I say you're fine," Dengler pushed back. "Besides, you have to get your strength back soon so together we can take on those bastards who did this to you."

With the Jeep now loaded up with everyone's gear, Hana pulled the car up to the hospital entrance. Dominic helped settle Lukas in the back seat with Karl, took the wheelchair back into the building, and returned, jumping into the shotgun seat.

"Let's hit it!" he said, aiming an arm toward the Autoroute.

CHAPTER

THIRTY-FIVE

Among the more respectable antiquities dealers in all of Rome, Vincenzo Tucci was a quiet, portly man, with a veal-white complexion made all the more spectral by a severe case of alopecia. Not even a hint of hair appeared on his face or head, and the lack of eyebrows and lashes gave him the one advantage of looking far younger than his seventy-five years, though it often earned longer than polite stares from the otherwise well-mannered set of affluent clients who entered his shop on the Via del Governo Vecchio.

Tucci was known throughout Italy as an expert in Etruscan art. His shop was packed with statues, bronzes, vases, jewelry, glass objects and numerous other fine antiquities appealing to discerning collectors worldwide, who often called for right of first refusal on especially rare and previously unseen artifacts that might fall into his hands.

But Vincenzo Tucci also wore another, lesser-known hat atop his bald pate—that of *capo zona* to the *tombaroli* of

Rome—the regional head of black market tomb raiders, whose work often kept Tucci busier than his legitimate business. He possessed a keen eye for ethical loopholes which had, up to now, kept him at arm's length from legal complications.

As it has been for generations, the black market for antiquities in Italy is a thriving enterprise. Long before artists of the Renaissance began producing renowned works on canvas and marble, artisans of ancient Greece and other old-world cultures before the common era spawned industries turning out works of stone and bronze, of terracotta pottery and marble vases. And while much of this heritage had found its way to museums, it had long been presumed that private collectors owned by far the vast majority of works, much of which possessed dubious legal provenance.

The *tombaroli* maintained a distinctly secret list of potential fences for items they acquired, and befitting his role as *capo zona*, Tucci usually got the first call when anything of particular intrigue came on the market. And he had the singular resources to whom he could turn for authenticating or effectuating the sale of such an item.

Extreme care had to be taken with these arrangements, naturally, for Italy has a proud tradition of protecting its cultural heritage, and penalties for trafficking in stolen antiquities are severe.

Leading this perennial effort is Italy's *Tutela Patrimonio Culturale*, a special unit of the Italian *Carabinieri* informally known as the Art Squad. Housed in a four-story baroque palazzo on the Piazza Sant'Ingazio—across from the Jesuit Church of St. Ignatius, with its magnificent Pozzo trompe l'oeil frescoes—the Art Squad is headed by Colonel Benito Scarpelli, a precise and orderly man in his sixties who, before the current post he has held for some twenty years, worked as curator for antiquities at Sotheby's in London. Scarpelli knew his world well, and his path had often crossed that of Vincenzo Tucci's.

In fact, Scarpelli had established a permanent wiretap on Tucci's phones, one that was well worth renewing every fifteen days as mandated by Italian law.

~

WHILE CARDINAL DANTE had returned to Buenos Aires following the end of the papal consistory, Ivan Govíc had decided to stay on in Rome for a while longer, declining the cardinal's generous offer of a free flight back to Argentina. There was work to be done before Govíc could return to his home and family.

It hadn't taken much effort at all to open the wooden chest they had taken from the cave before sealing the fate of Father Dominic and his friends. But since he planned to find a fence to sell it, Govíc needed to open the reliquary with great care, calling upon the services of an associate who specialized in safe cracking, and whose favored hobby went by the curious name of locksport.

The ancient warded lock gave little resistance as the craftsman worked with his collection of old skeleton keys, filing away all but two teeth on one full key blade until, when slid through the keyway, the wards lined up with the grooves in the newly-fashioned key, allowing entry to the lock cylinder without causing any damage to the ancient device itself. After turning the key, the lock clicked open.

As he started to lift the top of the object, Govíc placed his hand on it.

"I would prefer to open it myself, thanks." The man handed Gović the skeleton key.

Thanking him for his time, Gović paid the man and saw him out, then returned to open the reliquary and inspect its contents in the seclusion of his hotel room.

But what he found puzzled him.

CHAPTER

THIRTY-SIX

Dominic was grateful to be back in Rome, in the safety of the Vatican and the comfort of his beloved Archives for two reasons. First, Colombo believed Gović was on the run and no danger to Michael or his friends. He also assured Michael that the AISI had Gović in their sights and would capture him soon.

The other reason was, despite caving being Dengler's passion, his friend's rabid encouragement that Father Michael Dominic be included had run its course. He'd rather stay here and study, taking in the pleasures of his adopted city by running its colorful, bustling streets every morning. That would be enough adventure for a man more suited to reading than squeezing through limestone crevices or having guns pointed at him.

As usual, he found Simon Ginzberg deep in research in the Pio Reading Room. The old man was bent over the table, inspecting Guillaume de Sonnac's military orders from the Albigensian Crusade to the Seventh Crusade, his attention deeply focused on the battles of Damietta and Al Mansurah in Egypt—the papers Dominic had mentioned earlier to the scholar which had yet to be explored.

"*Buongiorno*, Simon," he said, taking a seat opposite his friend.

"Michael! So good to see you again." Ginzberg set down his pencil and stretched his arms behind his back.

"Sorry, but I don't have much time right now, and here isn't the place for this discussion anyway," Dominic said, his expression revealing excitement, "but we need to speak soon. Much has happened in the past couple of days that you will absolutely want to hear about."

"Well, as always, my young friend, you have my complete attention. How about tonight, my office at the university?"

"That works for me. Hana may be joining us if she's available. We just returned from France and have much to tell."

"Did you find what you were looking for, Michael?" Ginzberg asked in a whisper. "Was the reliquary there?"

Dominic looked around the room before answering, then whispered back, "Yes, we found a reliquary, but not the one we expected to find, something else entirely—but then we lost it. It's a long story, but we'll tell you more tonight."

Ginzberg closed his eyes and let out a long sigh. "These are the moments that try one's patience."

"Yes, but now you have something profound to look forward to! And I swear, it will be a story worth the telling. See you tonight."

∾

DOMINIC HAD BORROWED Dengler's Jeep for the evening, picked up Hana at her hotel, then drove to Zagarolo on the outskirts of Rome and on to Teller University, Rome's leading Jewish academy. Students were still milling about the campus at sunset, with a devout cluster of Hasidim reciting the Amidah as they stood around a reflecting pool, some moving their bodies back and forth, others lightly bouncing in spiritual contemplation, all holding prayerbooks.

Parking near the Caprioli Palace, Dominic and Hana headed inside to Dr. Ginzberg's office on the top floor, where he was just finishing up counseling a student.

"My dear Hana, what a delight to see you again," the old man said eagerly as he welcomed both of them into his small office. "I hear you've had quite the adventure, though I don't have a clue yet as to what it entailed."

Hana glanced at Dominic with a look of expectancy. Simon's eyes followed hers, as they both turned to the priest to begin telling the story.

"I guess that's my cue," Dominic said with a slight smile.

As they all took seats, he began by reminding Simon of the puzzle map he'd found, and of his later being mugged outside the Vatican wall and his attackers taking the backpack that held the map and his other notes. Ginzberg was deeply disturbed by such behavior, cursing the scoundrels as Dominic related the episode.

"Though we had little to go on at the time, we did suspect Ivan Gov*ć* to be behind the theft. Ivan is the son of Ustasha leader Petrov Gov*ć*, whom you'll recall from last year's episode in that warehouse when Hana was kidnapped, and who we were warned might be looking to take revenge on us for his father's killing."

"Yes, a sordid affair that ended well," Ginzberg noted with satisfaction.

Dominic continued apprising Simon of their trip through the cave, of finding the reliquary, and of the unforeseen intercession by Gović and his men.

"There we were, Simon, in the middle of what should have been an awe-filled moment, just about to extract the reliquary when, all of a sudden, we were prisoners! Our friend Lukas got shot in a scuffle, and Gović took the reliquary, leaving us tied up and doomed to die in a cave he was about to blow up.

"Fortunately, one of the men was a mole for the AISI and helped us escape. If not for that, we might not be here talking with you now."

"God be praised for that! But back to the reliquary, Michael," Ginzberg said impatiently. "Tell me more about it."

"We didn't have enough time to really examine it," Hana interjected. "But Michael should tell you what he found."

Nearly holding his breath with anticipation, Ginzberg eagerly turned back to Dominic.

The priest leaned forward in his chair, clasping his hands in front of him. He patiently described the appearance: its dimensions, the composition, the inlaid Byzantine ivory denoting sacredness, the Egyptian ward lock. "Simon, there was also an Aramaic epigraph on the side, much like those we've seen on ossuaries identifying whose remains lie within.

"And the epigraph read, '*Sarah, daughter of Yeshua and Mariam.*'"

Ginzberg leaned back slowly in his old wooden chair,

stunned at the unexpected disclosure. Apart from the creaking of the chair, silence filled the cramped room.

"Well, I was hardly anticipating that," the scholar muttered, a distant look in his eyes. "So, the legends might be true after all."

Dominic nodded. "That's what I thought, too."

"Which leaves us with yet another question, though," Ginzberg added. "Where is the Christ reliquary Magdalene spoke of in her papyrus?"

Dominic shrugged his shoulders. "I don't have a clue—yet. But our immediate goal is to try to find *this* reliquary before it ends up on the black market. Call it a hunch, but I'm sure that's what Gović would be planning."

"It's a good hunch, Michael. I agree," Ginzberg said, stroking his Van Dyke in thought. "I'll put out some feelers of my own. If anyone is shopping something this extraordinary, it's possible someone in my world will hear about it. From my experience, though, we won't have much time. These things tend to move rather quickly on the black market."

"Thanks, Simon, I was hoping you might have some influence in this."

"I am intrigued by this 'new' Sarah reliquary. We *must* find it, Michael. It is incredibly important."

"It is my only priority now, Simon. That and bringing Gović to justice. I'm not sure what Agent Colombo is waiting for, but I hope his operation comes to a close soon."

"Well, as for what you intend to do with Mister Gović, I leave you with a Yiddish proverb: 'Rejoice not at your enemy's fall—but don't rush to pick him up either.'"

"Hah! Duly noted, thanks."

After exchanging goodbyes, Dominic and Hana left Ginzberg's office.

"Are you free for dinner, Michael?"

"I was hoping you'd ask that!" he said. "I'm starved."

Returning to the Rome Cavalieri hotel, Hana reserved a table at La Pergola, and they spent the next hour in the Tiepolo Lounge, planning their next moves.

THIRTY-SEVEN

Vincenzo Tucci had, of course, seen many of the finest antiquities come through the doors of his gallery over the years. Apart from his expertise in Etruscan artifacts, he had developed an educated eye for objects from other cultures and eras, and though he always welcomed opportunities to find buyers for even the most exquisite of items, he was rarely moved by what he had seen, considering even the rarest objects as more or less simply commodities. He left the practice of fawning over such collectibles to his clients.

But when Ivan Gović set down the ancient reliquary on the spacious wooden table in Tucci's private back room, even he gasped on beholding it.

Though questions for establishing provenance were routine when it came to buying and selling legitimate objects, there were times when questions could not—or should not—be asked and answered. Yet, he couldn't resist in this case.

GARY MCAVOY

"Where did you find such an extraordinary object?" he asked.

Govič responded warily. "Um…in a remote cave in France. I am told it had been buried there for eight hundred years, and apparently, it has some relationship to Mary Magdalene."

Tucci was startled at hearing the venerable saint's name. "And how do you know these things?" the dealer asked, his eyes wide with amazement as he opened the reliquary and inspected its contents.

Govič then reached into his backpack and extracted the Vesconte puzzle map, along with Ginzberg's translation of the Guillaume de Sonnac journals. "These may answer your question," he said, laying the items on the table.

Tucci's gaze moved slowly from the reliquary to the map. He took hold of it, examining the intricate design, the clever construction, and then, picking up a magnifying glass from the table, he read the tiny print revealing its maker as 'Pietro Vesconte.' He well knew Vesconte's legendary work with medieval maps, which alone helped serve as convincing provenance for both artifacts.

"The map is what led us to find the reliquary," Govič noted, picking up Guillaume de Sonnac's pages. "And here you will find descriptions of the reliquary's history. I don't exactly know where these came from, but they accompanied the map."

Tucci examined the modern documents, leaning toward a clearer understanding of what he might be dealing with.

"I'll need some time to evaluate these materials, then make some calls to help establish authenticity. Are you in any particular hurry?"

"The sooner, the better," Govič said.

"Meanwhile, for your consideration should we come to

206

some understanding, there are two ways we might work together," Tucci began explaining. "One of them is consignment, where—"

"I would rather this not be a matter of public record," Gović interrupted. "I would prefer that it be completely confidential in all respects, if you understand my meaning. I looked into you and your business before coming here, Vincenzo. I have associates in the *tombaroli* community, and you come highly recommended for such discreet affairs which certain objects might require."

Tucci's demeanor changed from perfunctory to cautious. He carefully considered the stakes.

"I will, of course, insist on the name of your associate in this community you mention," Tucci said. "For obvious reasons, as you did with me, I must verify the bona fides of people I do business with."

"My contact in the *tombaroli* is Alfredo Moretti. He'll vouch for me."

"Yes, I know Fredo. Rest assured; I'll be contacting him. Until then, kindly keep our transaction private, consistent with your own wishes, and do not mention my name to anyone."

"Of course. And I'll expect the same of you."

AFTER GOVIĆ LEFT HIS SHOP, Vincenzo Tucci locked the door and turned out the lights of the front gallery. Returning to the back room, he reopened the reliquary for a better look at what it contained.

He found bones—a small skull and a pair of hands, both left and right, as well as several pieces of jewelry and a vial of myrrh, a traditional burial spice symbolizing suffering and affliction—along with an aged parchment written in what appeared to be Koine Greek, a brief page of text filled with ancient symbols.

He also noted the epigraph on the outside front panel and took a photo of it, along with photos of everything else Gović had brought him.

He then picked up the telephone, calling a private mobile number in Russia.

"*Da*?" the voice answered.

"Good evening, Mister Zharkov, this is Vincenzo Tucci in Rome. I have an incredible object here that may be of particular interest to you—an ancient reliquary of major biblical significance. We're going through the preliminary validation processes now. By any chance will you be in Italy soon? I assure you it will be worth your while."

There was a long pause. "I'm afraid that will not be possible, Vincenzo," Zharkov said. "Italy has revoked my ability to obtain visa. I have been banned from entering country for some time now, sadly, owing to some past dealings there.

"But I assure you, based on my respect for your discerning eye in such matters, that my interest is strong. Please continue with your process, and we can discuss how to proceed from there. In meantime, can you send me photos of what it is you have?"

"Of course, signore," Tucci said excitedly. "You shall have them by email shortly."

CHAPTER

THIRTY-EIGHT

Dmitry Zharkov's penthouse, located on the top floor of the fifty-eight-story Imperia Tower on Moscow's Golden Mile, ranked among the city's most prestigious real estate. And its most secure.

Situated near the Zachatevsky monastery with views of the Kremlin and the radiant, brightly-colored domes of Saint Basil's Cathedral, the Moskva-City penthouse—for it was just one of several he owned in the world—housed part of Zharkov's vast collection. This included Russian iconography, early works of Picasso, Braque and Matisse, exquisite vases and stone dragon turtles from the Ming Dynasty, and so-called "trophy" artworks seized by the Nazis during the war, which were technically the legal property of the Russian Federation—though little was denied close friends of the Russian president. He had also just acquired his third Fabergé egg, of which only fifty-seven were known to exist.

As one of Russia's wealthiest oligarchs, Dmitry Maksimovitch Zharkov ranked among the aristocracy of collectors, and little stood in the way of his getting what he wanted. Money was hardly a consideration. But he had a particular taste for objects that were, for the sake of little more than bragging rights among his peers, impossible to obtain through legitimate channels.

His latest passion was the acquisition of objects from the Holy Land: ancient religious artifacts, Bronze Age pottery, rare Etruscan busts … prized treasures the world's most prestigious museums could only dream of obtaining.

Zharkov's elite standing in the world of antiquities collections was well-known by prominent dealers in major international markets, not to mention leading traffickers in global black-market operations—and this is often where the most desirable objects were to be found. Zharkov didn't much care, either way.

When he got the call from Vincenzo Tucci, among his more reliable purveyors, Zharkov knew that whatever Tucci was offering would be of the highest pedigree and likely something so excessively rare it merited a late-night call to his personal cell phone.

Complicating things, though, Dmitry Zharkov was persona non grata in Italy, thanks to the Art Squad banning him from ever entering the country again based on his well-known shady dealings in stolen antiquities. But he had no need to personally enter the country anyway, for Zharkov always had ways of getting what he wanted. He even had a well-placed mole deep inside Interpol, who often passed on classified knowledge crucial to the oligarch's acquisition operations.

There were few things more intoxicating in life, Zharkov believed, than owning exquisite, one-of-a-kind rarities that no one else could ever possess.

And Tucci now had his full attention.

CHAPTER

THIRTY-NINE

" I assume you know why you're here, Sergeant Koehl?" Massimo Colombo sat across the table from Dieter Koehl in Interview Room 2 at AISI headquarters, accompanied by that agency's specialist in bombs and military ordnance. The room was hot, made more so by the hanging overhead light above the table and no vents for air conditioning.

"I honestly have no idea," Koehl said defensively. "The *poliziotto* who picked me up only said it was a matter of national security."

"Do you know a man named Ivan Gović?"

Tiny beads of sweat began forming on Koehl's upper lip as he heard the name of his Ustasha comrade.

"Yes, I know Ivan. Why?"

"How long have you known him, and what is the nature of your relationship?" Colombo asked quietly.

"I don't recall when or where we met," Koehl said, "but it was some time ago. We're not especially close if that's what you mean."

"I understand you are an expert in demolition, is that correct? That you know your way around bombs from your time in Afghanistan?"

"That's right. I served in Army Reconnaissance Detachment 10 with the Swiss Army before I became a Swiss Guard. May I ask what this is all about?"

Colombo considered his next words carefully.

"We have reason to believe that Signor Govié recently used a bomb, a plastique device to be exact, to carry out a criminal act in the south of France. Do you know anything about such a bomb?"

Koehl's composure started to crack. All at once, he felt he had been used, exploited for nefarious purposes, his worst fears now confirmed about what he had inadvertently done for ostensibly good reasons.

"Agent Colombo, I had no idea whatsoever that was what Govié had intended for the plastique I prepared for him," Koehl said, a flurry of words now pouring out of him. "He told me it was to be used on a farm outside Rome, for the removal of a large boulder on his cousin's farm. I swear I had no involvement in whatever sinful acts he carried out with it. You must believe me! I have a wife and daughter and would never put them or myself in jeopardy!"

The interrogation continued for another hour, with Koehl, now sweating profusely as he roasted in the small room, nearly breaking down in tears at certain points while distancing himself from Govié time and again.

"Thank you for your candor, Sergeant," Colombo concluded. "You are free to go. Please say nothing about our meeting to Signor Govié should you encounter him again. We will attend to him ourselves."

. . .

"HIS STORY CHECKS OUT with what Jean-Claude told us," Colombo said to his colleague as they returned to their offices. "Koehl was, in fact, told that the bomb was to be used on the farm. I don't think his conscience would accept knowing participation in what Govic really intended it for. We can clear him for now.

"It's time to set up the sting on Govic, though. Get the team together tomorrow morning to start planning the operation. Call Benny Scarpelli at the Art Squad and have him join us. The stolen reliquary now puts this within his purview as well."

LEAVING THE AISI BUILDING, Dieter Koehl had worked himself into a blind fury over Ivan Govic. He'd been such a fool, betrayed, left as the fall guy. That he even fell for the supposed prospect of a promotion for his vile participation —with the lure of even getting the Benemerenti Medal itself!—was beyond humiliating.

And for that, there would be consequences.

CHAPTER

FORTY

I n the course of his long career in antiquities, Vincenzo Tucci had, naturally, established connections with others in many fields, people he could turn to for assistance with various projects as the need arose.

In the case of this reliquary and its parchment, though, there was only one person he knew he could trust to produce a worthy translation of such a document and do so quietly: Brother Calvino Mendoza, prefect of the Vatican Secret Archives.

He reached for the telephone.

"*Buongiorno*, Calvino, this is Vincenzo Tucci."

"Ah, Vincenzo, to what do I owe this pleasure?" Mendoza responded in his hushed, lyrical manner. "It's been a while since we've spoken."

"Yes, and that is entirely my fault," Tucci said apologetically. "But I come to you today asking a special favor. I have come upon an exceptional parchment, written, I believe, in Koine Greek, and I have an urgent need for it to be translated. Is that something I can count on you to do for me?"

"How long of a document are we talking about, Vincenzo?"

"Oh, quite short. It appears to be maybe a hundred characters."

Mendoza thought a moment, considering his workload and available staff.

"There is one *scrittore* I have in mind who would be ideal for such a task. How soon can you send it over?"

"I will hand-deliver it myself this afternoon if that's convenient."

"I look forward to seeing you then, Vincenzo. *Ciao*."

MICHAEL DOMINIC HAD BEEN WORKING with Toshi Kwan on the *In Codice Ratio* project for the better part of the day when Brother Mendoza approached him. At the monk's side was a stout, bald man dressed in a fine white Zegna linen suit, a pale pink Rubinacci shirt with Saint Tropez collar, and a narrow Canali white silk tie fastened around an ample neck. The unusual thing Dominic noticed most, apart from the man's extraordinary taste in clothing, was his hairless face. As Mendoza introduced him, Dominic's eyes wandered to the man's hands as they exchanged a handshake, noticing his fingernails were severely ridged and discolored. He had never seen such an acute case of alopecia before, but he knew the symptoms.

"Miguel, Signor Tucci is a fine antiquities dealer of some repute here in Rome, and from time to time he turns to us for assistance with the translation of certain documents he comes across. He has requested that we apply our skills to this parchment. As you can see, it is quite old."

Having already encased the parchment in an acid-free folio, Tucci handed the document to Dominic, who, as usual, marveled at the enigmatic history he held in his hands. The parchment itself was complete and in superb condition, clearly well-preserved. He looked at the carefully scripted glyphs.

ΕΔΏ ΒΡΊΣΚΟΝΤΑΙ ΤΑ ΙΕΡΆ ΛΕΊΨΑΝΑ ΤΗΣ ΣΆΡΑΣ: ΚΌΡΗΣ ΤΟΥ ΙΕΣΙΟΎΑ ΓΙΟΥ ΤΟΥ ΙΩΣΉΦ ΚΑΙ ΤΗΣ ΜΑΡΙΆΜ ΤΗΣ ΜΑΓΔΑΛΆ

Toshi Kwan, already seated at the computer used for *In Codice Ratio* translations, offered a suggestion. "This is easily something we can run through the ICR system, Michael. It's built for quick translations like this."

"Great, Toshi, I'll leave it to you then," Dominic said, handing him the folio.

Kwan carefully extracted the parchment from its enclosure and placed it on the glass plate of a customized flatbed scanner, then closed the cover. He tapped in a few commands on the keyboard, and a specialized cold cathode fluorescent lamp lit brightly as the lamp head moved slowly beneath the glass plate. It then repeated the process two more times, each pass picking up a different color spectrum at a dense resolution of 9600 dots per inch.

A few moments later, the translation appeared on the display.

HERE LIE THE SACRED REMAINS OF SARAH,: DAUGHTER OF YESHUA, SON OF JOSEPH, AND MARIAM OF MAGDALA.

Everyone in the room gasped. Dominic, staring at the screen, froze. *Sarah?! This can't be coincidental.* Further confirming his suspicion was the fact that Yeshua was the Hebrew name for Jesus, and Mariam of Magdala was, of course, Mary Magdalene!

That document must *be related to the stolen reliquary! And if so, did Tucci have it in his possession?*

"May I ask, Signore, where you acquired this parchment?" Dominic asked the man in white, his voice unsteady.

"Normally I do not discuss such business details, Father Dominic, but as you have been so kind as to translate this for me—well, I discovered it inside a reliquary I have taken on consignment."

It was all Dominic could do to maintain his composure. He couldn't very well accuse a prominent antiquities dealer of theft, but obviously, the man was at least an accomplice in a black-market transaction, unintended or otherwise.

"Signor Tucci, as it happens, a wooden reliquary with inlaid ivory, iron ornamentation with dual handles, and an Aramaic epigraph on the front reading '*Sarah, daughter of Yeshua and Mariam*' was stolen from me just as I discovered it in a cave in France this past weekend, at gunpoint by a man named Ivan Gović. May I ask, is that who brought you the reliquary?"

Tucci was visibly shaken, uncertain how to deal with this sudden change of events. "I … I am afraid I'm unable to confirm one way or the other, Father Dominic. For obvious reasons my clients rely on complete confidentiality in our dealings."

Mendoza, as stunned as Tucci was, began to ask his own questions, but Michael held up his hand for patience. The monk huffed a bit but took his cue to let it play out.

"Signore, may I see this reliquary?" Dominic asked firmly.

"I'm sorry, gentlemen, but I really must be going," Tucci said abruptly. "Thank you for your assistance, but I'm afraid a viewing will not be possible, Father Dominic. I doubt this is the same reliquary of which you speak, for my client is a man of dependable standing in the world of antiquities, and I seriously doubt he obtained this object under dubious circumstances."

With that, Tucci reclaimed the parchment from Toshi Kwan's scanner and asked Brother Mendoza if he would be so kind as to escort him out of the Vatican. Dominic fumed and wanted more than anything to restrain the man, who obviously was well aware now, if not prior to this, that his "merchandise" came to him in a black-market deal. Did the man know that four people had nearly lost their lives in that theft? But Michael couldn't very well strong-arm the man in the middle of the Vatican to hold until the police arrived.

But one thing was now certain: He had to act fast before losing the reliquary forever.

FORTY-ONE

I t was nearly midnight in Moscow when Dmitry Zharkov's private mobile phone chimed with the arrival of new email—an encrypted ProtonMail message dispatched from Vincenzo Tucci in Rome.

There was a brief introductory note, along with several attachments: photographs of the reliquary and the bones it contained, both from various angles; the parchment written in Koine Greek included within the artifact; and the handwritten translation Tucci had prepared on a sheet of blank paper, with a postscript indicating the translation had been verified by the Vatican. Assuming his telephones might be tapped—always a precaution in his more esoteric line of work—the less chance of him being identified, the better.

The content of the message itself was brief and to the point:

· · ·

EXTRAORDINARY BIBLICAL RELIQUARY **just discovered in a cave in France. No other like it exists. The price is €100 million.**

ZHARKOV EXAMINED THE PHOTOGRAPHS EAGERLY, his collector's arousal growing. He gave no thought to the quoted price, but as a prudent buyer he preferred as much provenance as possible, and professional authentication— or at least scrupulous inspection by a highly seasoned eye —from a trusted third party.

And for that task, there was one man in all of Rome whom he knew well and trusted implicitly: Dr. Simon Ginzberg of Teller University.

Fellow Jews, the two men had known each other for decades. Zharkov was honorary godfather to Ginzberg's daughter, Rachel, even though Jewish tradition does not recognize the concept of godparents. But it was one of Zharkov's greatest joys to provide for Rachel's education— paying her tuition for Harvard Law School—which is not something Ginzberg could have offered his only child on a scholar's salary. He was honored to accept his wealthy friend's generosity.

Yes, he would call Simon in the morning, certain that his friend would help him.

❧

"*SHALOM ALEICHEM*, SIMON," Zharkov said after placing the call to Rome.

"Dmitry! *Aleichem shalom, yedidi*," Ginzberg replied, happy to hear his old friend's voice.

The two exchanged pleasantries and talked briefly

about their families and their respective health. Then Zharkov got down to business.

"My friend, I need special favor," Zharkov said.

"Anything for you, Dmitry, you have but to ask."

"I am in the process of acquiring an extraordinary object from a respected antiquities dealer in Rome by the name of Vincenzo Tucci. And as I am not there to inspect it myself—nor would I even know what to look for—would you mind meeting with Signor Tucci on my behalf?"

"Of course, I wouldn't mind. What kind of object are we talking about?"

"Tucci described it as a sacred reliquary found in a French cave, quite old and very important. It is said to contain the bones of Sarah, purportedly the daughter of Jesus Christ and Mary Magdalene, though I leave it to you to determine that as best you can."

Ginzberg was stunned hearing the words Zharkov had just spoken. *It must be the same reliquary Michael lost to those barbarians!*

"I have heard of this reliquary, Dmitry, yes. But I understand there may be some issue of ownership at stake in the matter. I would tread very carefully here."

"We can deal with such matters at a later time if we must, Simon. Should I acquire it as offered, there are many options open to me for disposition, such as public display and historical appreciation, if those are among your concerns. As Tucci currently has possession, in my view that constitutes the right to pass ownership, regardless of the source of acquisition."

Ginzberg was all too aware that the ethics of wealthy collectors can be fluid, depending on their motivations— not to mention the fact that class entitlement rarely denied them anything they set their sights on. But he was now in the awkward position of having to choose between the conflicting ambitions of two friends, made more difficult by somewhat dubious moral grounds. He considered his position carefully. The historian in him wanted more than anything to experience this discovery for himself. But knowing that Michael and his friends had been nearly killed for it, brought a shiver of fear as well.

"I will do what you ask of me, Dmitry," Ginzberg said, "but given the ambiguous nature of possession over ownership—and you can understand my position on who should really 'own' such historically significant artifacts in the first place—I will only provide my analysis to you, and not offer any type of formal authentication to anyone else. Besides, there is far more to that process than I am able to do alone. It could take years for a thorough analysis, and much debate."

"That is all I can ask of you, my friend," Zharkov said. "Yes, I realize something of this nature cannot be so quickly appraised. But if there is even a remote chance, I have sufficient resources to take the risk.

"And, of course, I ask that this be done on a completely confidential basis. No one else must know of my personal interest in this object. I will send you the contact information.

"Oh, and please send my best regards to Rachel. I trust she is doing well at Harvard."

Faced with yet another complication, Ginzberg was now torn between two loyalties. Should he even tell Michael that he not only knows where the reliquary is, but that he might be involved in its fate?

FORTY-TWO

A t the end of his first day back at work, Sergeant Karl Dengler was sitting on a tall, wooden stool at a workbench in the Swiss Guard armory, diligently polishing his steel breast harness as his mind reflected on the events in the Trou la Caune cave the past weekend.

It had been a busy couple of days for him since then, having taken time off while attending to Lukas's care, and this was his first day back on duty. His mind ran through the possibilities of what could have happened had Jean-Claude not been there to free him, of who was responsible for the awful explosion, and, thinking like a soldier, considering how he handled the situation and what else might have been done if things had not turned out so fortunately. A halberdier must always be prepared, he reminded himself.

At that moment Dieter Koehl walked into the room. Still in full uniform, he silently looked Dengler in the eyes, an awkward look of discomfort on his own face. Koehl removed his plumed steel helmet and set it in its place on the shelf. As brothers in the Guard do, Dengler stood up reflexively to assist Koehl in removing his armor. Not a word was spoken by the two as they went through the elaborate procedure, the activity simply an assumed part of their end-of-day rituals.

"Karl," Koehl began quietly, "there is something I must tell you. It gives me no pleasure to confess what I have done, but it is the honorable thing to do."

Dengler, already aware of Koehl's murky involvement in the scheme, was stoic. "Go on," he said.

The words tumbled out of Koehl's mouth. "I know that you went caving in France with friends last weekend and that Ivan Gović set an explosion at the cave entrance, intended to seal you in. I know this because I figured out for myself what Gović's real plan for the bomb was—and I know about the bomb because I built it myself!"

Koehl's eyes glistened with emotion as he continued. "He told me that explosive was to be used on his cousin's farm outside Rome, to remove a large boulder in a crop field. I swear I didn't know he was going to use it for such an immoral act, Karl, you must believe me! If it weren't a mortal sin, I would kill Gović myself for lying to me, for manipulating me in his perverted scheme.

"I don't expect you to forgive me. I just had to get that off my chest. I haven't slept well in days knowing I was a part of such an abomination."

As he listened, watching Koehl's sincerity and obvious humiliation, Dengler began getting emotional himself. Looking Koehl in the eye, he held out his hand.

"Thank you, Dieter," he said. "I did know you had some involvement, though I wasn't aware of how much. I believe you, and I do forgive you."

Koehl reached out his own hand and the two stood there, a firm handshake locked between them.

"But sin or not," Dengler said angrily, "I will have my revenge on Gović for what he did. One of his *schweine* shot Lukas, and what he intended for all of us in that cave is unforgivable."

"Karl, I had no idea Lukas was shot!" Koehl exclaimed. "Is he okay?!"

"Yes, he's fine. The bullet went through his forearm with little damage. He'll be back on limited duty later this week."

"Well, for what it's worth, the authorities interviewed me yesterday," Koehl said, "and I am cooperating with them fully to bring Gović to justice, any way I can."

Dengler was grateful to hear this. "Perhaps we can work together on that. I'm sure we can come up with a suitable punishment."

FORTY-THREE

incenzo Tucci's antiquities shop was closed when Simon Ginzberg arrived early the next evening, but seeing a light on in the back room, the scholar knocked firmly on the door.

A figure emerged from the dark recesses of the back of the gallery, approaching the door. As Tucci unlocked then opened it, Ginzberg smiled kindly and entered.

"*Buona sera*. Signor Tucci, I presume?" he asked.

"Thank you so much for coming, Doctor Ginzberg. I truly appreciate it. My client, Mr. Zharkov, recommends you highly."

"Yes, Dmitry and I go back a long way. I suppose I should make it clear that I am here as a personal favor to him, so, as you can understand, my evaluation will be for his purposes only."

"Of course, understood completely," Tucci responded.

Locking the door, Tucci led Ginzberg to the back of the shop. On a broad wooden table beneath a French Victorian bronze chandelier sat the reliquary, draped with a burgundy red damask cloth aglow from the lights shining above it. Tucci removed the fabric, and at once, Ginzberg was spellbound.

His hands shook as he reached out to touch it, the weight of its presumed history taking hold of his mind as few things could.

"Simply extraordinary," he whispered absently, taking in the ancient inlaid ivory and the Aramaic inscription carved on the front, caressing the object respectfully.

He looked up at Tucci, his eyes wide behind the thick lenses of his spectacles. "May I look inside?"

"Of course," Tucci replied, slowly opening the top of the reliquary as if unveiling a chest full of treasure. He then handed Ginzberg a pair of white cotton gloves.

As he pulled on the gloves, Ginzberg couldn't take his eyes off the relics inside. Already, questions swarmed the scholar's mind. If these were, in fact, the remains of Sarah, daughter of Jesus and the Magdalene, did she have siblings? Could she have been the progenitor of others in the holy lineage? And where were *they* now? How did they fare throughout history? *So much yet to know!*

First, he picked up the parchment lying on top of the bones and scanned its content. Fluent in Koine Greek, he read the document without effort and absorbed the assumed provenance and its implications. Setting that down, he toyed with the ancient jewelry, inspecting its simple finery, common for the era. He picked up the thick glass vial of myrrh but dared not try to open it lest it shatter from age. Any residual scent had long since vanished, though he held it to his nose instinctively.

He chose not to disturb the bones, leaving them to lie where they rested.

"As a start, Signor Tucci, I recommend we have these

items carbon dated. We can do that discreetly in my lab at the university, and since Mr. Zharkov seems to want things to progress quickly, I suggest we start immediately. Can you bring the reliquary to Teller University first thing in the morning, say eight o'clock?"

"Yes, that can be arranged," Tucci said, a nervous edge to his voice. Ginzberg gave him directions to his office, and Tucci thanked him for his time.

~

TUCCI ARRIVED at the Caprioli Palace, as expected, at eight o'clock sharp the following morning, with the reliquary again draped with its red damask covering.

Ginzberg had been chatting with a young technician in his office when Tucci walked in, and after greetings were exchanged the three walked down the hall to the Accelerator Mass Spectrometry Laboratory.

"Noah here will be running the tests for us today," Ginzberg said to Tucci of the technician, "and we should have results fairly quickly."

Once they were in the lab, Noah dispassionately set the reliquary on an examining table, opened the top, and carefully extracted each of the items, laying them on a stainless-steel utility tray. It was not his business what the materials were. It was just a job, but one he did well.

Using a miniature shaving plane, he first extracted a tiny sample of the wooden reliquary itself and placed it in an agate mortar, where he ground it into dust using a pestle to speed up the chemical reaction with the next ingredient in the process, hydrochloric acid. After filtering out contaminants, he freeze-dried the sample to remove excess water. As he went through the procedures, Noah explained how it worked.

"Radiocarbon dating relies on the decay of nitrogen in carbon-14," he began. "C-14 is a natural process formed by interacting with nitrogen-14 found in the atmosphere, which in itself is comprised of neutrons produced by the sun's rays as they interact with the air around us.

"As plants, trees and animals take in air or food, they absorb these molecules of carbon dioxide, which are then passed on to other organisms by way of nature's food chain. The decay of radiocarbon is very slow, and once an organism dies the amount of radiocarbon in its tissues gradually declines.

"We know that carbon-14 has a half-life of 5,730 years, give or take, meaning half of the radioisotope found in the organism will disintegrate over the following span of 5,730 years. Since carbon degrades at such a constant rate, we can estimate the date when, for example, a tree or a person died by calculating the residual radiocarbon present in the organism—in this case, the wood from the reliquary or the bones found within it."

Finishing the process, he inserted the mixture into a liquid scintillation spectrometer, and a computer provided a radiocarbon age for the sample. Having that, Noah compared it against samples of known age using a terrestrial calibration curve with specialized software, which then produced the calendar age of the sample.

Looking up at the two men, Noah offered his evaluation. "It's safe to say the analysis of the wood gives us a calendar date range of 25 to 60 CE, or AD if you prefer."

Ginzberg was quietly ecstatic. That certainly placed it in

the radius of the thirty-third year, around when Sarah would have been born. And since the skull and hands were so small, it's likely she died young, perhaps in her teen years.

He revealed nothing to Tucci about his excitement, nor of his speculation.

Noah went through the same thorough process for the bones, coming up with nearly identical data for the human organic material. Ginzberg was now satisfied they were dealing at least with someone from the appropriate era.

Now he just had to decide what to do with this information. He had to pass it on to his old friend Zharkov, of course.

But should he also inform Michael Dominic of his collusion? His dear friend had nearly lost his life because of this. How safe was anyone, including himself now, involved in this deceitful act?

FORTY-FOUR

From his apartment in the Vatican's San Carlo Palace, Enrico Petrini sat in deep reflection, alternately drawing on his pipe and sipping Puni Alba Scotch whiskey. The rich cherry aroma of the toasted Cavendish and Burley tobacco blend drifted throughout the lavish sitting room overlooking the gardens of Saint Martha's Square, but his enjoyment of these pleasures was tempered by Cardinal Dante's dismal ultimatum. He was unsettled.

Such moments turned his mind to better days—not better for the circumstances surrounding them, for they revolved around the dark period of World War II and Petrini's role as a leader of the Maquis, a shadowy arm of the French underground resistance movement. No, what came out of that period most for him was the deepest of friendships, the mutual dedication and devotion of his two comrades-in-arms, Pierre Valois and Armand de Saint-Clair. The three had been known then as Team Hugo, and their discreet successes in Operation Jedburgh had helped turn the war to the advantage of Allied forces, obstructing the Nazis from achieving many of their darkest ambitions.

Petrini's second-in-command at the time, Armand de Saint-Clair, was the scion of a 300-year-old banking family in Switzerland. Banque Suisse de Saint-Clair was among the most respected institutions in that country, and one of the few to remain unscathed in the aftermath of the war, when countless investigations of German complicity hounded every bank in Switzerland. Though officially neutral politically, Swiss bankers, by and large, knew Hitler's war machine required extensive and ongoing funding, and the stakes were too great on either side of an unwinnable equation. If you incurred Hitler's wrath by not taking his business, you were vulnerable to the Führer's retaliation. Those who did comply enjoyed both freedom from Nazi persecution and the prodigious financial rewards of a continuous river of looted gold and currency. But their complicity with the Third Reich made them targets both during and after the war, and post-war investigators were hardly timid in meting out full measures of justice to Nazi collaborators. Owing to his aristocratic legacy and multi-generational sphere of influence, the young Saint-Clair was able to adroitly escape having to take either of the two worst options, keeping his bank clear of Nazi collaboration and Hitler's vile retribution.

Saint-Clair and Petrini, also of noble European blood, became fast friends in the Maquis, along with Team Hugo's radio operator, Pierre Valois, who was now president of France. The three had fostered close connections since the war and turned to each other when any of them needed counsel or support in any form.

It was Armand de Saint-Clair to whom Petrini must now turn, he considered, as he drew on his pipe, absently looking out over the gardens. Armand was an old friend of the Holy Father, knew the stakes and the players in the dilemma he now faced, and would surely give him the wisdom of his counsel.

He took a sip of the fine Scotch, then picked up the phone.

~

"GRAND-PÈRE!" Hana said cheerfully as she answered her phone the next morning. "I've been meaning to call you. There's so much to tell you! Where are you now?"

"Ah, mon petit Hana," Armand de Saint-Clair said soothingly when he heard his granddaughter's voice. "I am in Geneva, my dear. And you shall have your chance to talk in person. I'll be coming to Rome this evening and wanted to make sure you were still there. How is your work going?"

"Actually, I'm here for a week-long conference, but I've also taken some holiday time off, so I'll be here a while longer."

"Your editors at *Le Monde* are very generous, Hana," he said. "But then, I'm sure they appreciate your value."

"It will be good to see you tonight, pépé. What brings you to Rome? Another meeting with the pope?"

"Well, I will be seeing His Holiness while I am there, yes, but Enrico is in need of my assistance on a matter of some seriousness. I'm afraid I cannot go into details, my dear, but it will be resolved one way or another. I assume you're staying at the Cavalieri?"

"Yes," she replied. "I'll make sure the staff has your room ready. *Au revoir* until then, pépé."

~

THE GLEAMING white Dassault Falcon 900 touched down on runway 33 at Rome's Ciampino Airport just as the sun was setting. It was a brisk evening, and a light rain had begun to fall.

As the pilot taxied to a private hangar adjacent to the elite Signature terminal, Baron Armand de Saint-Clair stowed the papers he had been working on in his attaché, then accepted his jacket from Frederic, Saint-Clair's personal assistant who also served as flight attendant, chauffeur and bodyguard.

"Will we be in Rome for long, baron?" Frederic asked as he brushed down the jacket.

"I think it may be a few days, Frederic," Saint-Clair replied. "You should take some time with your family here. I'll call you when my business has been completed."

"Thank you, sir. Have a pleasant visit."

With Cardinal Petrini's compliments, a white Mercedes S500 papal limousine was waiting beside the jet, its motor thrumming as Saint-Clair descended the steps of the aircraft. A tall, fit chauffeur who doubled as a bodyguard stood beside an open rear door waiting for the baron.

"*Buona sera, barone,*" the chauffeur said. "Would you like to go directly to the Vatican, or your hotel?"

"To the hotel, please, the Cavalieri."

As the vehicle exited the airport and moved through the rainy streets of Rome, Saint-Clair wondered what it was his friend had been so worried about when he called. Obviously, the matter was of such grave importance that he could not discuss it by phone, and to insist on a personal visit hinted that Petrini was likely in some sort of trouble.

Whatever it was, he would be there for his friend, as he always had been.

CHAPTER

FORTY-FIVE

"Welcome, Grand-père!" Hana said as she hugged her grandfather at the door of their Palermo Suite.

"Hello, my dear. You look very well. Time off agrees with you, I see!"

Behind them the porter wheeled the luggage rack into the foyer and on through to the baron's bedroom, hanging the garment bag in the closet and setting the bags on the bed. He then prepared the fireplace in the sitting room, and within minutes a warm blaze began toasting the room. Hana thanked the man, then saw him out.

"Get settled in, pépé, I have much to tell you. Would you like a drink?"

"In a moment, my dear, do let me get my bearings first." For a man approaching ninety, Saint-Clair was remarkably spry, with a quick mind and an agile memory.

As one of Europe's leading bankers accustomed to the wealth, privilege and power of a noble aristocratic family,

Armand de Saint-Clair's lineage traced back to Henry de Saint-Clair, Baron of Rosslyn in Scotland, who accompanied Godfroi de Bouillon on the First Crusade in 1096. The Saint-Clairs had a long, rich and influential history.

For centuries, certain of Europe's upper-class families have been called on to provide personal service to popes, an elite circle known as the papal *Consulta*. Saint-Clair's own family had for generations maintained powerful links to the papacy, and the baron himself had served on the *Consulta* of three popes, ensuring him virtually unrestricted access to the Holy Father, day or night.

Having freshened up, Saint-Clair emerged from the bedroom. "You know, Hana, I think I will have that drink now. Brandy, please, if we have it."

While Hana prepared the drink, her grandfather stood looking out over the rain-glistened city, the darkening sky contrasted by thousands of dimly lit homes spread out below him.

"What is it do you suppose Cardinal Petrini needs your advice on, pépé?" Hana asked.

Her grandfather took a seat and a sip of brandy before he answered. "I wouldn't presume to know at this point. He was quite guarded on the phone, but he did mention that Cardinal Dante has a hand in it. If that rogue is involved, it can't be good for anyone. Dante is only out for himself."

Hana shuddered at hearing Dante's name. *'Rogue' is the right word for that godawful man*, she thought.

"Well, you'll know more when you meet with Enrico tomorrow," she said. "If I can be of any help, do let me know."

"Of course, my dear. Now, tell me all about your adventures of the past week. You have my undivided attention."

Sitting next to the fire, Hana took a sip of the martini she had prepared, then began her story with Dominic's discovery of the Pietro Vesconte puzzle map, the mention on it of a cave in France, and her role in deciphering it.

She took him through the exploration of the Trou la Caune cave, of their being surprised and held captive by Gović and his men, of Lukas being shot, losing the reliquary, and finally, of the explosion that could have killed or at least trapped them all.

Saint-Clair sat there in stunned silence as Hana blithely laid out the complex tale.

"This is terrible news, Hana!" he exclaimed. "It seems trouble has a way of seeking you out, does it not? Is this Gović fellow any relation to last year's adventure? I recall there was a Gović involved then, too."

"Yes," she affirmed, "Ivan is the son of Petrov Gović, that Interpol agent who kidnapped me for personal gain. Like father, like son, as the saying goes."

"And what has happened to this reliquary now?" he asked.

"We have reason to believe it might end up on the black market, I'm afraid. Michael—Father Dominic—told me that an antiquities dealer here in Rome may have it in his possession. We're prepared to do whatever is necessary to get the reliquary back, Grand-père. Is there any way you might be able to help?"

"I don't know how I might be of service, my dear, but of course you have my complete support, should you need it.

"But now, I must retire for the evening. I meet with Enrico in the morning and want to be at my best. Goodnight, my dear."

FORTY-SIX

S imon Ginzberg stared at the phone on his desk, as if willing it to make the call itself, relieving him from the necessity. He picked up the receiver and dialed Zharkov's number in Moscow.

"Good morning, Dmitry. It's Simon," the old man said.

"Simon, *meyn guter fraynd!*" Zharkov responded in Yiddish. "All is well with you, I hope?"

"Yes, all is well here, thank you. I have some news for you about the reliquary."

"Really?" Zharkov said, an expectant edge to his voice. "Well, I am all ears."

"We went through a series of tests, carbon dating the wood of the reliquary and the bones inside it," Ginzberg began. "The process is complex but very accurate. Our technician gives both samples a date range of between 25 and 60 CE. This puts it squarely in the era during which Mary Magdalene was alive.

"As I'm sure Signor Tucci advised you, there also was

an accompanying parchment claiming that the bones were those of Sarah, daughter of Yeshua and Mariam. On this alone, I could be persuaded that it may indeed be authentic. But one cannot be one hundred percent certain in these things, Dmitry. Significantly more archaeometric investigation would need to be carried out—using such methods as dendrochronology, thermoluminescence, IR and UV light, and X-ray analysis, not to mention DNA examinations of the bones, all of which takes more time— and there would surely be hotly contested debate in many scholarly circles.

"But as time is a factor for you," he continued, "I can state with fair certainty that the objects do come from the appropriate period. As to its relationship to Jesus, that is only a possibility, and for all one knows, a remote one. I'm afraid I cannot confirm much more than that, my friend."

Zharkov, optimistic by nature and thus eager for validation, wanted to push Ginzberg for more. But he was right; time was of the essence. His instinct cautioned that the Italian Art Squad could already be sniffing around this anyway, so he had to make a decision one way or the other. And quickly.

Even at a hundred million euros, it was a pittance for him, and if there was even a remote chance the reliquary was authentic, he would be the envy of biblical scholars and collectors worldwide, a strong motivation for one so possessed. Once he had ownership of it, he could administer all the tests needed for establishing stronger legitimacy.

He had made up his mind.

～

"Vincenzo, this is Zharkov. I wish to proceed with the acquisition of the reliquary."

Tucci was momentarily speechless. He had just earned a €20 million commission on a few days' worth of effort.

"This is excellent news, Signor Zharkov! I assume Dr. Ginzberg's examination went well, then?"

"As well as it could under the circumstances. But I am satisfied with his preliminary analysis and am willing to accept the balance of risks involved. However, if further testing does not yield satisfactory results, Vincenzo, I will expect a full refund of the monies paid.

"Meanwhile, I have specific instructions for you in regard to delivery. You said the consignor was a young man named Gović, yes?"

"That's right, Ivan Gović."

"I would prefer that Mr. Gović personally deliver the artifact to me at the Geneva Free Port in two days' time. I want him to travel alone and not tell anyone of his mission or itinerary. He is to purchase a burner phone before he leaves, and I want him to *fax* me with the phone number. Faxing is more secure and virtually impossible to intercept. Have him do this immediately. I want that fax within the hour.

"I will today wire fifty million euros to your Swiss account as a deposit and will deal with Mr. Gović on the balance when I meet with him in Geneva. Tell him I will open a Swiss bank account on his behalf since he might have trouble doing that on his own. Is that acceptable, Vincenzo?"

"Most certainly, Signore, I will carry out your instructions to the letter. As always, it is a pleasure and a great honor doing business with you."

After giving Tucci his fax number and exchanging goodbyes, Zharkov ended the call.

Tucci sat at his desk, rocking in his chair, ecstatic at his good fortune. He only hoped, he prayed, that Zharkov's additional examinations of the reliquary proved it to be authentic—or at least to the degree that his client was satisfied. And if Tucci knew one thing, he knew that clients often let their desires exceed prudence. Such artifacts as biblical reliquaries were notoriously difficult to authenticate, but the mere thought of possessing one so historically seductive could be enough to satisfy this particular collector's hopes.

And a €50 million deposit! Surely Gović will be more than satisfied with his fifty million provided to him on delivery, Tucci considered, *since he wasn't aware of the full agreed-upon sale price or of a deposit....*

"Ivan, it's Vincenzo Tucci. I have good news: my client has just agreed to purchase your consignment!"

Tucci gave Zharkov's list of instructions to Gović, including acquiring a burner phone immediately and faxing the number to his client in Moscow within the hour, and that he would be paid fifty million euros by Mr. Zharkov personally once he got to Geneva—in his own newly minted Swiss bank account.

"I...I don't know what to say, Vincenzo," Gović said haltingly. "I am speechless! And so grateful to you for arranging this. I will do everything you say. When shall I pick up the package?"

"Be here first thing in the morning. I have yet to box it up, but I'll make it convenient for travel. Take the first train to Geneva you can get, allowing for pickup here and a taxi to the station.

"And do not take any unnecessary risks, Ivan. This is my most important client."

FORTY-SEVEN

The Operations Center at AISI headquarters in Rome was packed with blinking and humming electronic equipment for all manner of intelligence and surveillance missions, but Massimo Colombo stood over one desk in particular as the comms operator sat at her console. Both wore headsets as they listened to the conversation between Vincenzo Tucci and Dmitry Zharkov.

When the two parties had ended their call, Colombo removed his headset and placed it on the desk.

"So, we know Tucci now has the reliquary and Gović will be transporting it to Geneva," he said to the operator. "Please email me a transcript of that intercept, and get Colonel Scarpelli from the Art Squad on the line for me, will you?"

The operator set up the call. Colombo took a seat at a vacant desk in the back of the room. A few moments later the phone on that desk rang.

"Benny? Yes, it's Max. We have a lead on Gović and the

stolen reliquary. Dmitry Zharkov is the buyer, and he's asked Tucci to arrange for Gović to deliver it to him in Geneva, in the free port zone. You and I should assemble a team to intercept them together—and they *must* be together, sealing the transaction—then we can arrest them both. I'll coordinate the operation with Swiss authorities so we're in compliance with their laws."

Colombo leaned back in his chair, a feeling of optimism coming over him. After all this time, he was close. And to get both *bastardi* would be a huge win.

Tempering that, however, was another thought, one much less welcome.

What if they got away with it?

CHAPTER

FORTY-EIGHT

T he Vatican Secretariat of State offices were abuzz
with activity as various teams in scattered rooms
were planning their respective roles for the pope's
upcoming trip to South America.

Sergeants Karl Dengler and Dieter Koehl were
managing the security protocols for the Vatican secret
service, or *gendarmerie,* who accompany the pope while he
is immersed in crowds and aloft in the popemobile, as well
as the honorary Swiss Guard contingent for scheduled
ceremonial events.

Maps of all cities to be visited—São Paulo, Lima,
Bogotá and Buenos Aires—lined the walls of the secured
room, marked with heavy black lines depicting the path
the pope and his entourage would take in each city, and
thick red lines indicating positions where the Holy Father
might be exposed to possible attack.

Advance teams had already coordinated with local law
enforcement agencies to supplement the Vatican's security

detachment, but Dengler was still nervous about the reliability of forces not under his control.

The door to the room opened and Secretary of State Cardinal Enrico Petrini walked in.

"How is the planning going, Sergeant Dengler?" he asked.

"It's as good as we can manage, Your Eminence," Dengler replied. "I do have some concerns about the locals, it being South America and all. Do you have time to discuss this now?"

"I'm afraid I don't, not at the moment. I'm going into a meeting shortly. I just wanted to stop in and see how things were progressing. Let's go over your plans a bit later today."

"Of course, Eminence. Whatever time suits you."

Petrini glanced at the clock on the wall. *Armand should be here any minute,* he thought. "Thank you, sergeant. Carry on."

As PETRINI WALKED BACK to his office, Armand de Saint-Clair emerged from the elevator just as the cardinal passed the foyer. The two exchanged handshakes and greetings, then went into Petrini's private office.

Father Bannon brought in a tray of coffee and biscotti and set it on the low table between two Queen Anne armchairs near the window overlooking Saint Peter's dome.

"Please hold my calls for the next hour, Nick," Petrini said as his secretary quietly left the room.

"Armand," he began solemnly, "in our many decades of friendship I have never needed your advice as much as I do now. I have lived as good a life as any man in my position can hope for, and I am grateful for so much. There is, however, one significant part of my life that I have kept secret from everyone, with good reason, as you shall see. I fear the time has come for that secret to be revealed, for if I do not do it myself, it appears it shall be done for me in a most callous way."

Saint-Clair sat attentively, sipping his coffee as he looked into his friend's weary eyes. "This sounds serious, Enrico. Please, go on. You will have no harsh judgment from me."

"When I was a parish priest in New York, some thirty years ago now, I had a longtime housekeeper in my rectory. You may recall her. Her name was Grace Dominic."

"Yes, I do, actually. Wasn't she the mother of Father Michael Dominic?"

"Indeed, she was," Petrini replied, then looked down into his coffee cup, his hand shaking as he held it. "And as it happens, I am his father."

Saint-Clair's reaction was stolid as he set his cup down and reached for his friend's free hand, holding it gently. "Enrico, this comes as little surprise to me. I knew the two of you were close for many years, and to be candid, Michael does have many of your features. I've long suspected that might be the case, but of course it was none of my business to inquire, nor do I think any less of you for knowing the truth. But how is this a problem now?"

Petrini, his eyes glistening, took a deep breath and let it out slowly.

"It seems Cardinal Dante has gone out of his way to dig into my past for his own abhorrent gain. He's threatened to expose me if I don't relinquish my office back to him.

That's all he wants—this job!—and he's prepared to ruin me if it comes to that."

His anger building, Saint-Clair stood to pace the room, clasping his hands together. "Dante cannot get away with this, Enrico. Whether he knows it or not, he is putting himself at great risk attempting blackmail."

The baron stopped at the window, looking out over the Vatican gardens as he conceived a plan. He turned to look back at Petrini.

"I suggest we take this to the Holy Father, right now," he said confidently. "It's not as if you're the first priest to have had an affair in which a child came of it. And while the Church has taken ensuing action in such matters, both you and Dante have much more at stake here. I personally know the pope favors you over that scoundrel anyway. I say we petition His Holiness as a matter of confession, asking that he deal with Dante personally. He owes us that. He owes *me* that."

Saint-Clair did not elaborate on the conditions of such a statement, but Petrini well knew the two men had a long and affectionate history together. One was now pope, and the other was his closest advisor.

"If you think that is the best course, I will make the call now," Petrini said. They both looked at each other, acutely aware of the challenges such a confession might provoke. But the alternative was undoubtedly worse. At least this way they stood a better chance of potentially neutralizing Dante.

Sitting nervously at his desk, Cardinal Petrini picked up the phone and dialed the pope's private number.

∾

It was eight in the morning in Buenos Aires when the telephone in the archbishop's office of the Metropolitan Cathedral emitted two shrill rings. The ringing always irritated Father Bruno Vannucci, whose ear was more finely attuned to the pleasant ringtones of his cell phone.

"*Hola?*" he answered gruffly.

"Please stand by for the Holy Father," a female voice said. A moment later a more recognizable voice came on the line.

"Cardinal Dante?" the pope asked assertively.

"Pardon me, Your Holiness. No, this is Father Vannucci, His Eminence's secretary. Let me get Cardinal Dante for you. Please hold a moment."

Vannucci put the call on hold and then scrambled through the double doors leading into Dante's office.

"Your Eminence!" he said breathlessly, "It's the pope! He's waiting on the phone for you!"

"Don't be ridiculous, Bruno. It's got to be someone playing a joke. The pope never calls me."

"I swear it is, Eminence. The call came through the Vatican switchboard."

Dante sat up straighter in his chair, looked at Vannucci warily, then picked up the phone.

"This is Cardinal Dante," he said cautiously.

The familiar voice was firm and to the point. "Fabrizio, what is this I hear about you blackmailing Cardinal Petrini? Is this true?"

Dante stood up at full attention, his mind racing for a response.

"I…I, um…no, of course not, Your Holiness, I had merely a brief chat with Cardinal Petrini. I don't understand what you mean by blackmail. He misunderstood, of course. For the sanctity of the Church, I meant only to—"

"Don't be coy with me, Fabrizio," the pope said. "We just spoke with Cardinal Petrini about your proposition to him. We are aware of his past indiscretion, and he has our personal absolution on the matter.

"As for you, if you dare say a word about this to anyone—or if Father Dominic finds out in any way about Cardinal Petrini's role in any of this—there will be consequences. If Buenos Aires isn't to your liking, I am sure we can find a more suitable post for you."

Fully chagrined, Dante knew then he had been defeated. His back was to the wall.

"My deepest apologies for this misunderstanding, Holy Father. I never intended—"

"That is all for now, Fabrizio," the pope interrupted. "You may continue your work in Argentina."

The call ended with a harsh click.

CHAPTER

FORTY-NINE

fter a long morning working with Toshi Kwan on the ICR project, Michael Dominic's frustration about Govic got the better of him. Colombo might be handling this case in his way, but the reliquary— the most important religious discovery in a century or more—could be lost. The ticking clock echoed at the back of his mind. He pulled out his iPhone and texted Karl Dengler: **Can you and Dieter meet for lunch in the canteen now?**

A few moments later the response came back. **Perfect timing, we're breaking for lunch too. See you there.**

Dominic walked into the bustling cafeteria where Dengler had arrived earlier, securing them a table by the window. He and Koehl were sitting there, waiting, as Dominic approached. "Let's grab some food first, then we'll talk."

Standing in line amongst other Vatican employees, each of them took portions of various pastas, baked ling cod with spicy caramelized Andouille sausage coins, grilled

Roman tomatoes, and tiramisu, then made their way back to the table with overflowing plates.

After Father Dominic said grace, they dug into their meals. After a few minutes, Dieter Koehl spoke up.

"I want to help you any way I can to get Gović and return the reliquary," he said as he tugged on a piece of bread. "And as you said, Michael, it needs to be soon."

"Yes, I've been thinking of that, Dieter," Dominic said, setting down his fork and steepling his fingers. "You should call him today and ask for a meeting. Tell him it's something you must convey to him in person, and you need his advice. Play to his presumed power."

Dengler wasn't so charitable. "Why don't we just kill him and be done with it?"

Dominic studied him with astonishment, then looked around the room. "I don't much like the guy either, Karl, but we can't just do that. The goal is to get the reliquary back. It may already be too late. If Dieter can get him to meet, the three of us can force him to take us to it. He should be surprised enough that we survived the cave blast."

"Alright," Koehl said. "I'll give him a call, then depending on his timing, we can work on our plan."

FIFTY

The large rectangular block of solid gray foam lay on Vincenzo Tucci's worktable, removed from the black Pelican Protector Transport Case in which the reliquary would be conveyed.

Tucci's job now was to cut and shape the foam so that it gave full protection to the artifact while in transit, together with its skeleton key and the oblong Vesconte map. The Pelican case itself was large, with an interior of twenty-eight inches by nineteen inches by seventeen inches, and four strong polyurethane wheels for easy transport. Though hefty, it would serve to conceal the reliquary while Gović was traveling with it to Geneva.

He went about measuring the reliquary and map device, then drew outlines on the foam with a black marker. Using an electric carving knife, he carefully sheared away inside portions of the foam matching the measurements of the reliquary, then the map, retaining some for extra padding on the top when the base job was finished.

With the foam enclosure now complete and tucked back into the Pelican case, Tucci gently fit the reliquary inside, then the map in its own receptacle, and inserted the extraneous formed padding on top of each to keep its contents stable while in transit. He then closed the case and fastened heavy-duty Ingersoll padlocks on each of two double throw latches.

It was now ready for Govi<U+0107> to pick up.

~

It was ten o'clock on Friday night when Govi<U+0107> answered the phone.

"Hello, Ivan, it's Dieter. Have you got a minute?"

"Only a minute, Dieter, so make it quick." Govi<U+0107> put the phone on speaker while he continued packing his bag.

"There's something important I need to meet with you about, relating to that plastique I made for you. The Italian authorities have interviewed me about an incident they think is related. Can we meet in the morning?"

Govi<U+0107> was cautious but curt. "I'm afraid not. I have to catch the first train to Geneva for business. This will have to wait until I return."

"That's too bad," Koehl said. "Alright, please let me know when you return. We need to coordinate our stories."

"Well, there isn't much of a story beyond a crop field boulder clearance. Regardless, I must go now. Goodbye, Dieter." He tapped the red End button on his phone.

Finished packing now, Govi<U+0107> felt a bit anxious about Koehl's call and authorities being involved. How could they have traced the explosive to Dieter? No matter. But in a couple of days he would have no worries at all, and with so much money, he would fly direct from Geneva to Buenos Aires and never have to look back. He would hire lawyers to fight out whatever it was Italy had concerns about.

He dropped his Glock 19 pistol in the backpack, gulped down the last of his vodka, then lay down to sleep.

~

"HE'S LEAVING TOWN, Michael, taking an early train to Geneva tomorrow morning. What should we do?"

Koehl had conferenced Karl Dengler in on the call before phoning Dominic.

"Geneva?" Dominic asked. "What's in Geneva?"

"He said it was business," Koehl added. "Maybe he'll have the reliquary with him. Maybe he found a buyer for it. As Karl knows, too, Switzerland is a hub for black market traders. A lot of dark money goes through Geneva."

Dominic thought for a moment. He had to get Colombo involved, but would the AISI move quickly enough? He couldn't let Ivan escape. "You and Karl should follow him as a precaution. It's the weekend so you're both off duty, right?"

Dengler and Koehl said "*Yes*" at the same time.

"Okay, you two get to the *Stazione Termini* in Rome as early as you can, before dawn just in case. Watch for Gović and take the train he gets on. Don't let him see you if at all possible…maybe disguise yourselves somehow or keep your distance. Karl, do you still have that AirTag tracker I gave you last summer?"

"You bet, it's here in my locker."

"You must find a way to get it into Gović's luggage. Or,

if he has the reliquary with him, it's got to be packed in some kind of crate or box. Get into it somehow and find a hidden place for the tracker inside. Remember to register it to your iCloud, otherwise it's useless.

"Hana and I will find a way to get to Geneva and meet you there. I'll alert Colombo, too, and fill him in. We'll get this snake one way or another."

CHAPTER
FIFTY-ONE

On the Route du Grand-Lancy, an unremarkable avenue just off the southern tip of Lake Geneva in Switzerland, sits a drab gray and pale-yellow complex of warehouses called *Ports Francs*, also known as the Geneva Free Port zone to the global ultra-wealthy elite who store their priceless treasures there.

Reputedly stashed inside its climate-controlled, fire-resistant walls are over a hundred billion dollars' worth of exquisite art alone, including a thousand works by Pablo Picasso, as well as untold numbers of museum-quality Old Masters paintings. All told, more than a million pieces of the most magnificent art ever produced call the Geneva Free Port their permanent home.

The buildings also house other high-value collectibles such as gold bullion, Etruscan, Greek, and Roman-era antiquities, and an extraordinary collection of rare wines—some three million bottles. All are stored in secrecy while their owners enjoy tax-free privileges, since, while stored in its secure environment, all goods are considered "in transit" and despite their physical presence in Switzerland are deemed outside the Customs territory. Thus, all Customs duties and tax liabilities are deferred until the objects leave the well-protected property. But few things ever left the free port zone; indeed, there are even special rooms where owners of the objects can display, buy and sell their objects freely, without taxation and in complete secrecy, while they remain in the privileged shelter afforded by the zone.

Beyond its legitimate business, the Geneva Free Port— along with many economic free zones in other countries— also have the reputation of being the ideal place for transferring and storing looted black market antiquities, and the plunder gained from extensive money-laundering operations worldwide. Much of this exclusive inventory has been sitting there simply appreciating in value for decades. And few ever even see it.

Dmitry Zharkov was not just the largest shareholder of the company, he was among the free port's most active clients, positions he also held in free zones located in Luxemburg, Croatia, Belarus and Russia. Such standings gave him enormous latitude, extending his sphere of influence among other ultra-wealthy individuals along with the also-rich seedier elements of the illicit antiquities market, from whom Zharkov acquired much of his vast collection.

As HE STOOD at the long Dalbergia bar in his Moscow penthouse, Zharkov poured himself a glass of Beluga Noble vodka while crystalizing his change of plans for Ivan Gović.

Once he was on the train to Geneva, he would call the

young Croat on his burner and give him the details. There was the possibility of him being followed—whether by the Art Squad or somebody else—and Zharkov couldn't take any risk. Too much was at stake.

Turning to his computer, he arranged for his Airbus A319 to be ready to depart Moscow's Vnukovo Airport for Geneva in the morning. Then he alerted the staff at Les Rives d'Argentière, a five-star resort nestled high in the Alps at Chamonix-Mont-Blanc, to have his chalet prepared for his arrival the next afternoon.

He might even get in some skiing if there was time.

FIFTY-TWO

Ivan Gović knocked sharply on the door of Vincenzo Tucci's shop promptly at six o'clock Saturday morning, a backpack slung over his shoulder.

A moment later the door was unlocked and Tucci opened it wide, glancing outside to see if anyone else was lurking about as Gović entered the building. Few people were out this early on a weekend morning. The taxi Gović had taken stood waiting at the curb for his return, its motor humming.

Closing the door and locking it, Tucci escorted him to the back room.

"This special container is quite secure, and I've packed both items carefully," he said, handing Gović the keys to the padlocks on the Pelican case. "Don't let it out of your sight. Once you're en route, Mr. Zharkov wants you to call him directly for further instructions. When does your train leave?"

"I'm on the 7:15 to Geneva," the Croat said. "It's about a seven-hour trip with a stop in Milan."

"*Arrivederci* then, Ivan. Call me if you have any problems."

Gović set the Pelican case on the floor and wheeled it out to the waiting cab. The driver got out, opened the trunk, and dropped the case into the storage compartment.

"Hey, careful with that!" Gović hollered. *Estúpido tanos,* he fumed in Spanish. Then, in Italian, "*Stazione Termini, velocemente!*" To the train station and make it quick.

The taxi abruptly pulled away from the curb and raced up the street toward the heart of the city.

"GOVIĆ JUST LEFT, SIGNOR ZHARKOV," Tucci said diffidently into his phone. "He's taking the 7:15 train to Geneva. I told him to call you once he is on board."

"Thank you, Vincenzo," Zharkov said. "I'll take things from here now."

∼

THE COMMS OPERATOR AT AISI, having overheard Tucci's conversation with Zharkov, alerted Colombo of the intercept. Armed with fresh details, Colombo called Dominic.

"Father Michael, this is Max Colombo. Gović will be on this morning's 7:15 train to Geneva, leaving from the main terminal. Tell Koehl and Dengler he's traveling alone but will have the reliquary with him. If we assign agents to follow him, there's a risk of tipping him off, but we'll have a team standing by in Switzerland to take it from there.

"We must have Gović and Zharkov together to make the arrest, and that's probably going to happen in the free port. So, if you can have your guys keep an eye on him and maintain their distance, we should be okay."

"Thanks, Max," Dominic said. "Baron Saint-Clair has offered us a ride on his jet to Geneva, so we'll be leaving shortly as well. Will you be there?"

"Of course, this is not something I want to miss after all our work together. Hopefully, we'll have something to celebrate tonight. You have my cell number if there's anything you need from me in the meantime."

After exchanging goodbyes, they ended the call.

Dominic, having called from Hana's suite at the Cavalieri, turned to her grandfather.

"Baron, I can't tell you how grateful I am for your generous offer to take us with you to Geneva."

"Think nothing of it, Michael. I was heading home anyway, so it's hardly out of my way at all. And who knows, I may yet be of further service to you. The Swiss authorities do make certain accommodations for me. Keep that in mind as the situation develops."

CHAPTER

FIFTY-THREE

E ven this early on a weekend morning, Rome's central train station was a hive of activity, with early-risen tourists rushing to make their trains to destinations beyond the Eternal City.

Dominic had just called Karl Dengler with the details of which train Gović would be on. Dengler had reserved second class seats and purchased tickets for both Dieter Koehl and himself on the high-speed Frecciarossa 7:15 to Geneva, then stamped each of them at one of the many yellow ticket validation boxes dotting the terminal.

To make sure they didn't miss Gović, however, or that he might take another train, both Swiss Guards—each wearing casual street clothes, baseball caps, and sunglasses if they needed them—stood on opposite ends of the upper mezzanine looking down on the twenty-four train platforms, ticketing booths and surrounding vicinity. Since the reliquary was twenty inches long by fourteen inches high, it would be hard to miss a package like that being pulled behind a traveler.

True to its name, the Frecciarossa, or Red Arrow, was painted a glossy bright apple red, with a low pointed snout on the locomotives connected to each end of the train. At a top speed of three hundred kilometers per hour, they were the pride of Italy as its counterpart to French and Japanese bullet trains.

Parked on Track 3, the Frecciarossa to Geneva was just below where Dengler stood on the mezzanine, giving him a clear view of boarding travelers. He looked over at the massive clock hanging above the trains, its large Roman numerals easy to spot from any distance, and noted it was 6:50.

Just then he spotted Gović leaving the ticket window and heading toward the red train on Track 3. He was wearing blue jeans and a black hoodie, his long blond hair covering the hoodie which was lying flat on his upper back. He was pulling a large black Pelican case on wheels as he walked briskly toward the first-class seating section at the front of the train.

Dengler pulled out his phone and texted Koehl on the other side of the station: **He's here. Meet me in front of Track 3 now.**

As DENGLER and Koehl seated themselves in the second class section of the last car, they made themselves comfortable in window seats facing each other. Their backpacks—each holding their standard-issue Sig Sauer P220 pistols and other items—nestled between their hip and the window.

Conductors on the platform blew their whistles as the train slowly began to head out of the station. Next stop: Milan, where they would switch trains to Geneva.

FIFTY-FOUR

On newer high-speed trains in Italy, at the end of each car across from the restroom is a wide storage area for stowing luggage larger than what overhead bins can accommodate. Keeping such larger items with passengers in the seating area is forbidden by train regulations, so Gović had to park his Pelican case away from where he sat. But he made sure he had a direct line of vision from his aisle seat farther up the train. *It wasn't as if it had anywhere to go*, he thought, *being on a train, after all*.

He hadn't gotten much sleep the night before, his mind racing over the €50 million payday he was about to have. He still couldn't believe his good fortune. This was the easiest score he had ever made. And he was just twenty-nine. He'd be set for life!

The steady hum of the locomotive and the rocking of the train soon put him into a trancelike state. Yes, he did have to contact Zharkov, but it was still early in Moscow. He'd call the Russian after he took a quick nap.

. . .

"How will we get this AirTag into that Pelican case?" Dengler asked Koehl as he registered and synced the device with his iPhone.

"Well, between us I'm the only one who knows how to pick locks, right? So, I guess the decision's been made for us. I just have to make sure Gović doesn't recognize me. The best situation would be to wait for him to use the restroom, which has to happen sometime. We need to get closer to him and wait for the right moment.

"How do these things work, anyway?" Koehl asked, fiddling with the white disc in his hands.

Dengler laid out the schema for his friend. "AirTags are Bluetooth and ultra-wideband tracking devices developed by Apple. You can affix them to most any object you want to keep track of. Then, once registered, you can locate them from any distance— anywhere in the world, for that matter—using Apple's 'Find My' app. All the device needs to relay its low-energy encrypted signal is *any* iPhone nearby—even a phone belonging to a stranger in a crowd. The tag then sends its location signal to the home device using iCloud, and the object is found. This is how we located Hana when she was kidnapped by Gović's father last year."

"That is amazing!" said Koehl, clearly impressed. "Okay, so I'll wander up front wearing my hat and sunglasses, being careful to check out every passenger on my way. What's Gović wearing, by the way?"

"He had on a black hoodie when I spotted him, with the hood down, at least it was down in the station. The case is too large for the overheads, so it has to be in the storage area across from the restroom. I'll come with you and stay nearby in case you need help. Ready?"

"It's now or never," Koehl said. "Give me your knife."

"*My* knife? Why?" Dengler asked.

"Because I need the tweezers separate from mine to use as a tension wrench, while I use the toothpick on mine to fit into the keyway and manipulate the pins in the padlock. Any halfway decent Swiss soldier knows that."

Dengler smiled, accepting the barb gracefully. Once distant from each other and hardly speaking, the two had formed a tighter bond after the bombing incident, and Koehl's heartfelt apology over his role in it. Now they were on the same side—with a mutual goal of getting even with Ivan Gović. And now was their best chance.

Dengler handed over his Swiss Army knife, then watched in horror as Koehl extracted, then bent, one prong of the extended tweezers at a ninety-degree angle. "Sorry, my friend, it's all for the cause," he said with mock sincerity. "We'll get you a new one."

LEAVING their car and heading toward the front of the train, they peered through the glass windows of each adjoining car door before entering the next car, Dengler looking on the left side of each car while Koehl scouted heads on the right. Before boarding Dengler had counted nine passenger cars in total. They had made it through six cars before seeing the Pelican case sitting in the storage area of the next car they were about to enter.

There were several first-class passengers standing in line to use the restroom, which to the Guards' great fortune helped to hide their activity in the storage area.

Looking past the standing passengers, Koehl saw Gović

in an aisle seat, nine rows back, apparently sleeping. He pointed him out to Dengler.

"We have to act fast," Dengler whispered. "Our timing looks good as long as whoever's using the restroom takes their time!"

Pressing his hand against the large button to open the car door, Koehl slipped through and knelt down next to the Pelican case, Dengler following behind him. While Koehl worked on the locks, Dengler stood with his back turned to Gović, as if he were also waiting in line, providing some blockage to Gović's view of the reliquary.

Koehl was remarkably skilled at picking locks, Dengler thought, as he watched his friend deftly unlock one, then the other Ingersoll padlock on the Pelican case using two Swiss Army knives.

Inserting the bent tweezers at the bottom of the padlock as a tension wrench, Koehl then inserted the toothpick tool into the top of the keyway space and continually pulled up to push the pins into upright positions.

Though to Dengler it seemed to take forever, it took Koehl only about fifteen seconds to unfasten each lock. In the meantime, Dengler pulled out his phone and took a photo of the Pelican case in the event it might be needed later.

Dengler chanced turning his head slightly to see if Gović was still sleeping. He was. But the line to the restroom was moving more quickly than he was comfortable with. There were only three people left standing. Soon anyone would be able to clearly see what they were doing!

With the top of the case now open, Koehl took the AirTag out of his pocket, but as he took it out, it fell out of his hands and onto the floor. He was now sweating profusely. Snatching it from where it landed near the car door, he buried it deep beneath the interior foam, as far under as he could reach without dislodging the items it contained.

The restroom door opened, and as one person left, another took her place in the restroom. Only two passengers were left standing now—and Gović was waking up!

Peering through the legs standing next to him, Koehl watched as the Croat stretched his arms and looked out the window. They had to get out of there—now!

Closing the top of the case, his hands now shaking from the adrenaline coursing through his body, Koehl refastened the two padlocks, then turned around and pressed the large door button next to his head. The door slid open, and he stood to calmly exit the car, with Dengler walking nonchalantly behind him.

Back at their seats now in the last car, breathless from the obvious risks they had taken, Dengler took out his iPhone and opened the Find My app. Refreshing the *Devices* option, there it was: the location of the Pelican case was shown blinking on a full-color map just 125 meters ahead of them.

They had done it!

As THE TRAIN's vibrations lulled some to sleep, that same vibration jiggled the locking latch on one of the padlocks on the Pelican case, the one that Koehl, in his haste, had not fully engaged. A moment later, that one padlock snapped open.

FIFTY-FIVE

"Would you care for a beverage, Father Dominic?" the flight attendant asked.

"Sure, I'll just have a bottle of sparkling water if you have it, thanks."

"And you, Miss Sinclair?"

"I'll have the same, Frederic, thank you."

"And baron, what can I get for you, sir?"

Saint-Clair glanced at his Patek Philippe. It was eleven in the morning.

"I'll have a wee dram of whiskey, Frederic."

Hana looked at her grandfather in mock reproach.

He winked at her. "It's my damn plane, I'll order what I please, thank you very much."

Dominic laughed. "It's good to be king," he said, tossing his head back jovially.

"We should be in Geneva in about an hour," Hana said, looking at Dominic. "What's our plan?"

"Well, Gović won't be arriving until four o'clock, so we have a few hours to kill. Max said he has a team at the

Geneva Free Port ready to intercept him. I assume they're undercover, or however they do these things. I'm not sure there's really anything we have to do except wait."

"We can stay at Grand-père's château until Max calls us. Is that alright, pépé?"

"Of course, my dear, you are both welcome at La Maison des Arbres for as long as you wish."

"If you're sure it wouldn't be an imposition," said Dominic.

Hana smiled at him. "The château has twelve bedrooms, Michael, I'm sure there's plenty of room. It even has a chapel, so you'll feel right at home."

$\sim$

NOW FULLY AWAKE, Gović went into the café-bar car for a cold sandwich and a beer, then returned to his seat. It was time to call the client. He pulled the burner phone out of his pocket and dialed the number given to him by Tucci.

"*Da?*" answered the Russian.

"Mister Zharkov? This is Ivan Gović."

"Yes, Ivan, thank you for calling. The artifact is with you, correct?"

"Yes, sir, I am looking at it now." He glanced down the aisle at the Pelican case.

"Good," Zharkov said. "There has been change of plans. I have reason to believe you may be intercepted by police when you arrive in Geneva, so I have made alternate arrangements.

"I want you to discreetly exit train in Milan, then pick up car I have reserved in your name at the Europcar desk in Milan Centrale station. You will then drive to Chamonix-Mont-Blanc in French Alps, it shouldn't take you more than four hours, and it is most pleasant drive. I will meet you at my chalet in Chamonix; I will text you directions to it.

"Once I have concluded my inspection, I will arrange for your payment, then you will take object on to Geneva Free Port. Is that understood?"

"It is, Mister Zharkov, yes. Off at Milan, rental car to Chamonix, then on to Geneva from there."

"*Da*, very good. And tell no one of this new plan, nor should you make any calls other than to me. I will see you soon, yes?" Zharkov ended the call.

Looking down at the burner, then up at the Pelican case in the distance, Gović was rattled by the thought of police after him. *Who would know I'm even on this train?* He could trust no one now.

CHAPTER

FIFTY-SIX

T he Milan Centrale train station is, as architect Frank Lloyd Wright himself proclaimed, "the most beautiful station in the world." Its grand Art Deco glass-domed facade measures 200 meters wide and seventy-two meters high, a breathtaking architectural feat covering twenty-four tracks whose trains accommodate well over a hundred million passengers per year.

On his first visit to Milan, Ivan Gović was filled with awe at the monumental beauty and history surrounding him. Though he would have loved more time to explore the city, he was on a tight deadline. He could come back when he was rich—which should only be a few hours from now.

As the bright red Frecciarossa slowly nosed into its station track, Gović and other disembarking passengers rose to gather their things. Tossing his backpack over his shoulder, Gović went to fetch the Pelican case by the door. As he was extending its handle, he noticed one of the padlocks was unfastened, hanging open on the clasp. Unnerved, he knelt down to examine it more closely.

He didn't find anything noteworthy, but then he couldn't recall if he'd noticed before whether they were fully locked or not. He was sure he would have observed something like that.

Suddenly a chill rose on his spine. He looked around at the other passengers to see if he might recognize anyone, alert to suspicious behavior. *Could it have just popped open on its own?* he wondered. *Maybe Tucci didn't fully close it himself.*

Taking out the keys, he opened the other padlock. Looking inside he found both the reliquary and the Vesconte map properly encased in foam, apparently intact. He sighed in relief.

Figuring it was nothing, he closed the case, then firmly secured both padlocks, pulling on each one to test its resilience. They seemed fine.

"WHICH TRAIN GOES ON TO GENEVA?" Koehl asked Dengler as they got up to depart, standing in line behind other passengers heading toward the door.

"The Eurocity Express on Track 12," he said, referring to his ticket.

Just then Dengler looked up to see Gović dragging the Pelican case behind him on the platform outside their car's window. The darkened glass prevented them from being seen, but still, they reflexively turned their heads in the other direction.

"I don't want to lose sight of him, Dieter," Dengler said. "Let's get a move on."

Pushing past the other departing passengers, both men

quickly exited the train and searched for Govič in the general area of Track 12 and among the many boutique kiosks planted throughout the station. The large Pelican case was hard to miss, though, and they easily found him —not heading toward Track 12, but walking deeper into the station toward the exits.

"Where the hell is he going?" Koehl asked rhetorically.

"We won't know unless we follow him. Put your scarf and sunglasses on." They pulled neck scarves and sunglasses out of their bags, and with baseball caps pulled down they felt confident they were as disguised as anyone could be.

Govič was about ten meters ahead of them now. It wasn't even noon, and the chaotic station was packed with commuters and tourists—everybody moving in different directions, wheeled luggage trailing in their wakes, children screaming and running amok, pickpockets lurking among the crowd seeking easy marks—all under a constant stream of loudspeaker announcements in Italian, directing travelers to departing trains.

Dengler and Koehl watched anxiously as Govič entered the Europcar rental office. Instinctively Dengler said, "Wait here!"

He followed Govič into the office where four short lines of travelers were queued up. He got in line behind Govič, one person in front of him as a barrier, his head down.

When Govič got to the desk, Dengler listened as best he could.

"Yes, I have a reservation, please. Ivan Govič," he said to the attendant as he handed her his passport.

"Yes, Signor Govič, I see you're going to Chamonix-Mont-Blanc and on to Geneva. Signor Zharkov has made the reservation for you requesting an Audi R8. And since you're entering Switzerland, you'll require the Swiss Motorway Vignette, which has already been placed on the car's window for you. If you'll just sign here…and you're all set. The car is being brought to you now, if you'll just wait outside at the marked Europcar section by the curb and show the valet your papers. Have a safe journey, sir."

Dengler looked the other way as Gović passed him by, then jumped to a counter that had just opened up.

"I need a car to France and possibly Switzerland, please."

"Have you a reservation, sir?"

"No, it's a spur of the moment thing."

"I'm afraid we only have one car left with a Swiss Motorway Vignette, signore. But it is a fine vehicle—a Porsche 911. Will that suffice?"

Dengler smiled. "Yes, that will be fine, thanks."

While the attendant prepared the paperwork, Dengler shifted nervously, hoping it wouldn't take much longer. He turned to look at Koehl standing outside the window, perplexed, then shrugged his shoulders and held up a hand to be patient.

Having completed the paperwork and finally gotten the keys to the vehicle, he rushed out of the office.

"Zharkov rented a car for Gović. He's heading to Chamonix. We'll follow him in a car I just rented. They gave Gović an *Audi R8—mein Gott*, that's a top-of-the-line car. It sells for something like one hundred and eighty thousand euros!"

"Well, it *is* Zharkov we're talking about. That's nothing for a billionaire. What did we get?"

Dengler looked up at his taller friend with a wide grin. "*A Porsche 911!* Dieter, we'll be *flying* to Chamonix!"

FIFTY-SEVEN

"Apparently there's been a change of plans, Michael."

Dengler was behind the wheel of the blue Porsche 911 Carrera, cruising east on the A4 Autostrade toward Chamonix as he held the iPhone to his ear.

"Zharkov arranged for Gović to get off in Milan and take a rental car to Chamonix-Mont-Blanc, high in the French Alps. Dieter and I know it well, it's a famous ski resort and hangout for the wealthy jet-set. I've skied there myself, so I know it pretty well. We're following Gović now."

Dominic, now settled in with Hana at her grandfather's La Maison des Arbres château, was disturbed by the news.

"If Zharkov changed from the original plan, it could mean he knows the authorities are waiting for him in Geneva. I'm sure a man with his resources has connections. This isn't good, Karl. I'll inform Colombo and Scarpelli. They need to know."

"We did manage to get the AirTag inside the reliquary

case, by the way, we're good on that score. That was how we were able to catch up with him. We should be in Chamonix by three this afternoon. Will you be meeting us there? How's this all going to play out now? I mean, I have no problem dealing with Gović myself—but you can imagine what I'll do to him, given the chance."

"No, I don't think that's wise, Karl. He needs to be brought to justice, along with Zharkov for trafficking in stolen antiquities. Let Colombo deal with him. I'll get back to you after I speak with Max, but let me know if anything else changes, okay?"

"You got it, Michael. Take care."

Hana and Armand had been listening to one side of the conversation as all three sat in the great room of the house overlooking Lake Geneva.

"It sounds like Zharkov has changed plans. Gović is now heading to Chamonix. Do you think he's meeting him there?"

"Yes, I imagine so," Saint-Clair said, "Zharkov has a large chalet up there, more of a manor house, really, in Les Rives d'Argentière resort. I read about it in *Billionaire* magazine."

"You guys even have your own *magazine?!* I picked the wrong line of work."

"Well," Saint-Clair said, "I certainly can't include myself in *that* exalted circle, but as a banker, I do keep up with how my clients spend their money."

While the two men spoke, Hana had been contemplating alternatives, herself. "What if Zharkov is going to take the reliquary back to Moscow himself, without going to the Geneva Free Port? That presents a dilemma of its own. Max and his team won't be able to get their hands on him, nor catch Gović in the act."

"I'm calling Max now, let's get his thoughts."

Dominic picked up his phone and tapped Max's contact number. A moment later the agent answered.

"Max, this is Michael Dominic." He laid out the new facts as Dengler had reported them, then listened as Colombo responded, switching to speaker so all could hear.

"*Merda!* This makes things much more challenging. Tell Sergeants Koehl and Dengler not to take any action with Gović, just to keep him in their sights. We're in Geneva now, so we'll head down to Chamonix shortly. It's only ninety minutes so we should be there before they arrive."

"Actually, we're in Geneva, too, Max. We'll leave now and meet you there." After he ended the call, he looked at Hana. "Do we have a car that might be available to us?"

Saint-Clair answered for her. "We'll go in mine. Frederic is also my chauffeur; he'll get us there quickly and safely." Then, shouting for his aide, "Frederic, get the Rolls ready. We're going to Chamonix."

Dominic just rolled his eyes and stared at Hana. "A Rolls-Royce?"

"But of course," she said, affecting a mock air of entitlement. "Can you see us all cramming into a Fiat like a clown car?"

FIFTY-EIGHT

Nestled in the alpine shadow of the majestic snowcapped peaks of Mont Blanc lies the charming French village of Chamonix, a quaint hamlet of shops, inns, bistros and historic churches serving a resident population well below ten thousand.

But during peak winter season the flood of tourists and skiers alone can number more than twenty thousand, mostly rich Europeans and Russian oligarchs who can afford the most luxurious resort amenities in the world. Dior, Hermès, Prada and other top designers all have chic shops throughout the Auvergne-Rhône-Alpes region, and business is brisk year-round—especially among Russians who, if they don't understand French, will simply order the most expensive dish on the menu, assuming it must be the best the house has to offer. Locals view Russians as sturdy folk who can survive a weekend at altitude without sleeping, surviving on a regimen seemingly comprised of coffee, cigarettes, vodka and women.

With his Airbus parked that morning at Genève

Aéroport, Dmitry Zharkov's two-vehicle motorcade entered the Chamonix area at noon and proceeded through the gates of Les Rives d'Argentière resort on the banks of the Arve River. Arriving at his chalet, the security team checked the house for bugs and other surveillance devices, clearing the way for Zharkov and his entourage to enter the home.

With a few hours yet before Gović was to arrive, he decided he'd take a steam bath and relax after the four-hour flight from Moscow.

"Tatiana, Katerina, join me in *banya*, yes? And bring two chilled bottles of Stoli Elit and some glasses. We need to rest from our long trip."

~

THE PORSCHE 911 Carrera handled the twisting mountain roads beautifully, as Karl Dengler expected it would. This was his first experience with a Porsche, and if he weren't following Gović at a decent distance—allowing cars to pass so they could remain as inconspicuous as possible—he would have opened her up for a real exercise on the effects of speed and gravity.

As it was, the Mythos black Audi—a steady thousand meters ahead of them—was making good time as Gović put it through its paces on the serpentine alpine roadways.

"It would be good if he slowed down a bit," a nervous Koehl said as he gripped the dashboard. "I have a wife and daughter who depend on me staying alive."

"Relax, Dieter, we're only going a hundred and thirty kilometers per hour. This beauty is built for these roads. We should be in Chamonix in another hour or so."

~

FREDERIC SMOOTHLY GUIDED the silver Rolls-Royce Phantom southeast on Autoroute A40 as Saint-Clair, Hana, and Dominic took in the sights. One could barely hear any road noise from inside the luxurious car's cabin, much less the sound of its powerful V12 engine as it sped through the craggy mountain passes.

"Too bad we don't have any Grey Poupon," Dominic said, hoping someone would grasp the old trope.

"Pardon?" asked Hana.

"Never mind. You had to be there…"

"I'm afraid we would need another Rolls-Royce for that to work, Father Dominic," Frederic said, smiling meaningfully in the rearview mirror.

Dominic winked and smiled back. "Thanks for rescuing my dignity, Frederic."

"I wish we knew how this is going to play out," Hana said, clasping her hands nervously.

"It's really in Max's hands now," Dominic said, setting his hand on hers to suppress the fidgeting. "The best we can hope for is that they let us take the reliquary back to Rome. Finders, keepers, and all that. But I expect the French may have some say in any antiquities found on their soil." Then, turning to Saint-Clair, "Armand, do you think President Valois might be able to help us in that regard if it comes down to it?"

"Perhaps," Saint-Clair replied, "but I'm not without my own influence in such matters. We'll do what has to be done, Michael. But as you say, Agent Colombo may be the linchpin in all this."

Just then Hana's phone chimed with an incoming call.

"It's Max," she said, tapping the green button and putting it on speaker.

"Hana, we're about to enter Chamonix, as I expect you should be, as well. When you arrive please meet us in the lobby of the Grand Hotel des Alpes at 75 rue du Docteur Paccard. We'll use that as our operations center."

"Thanks, Max, we'll see you there."

CHAPTER
FIFTY-NINE

The black Audi R8 pulled up to the security gate of Les Rives d'Argentière just as a uniformed man stepped out of the guard shack to greet the driver.

"Good afternoon, sir. Do you have a reservation, or are you visiting a guest?"

"Visiting. Dmitry Zharkov," Govic replied. "My name is Govic."

The guard went back into the shack, checked a clipboard, and returned to the vehicle with a piece of paper. "May I see your passport, sir?"

Govic handed the man his identification. The guard inspected it carefully, comparing the photo with its holder, and handed it back to him.

"Monsieur Zharkov is expecting you, sir. Here is a map to his chalet. Please proceed directly there and observe the marked speed limit while you are on resort property. *Au revoir.*"

The gate raised and Govic drove through, following the map. The resort was large, and he passed several large chalets set back off the road. Snow on both sides of the drive was thick, two feet in some places, but the road was clear.

After several minutes Gović found the address and pulled into the wide driveway, noting two vehicles already parked there. As he pulled in, two burly men dressed in thick black jackets, one carrying an FN P90 submachine gun, approached him. Gović got out of the car. While the armed man stood by, the other approached the Croat and frisked him. He then reached into the Audi and fetched the keys from the ignition. Not a word was spoken by either man.

Once he was done, the frisker placed his arm behind Gović, guiding him into the open door of the chalet, then closed the door behind him. The two men remained outside.

Gović stood there, alone in the foyer, waiting for someone to greet him. Although he felt edgy about leaving the Pelican case in the car, he recognized this powerful man would play out this transaction however he saw fit. Which failed to make him feel any more at ease. He looked around. Ahead of him was an immense great room, easily two stories tall in the peak of its lofty, gabled roof, one wall of thick floor-to-ceiling glass (*probably bulletproof*, he thought) overlooking the Chamonix Valley, the other walls featuring heads of trophy animals—antelope, springbok, Roe deer, even a Siberian tiger—all amid the classic rustic architecture one expects to find in the Alps.

"Ivan Gović, I presume?" The booming voice startled Gović, seemingly coming out of nowhere. Looking up, he saw a heavily built man likely in his fifties, descending from the upper landing of a wide, half-log staircase.

"Mr. Zharkov, *I* presume?" Gović replied, holding out

his hand as Zharkov approached him. Instead of shaking hands, though, the Russian pulled him into a tight bear hug.

"Welcome to my home, Ivan Govíc. *Tatiana!*" he bellowed. "Vodka in great room, now! Bring herring and pickles, too, my love. Our guest must be famished. How was trip, Ivan? No problems along way?"

"No, sir, it was a great drive through the Alps. And thank you for renting such an incredible automobile. It drives like a dream."

"You are welcome. You have done me great favor by bringing artifact to me personally."

As he said this the two men who had met him outside brought in the Pelican case and set it down on a massive oak table in the adjacent dining room.

Looking around, Govíc observed that antique weapons of all sorts covered the walls of the chalet: long swords, wicked-looking daggers, Bavarian saber halberds and other pole arms, along with the mounted heads of various wild animals. Death and its implements surrounded him.

"First, we drink, Ivan!"

A beautiful young blonde wearing a shiny gold jumpsuit with golden high heels appeared from the kitchen, carrying a silver tray with a tall bottle, two glasses, and bowls of herring fillets and tiny dill pickles.

"Eat *zakuski*, Ivan, it is Russian tradition with vodka— and this is Russo-Baltique we are drinking. Very best vodka money can buy. You can afford your own now, yes?" He looked knowingly at Govíc and grinned.

Tatiana poured two glasses of the pure, clear liquid, then set the tray down on the dining table next to the Pelican case and left the room.

"Let us look at what you bring me."

Gović removed a key from his pocket. He opened the padlocks, then raised the lid of the case.

"Extraordinary," Zharkov whispered to himself as he looked at the contents. "The daughter of Jesus Christ and Mary Magdalene. No one else could ever possess such sacred objects."

Zharkov lifted the reliquary out of its molded foam enclosure and set it on the table. Then he plucked out the skeleton key from its foam mold. He unlocked the artifact and raised its lid.

The Russian gazed in amazement at the items within— the skull and hand bones, the ancient jewelry, the dark-tinted bottle of myrrh, the parchment, and, set in the adjoining foam enclosure in the Pelican case, the Vesconte map, which he picked up with shaking hands. Zharkov carefully examined the puzzle with curiosity.

Trying to be helpful, Gović noted, "This was the map used to find the reliquary. From what I understand, it goes back to the thirteenth century."

"Yes, Vincenzo told me about map, a treasure on its own."

While the Russian sat with a gaze of lustful wonder, Gović's mind swirled with visions of the fifty million euros that, in moments, would be his. He struggled to keep himself composed. The titillation Zharkov felt about this new addition to his collection, Gović felt about scoring this enormous windfall.

Zharkov stood up and sauntered around the room, considering his new prizes.

"You have done well, Ivan," he said, examining the puzzle map in his hands. "But I have one more job for you."

He turned to look at Gović.

GARY MCAVOY

"My informant at Interpol tells me Italian Art Squad is already here in Chamonix, waiting for me to take possession of artifact so they can arrest me for possession of stolen antiquities. Unfortunately for them, this will not happen."

Gović's face fell, shocked that the authorities would even know he had brought the object to Zharkov in the first place. How could they possibly know this?! It had to be Tucci. He was the only one who knew.

"What is it you require of me, Mr. Zharkov?"

"*Tatiana*," Zharkov shouted over his shoulder. "Bring me computer."

Then, turning back to Gović, he said, "I want you to take reliquary to Geneva Free Port, as originally planned. When you arrive ask for Herr Heinrich Becker. He will be expecting you.

"You must leave now, Ivan, and you will leave Audi here. I am giving you different car in case you were followed. Call it a bonus for your work: a nice BMW. It is being prepared for you now."

Tatiana entered the dining room with an iPad Pro, handing it to Zharkov. After logging in to his bank account, in a matter of moments he had transferred twenty-five million euros into Gović's new Swiss account, showing the Croat what he had just done.

"€25 million now, the balance of €25 million when job is complete, and reliquary is safe in free port."

He then reached into his breast pocket and handed Gović a small plastic card. "This is Carte Maestro, a special debit card for your account, so you have immediate access to funds." The Russian smiled. "How does it feel to be rich, Ivan? Very good, yes?"

Gović's entire body tingled with exhilaration. "Yes, it feels *very* good, Mr. Zharkov! Thank you!"

As if Zharkov had willed them to appear, his two men came back into the room, repacked just the reliquary into the Pelican case, then left the room, taking it with them. Zharkov still held the Vesconte map.

"I cannot have reliquary here, as I expect Italians to arrive any time. You must go now. Take extreme caution, Ivan. I am trusting you to complete job. Herr Becker will contact me this afternoon once he has reliquary in my vault at free port, at which time I wire you balance. Yes?"

"Absolutely, yes. Thank you again, Mr. Zharkov."

Zharkov led Gović out of the chalet and into the wide, six-car garage and motioned to a gorgeous white pearl BMW i8 Roadster with its top down.

"Look, it is white, like virgin bride!" Zharkov laughed. "She is all yours, Ivan. Drive careful now. 'Precious cargo aboard.'" Zharkov gave him air quotes as he said this.

Trembling over his newly gained wealth and a brand-new BMW to boot, Gović felt like a rich man might feel, emboldened and invincible. He was free! He had finally made it.

The Pelican case had already been placed in the trunk by Zharkov's men, and the keys were in the ignition. Getting into the car, Gović looked around, acquainting himself with the various controls and breathing in that new car smell. He especially liked that the windows had a dark tint to them, but as it was cold outside, he found the correct button to raise the roof of the car, sealing him in. He started the ignition and listened to the powerful German engine. Heaven.

Opening the door and stepping back out, he earnestly

shook Zharkov's hand, and they exchanged goodbyes. Then he got back in and left the compound.

Observing the slow speed limit, a few minutes later he had reached the resort's security gate. As he exited, he noticed two black vans and a Rolls-Royce entering on the opposite side of the guard shack.

Maybe I should get a Rolls-Royce, too, he thought.

Meanwhile, Zharkov placed the Vesconte map inside a small hidden safe behind a painting in his office. He expected visitors, soon.

"We are here on official business to see Monsieur Dmitry Zharkov," said Inspector Émile Boucher of the French Sûreté. Showing his official credentials to the security guard at the gate of Les Rives d'Argentière, he added, "and these two vehicles are with me. Let us pass immediately."

"I must first call Monsieur Zharkov, sir," the guard said.

"You will do no such thing unless you wish to be taken into custody for obstruction of justice. Open the gates now and do not inform Monsieur Zharkov of our presence."

"*Oui*, monsieur." The guard opened the gate and let all three vehicles pass. After they had gone through, the guard picked up the phone and called Zharkov's chalet anyway, notifying the woman who answered that *le gendarmerie* were on their way up.

A few minutes later Colombo and Scarpelli, along with their respective teams including the Sûreté officers, as well as Dominic, Hana and Saint-Clair, all paraded up into the driveway of Zharkov's chalet, passing the parked car Gović had rented in Milan. Everyone got out of their vehicles, but the Rolls-Royce contingent stayed behind while Boucher and Colombo handled the interaction with Zharkov.

There was no one present to greet them, so Boucher rang the doorbell. After a few moments, a heavyset Russian woman opened the door.

"*Da chego ty khochesh'?*" '*Yes, what is it you want,*' she said gruffly in Russian.

"Does anyone here speak French or English, or even Italian?" Boucher asked the woman.

She shrugged her shoulders, as if not understanding, nor even caring.

"Monsieur Zharkov!" Boucher shouted in English. "We know you are here, monsieur. Will you present yourself?"

The sound of heavy footsteps descending a staircase was heard as the maid walked away from the door, leaving it ajar.

Zharkov appeared and walked toward the door. "Yes, gentlemen, what is it I can do for you?"

"I am Inspector Boucher of the Sûreté. With me are Messieurs Colombo and Scarpelli, Italian authorities involved in the theft of a most valuable stolen reliquary. We are of the understanding that this artifact may be in your possession, monsieur, and we have a search warrant to inspect your premises."

"I have no idea what you are talking about, inspector, but I have nothing to hide," the Russian said confidently. "Come in if you wish but be assured. I will register my complaint with French Minister of Justice, who I happen to know very well."

Colombo's expanded team fanned out through the

house, using photographs provided by Dominic in search of the reliquary, the Vesconte map, or even the black Pelican case, which Dengler had taken a shot of on the train.

This being a large chalet with many cabinets and hiding places, Colombo did not expect to find it. The search was carried out mainly to spook Zharkov, to make him aware that they were on to him. If they got lucky, they *might* find something.

"Where is Signor Govié?" Colombo asked. "Is he not here with you?"

"I do not know anyone named Govié. There is no one else here but my employees, who came with me from Moscow. As for this—what did you call it, reliquary?—you must have your facts wrong, Agent Colombo."

Twenty minutes later Colombo's team had reassembled in the foyer, empty-handed. "Nothing here, boss," one of them said to him, "we even checked all the vehicles."

Colombo clenched his jaw. Catching the two together during their transaction had been his goal. He could expect the reliquary might be deeply hidden but where was Govié? Finding a wanted criminal here was all they would have needed to warrant their arrest plus a more thorough inspection. But without Govié...

"Signor Zharkov, I must inform you it is an international crime to both harbor criminals—I refer to Signor Govié in that regard—and to deal in stolen cultural antiquities. If you are found to be culpable in either of these crimes, you will be seeing us again. Then we will have different documents altogether."

"May I now return to my work, gentlemen? As you have seen, I have nothing here of interest to you."

Colombo and his team, including Dominic and his

friends, left the resort and returned to the Grand Hotel des Alpes to discuss their next steps.

~

HANDLING the agile roadster along the winding alpine roads, Ivan Gović felt a mix of intense joy, even privilege, along with barely subdued anger. Joy because he was now an instant multimillionaire, with sweeping latitude to do and buy whatever he wanted. And anger because Zharkov implied the authorities were now involved, creating a nuisance that tempered his exuberance.

But there was no way the Russian would give him up, there was too much at stake for both of them. Besides, he had the reliquary.

He needed a break. As he slowly motored through the little town of Chamonix, with its rich array of boutique designer shops, he spotted a fine jewelry store on the corner. He turned onto a small side street, pulled over to the curb, and stopped the car. He took a deep breath of the newness of his first new automobile, a BMW i8 at that, smelling of fine leather. He leaned back in the seat, soaking it all in.

His hand reached for the platinum Carte Maestro Zharkov had given him. Looking at it, he envisioned the €25 million just sitting in his own Swiss bank account. He had to see if it worked, if he actually had that much buying power.

He got out of the car, pressed the lock button on the key fob, and crossed the street to the jewelry store on the opposite corner. He would just give the card a little test, that's all. After all he'd done, he deserved a little splurge.

. . .

"THIS ROLEX SUBMARINER looks *fantastique* on you,
monsieur," said the clerk, a lovely older French woman
who knew the newly rich when she spotted one. "The
band is a blend of solid stainless steel interwoven with
eighteen-karat gold, and beautifully sets off the deep ocean
blue of the Submariner face. It is a watch that makes a
statement. One that says, 'you have arrived.' And it is only
twenty-four thousand euros."

"I'll take it," Gović said, smiling at the woman. He
proudly handed her his Carte Maestro, holding his breath
as she ran the card. A moment later she handed him the
receipt, then placed the Rolex box in a richly laminated
white bag.

"*Merci beaucoup*, monsieur. Have a lovely evening."

Having spent twenty minutes in the shop looking at the
many options, Gović was elated with his ultimate
purchase. The sheer weight of it on his wrist was a visceral
delight, and as it sparkled in the late afternoon sun he
thought, *Could life be any better?*

There was hardly any traffic as he crossed the road, still
admiring his new Rolex, and he decided he needed to find
someplace to eat before heading to Geneva. Just a quick
bite, then he'd be on the road again. *And there's another
twenty-five million waiting for me there!*

Reaching the opposite side of the street, he headed to
where he had parked the car, glancing at the other shops
along the way to see if anything else struck his fancy,
shaking his wrist to feel the heft of the expensive watch.
Then he turned the corner to the side street.

The Rolex no longer held his attention.

The BMW was gone.

CHAPTER
SIXTY-ONE

On the distant outskirts of Chamonix-Mont-Blanc lies the tiny hamlet of Les Pèlerins, a picturesque alpine village off the beaten path of most tourists, but close enough to serve as overflow when the more popular inns and restaurants of Chamonix are fully booked during peak season.

On the southernmost fringe of Les Pèlerins, at the very base of the Alps, several squalid camps of lean-tos and plastic-sheeted tents served as home to a ragged band of nomadic gypsies, more formally known as Roma, but generally called "travelers" throughout much of Europe.

Originating from India, the Roma arrived in Eastern Europe around the tenth century, mainly settling in Romania and Bulgaria but migrating to many other European countries as travelers simply seeking work and freedom from persecution. They are considered outcasts in every country they go to, and when their camps and populations grow large enough to be a distraction to locals, police are sent in to evict them and destroy their shabby homes, often deporting many back to Romania. It is estimated that up to 400,000 Roma live in France alone, and though many claim Islam as their main religion, French Roma are deeply Catholic, though they have few places to practice their faith outside of their rat-infested encampments.

Shandor and Milosh Lakatos, two brothers born and raised in various nomadic communes in the Alps, did what work they could find to support their parents and the community. But gainful work opportunities were hard for them to find. No one wanted their kind, for Roma were widely perceived as filthy beggars and thieves, not to be trusted, and thus, unemployable. So, as for many underprivileged and oppressed cultures, crime was their only option to survive.

Shandor's younger brother Milosh was the clever one in the family. His tactics for begging and eliciting handouts from tourists were always the best, and they paid off handsomely. He had learned to easily pick the pockets of tourists on the streets of Chamonix, where he and Shandor did most of their work. He fielded a constant supply of cell phones, watches, wallets, and other items people kept on them and which were easily liftable, all of which they fenced through a network of other Roma operators higher up the chain who worked the larger cities. They often kept many of the treasures they "found," such as the new unlocked iPhones both brothers now enjoyed after working a particularly rich crowd in one of the ski lodges.

Milosh was also mechanically inclined, able to fix broken radios and other electronics he and his brother found in trash bins. He also knew something about cars— mainly how to break into them and score their biggest trophies: choice vehicles they quickly fenced through the upline Roma syndicate.

As Gović was fulfilling his retail fantasies in the jewelry store, he failed to notice Shandor hanging around outside the shop window, holding what's known as a relay scanner. As with all keyless entry cars, the BMW's key fob in Gović's pocket emitted a constant low-energy signal seeking a compatible receiver, at which point—in practical usage—it would unlock the vehicle, allowing the driver to fully operate it.

Milosh, standing next to the BMW, held a booster receiver. Once the signal from Gović's key fob found Shandor's scanner, it bounced the signal to Milosh's device, instantly opening the car and allowing the ignition button to operate.

Once Shandor heard his brother's loud, sharp whistle, he knew Milosh had finished the job. Running across the street and around the corner, he jumped into the BMW, which raced away from the curb and up the street, heading back to Les Pèlerins and their family's camp.

⁓

"SO WHERE IS GOVIĆ NOW? And who really has the reliquary?" Dominic asked the others now gathered in the lounge of the Grand Hotel des Alpes. Colombo, deep in thought, was fuming. So many resources dedicated to this operation and nothing to show for it. They had waited until they knew Gović's car had arrived at the chalet. Everyone was exasperated.

"Wait a minute," Dengler said to the group as he launched the Find My app on his iPhone. "We saw Gović's Audi was still at Zharkov's when we left, right? But there was no sign of him there. And yet the AirTag tracker is in motion, right now heading east of here and at a fairly quick pace. Do you think Zharkov might have given Gović another vehicle?"

"It's the only reasonable explanation," said Hana, looking over Dengler's shoulder at the app. "Or, he could have given it to someone else, though that seems unlikely. We should follow the signal anyway, don't you think?"

"Absolutely!" said Dengler vigorously. "I want that mother—oh, pardon my French, Father—I want that sonofabitch badly."

"That's okay, Karl, I speak French, too," Dominic quipped. "Max, you and Benny and a few of your guys should take us with you to follow the tracker." Then, turning to Saint-Clair, "Baron, if you don't mind staying here, I think a Rolls-Royce might be in the way of whatever's about to happen."

"Of course, Michael, it's time for my cocktail anyway. You two, all of you, stay safe. I'll be right here when you return."

Taking the two black Citroën vans of the Sûreté, Dominic, Hana, Dengler, Koehl and Colombo got into the lead vehicle, while Scarpelli and several armed agents loaded up in the second, both heading out in search of the AirTag.

CHAPTER
SIXTY-TWO

Ivan Gović was both furious and terrified, and he didn't have a clue what to do with either emotion.

How could someone steal a state-of-the-art BMW?! he wondered aloud as he paced the sidewalk. *What was I thinking, stopping to buy anything without going on to Geneva? If Zharkov finds out about this, I'm a dead man!*

Thoughts tumbled out of his head now. *He can't find out, plain and simple. But how to locate the car—and the reliquary?! I don't know this place at all. And I can't call the police! Oh God, what have I done? What should I do?*

I have to run.

He went back across the street to the jewelry store and asked the woman if there was a car rental agency in town.

"*Oui*, monsieur. Just three blocks south of here, there is a Europcar agency," she said.

Gović ran the three blocks, finding the agency on the main street through town. He pulled open the door and rushed up to the counter.

"I need a car, please. I'll return it in Geneva."

"All we have left is an Economy Class Ford Fiesta, monsieur. Will that be acceptable?" the clerk asked.

Gović groaned. *The irony,* he thought. "Yes, that's fine. I'll take it."

After copying his passport, the clerk prepared the paperwork and handed Gović the keys to his new ride. He left the shop, got into the car, and headed out of Chamonix-Mont-Blanc as fast as he could. Once he got to Geneva, he would catch a direct flight to Buenos Aires and be done with it. He would still be rich.

But he would always be looking over his shoulder.

$\sim$

"François," Colombo said on the phone to his assistant at headquarters, "I want you to immediately file an Interpol Red Notice for Ivan Gović. Make sure all train stations, airports and border patrol posts get word of this. We no longer have the option of getting him together with Dmitry Zharkov."

Dengler was frustrated hearing this. "You know this denies me my revenge, Max. Honor is at stake here. Gović must pay for what he did to Lukas and to Michael."

"Yes, I'm aware of that, Sergeant," Colombo responded, "but trust me, he will pay for that and more where he is going. Rome's Regina Coeli penitentiary is often compared to the worst of Turkish prisons, where only the most hardened criminals are sent. Gović will be a most welcome addition to their population—he will be someone's girlfriend in no time. And *that* is surely more punishing than anything you might do to him."

Dengler smirked at the thought of it. Then, checking his phone, he noticed the red marker for the AirTag had stopped moving and was centered on the edge of a village on the map marked Les Pèlerins. He notified the driver of the van, holding up the phone so the agent could see the route for himself.

"It's only fifteen minutes from here," the driver said, then radioed the information to the van behind him.

HAVING PASSED THROUGH THE VILLAGE, both vans pulled off the main avenue and onto a dirt road leading into the forest. A few minutes later they found themselves in what clearly was a gypsy encampment, with ramshackle tents, metal bins afire to keep the camp's inhabitants warm, and several dozen shabbily-dressed people—men, women and children, along with a few dogs, cats and chickens—milling about the grounds or huddled in circles, talking and eating.

The one thing that stood out from the drab surroundings was a shiny-new white BMW, an odd spectacle in an otherwise meager landscape.

"This is a Roma commune," Dominic said, then asking no one in particular, "What would Gović be doing here?"

"The AirTag is in that Beamer!" Dengler nearly shouted, pointing to the BMW.

Colombo and Scarpelli and their men slowly exited the vehicle with weapons drawn while the others stayed put for the moment.

While attending the University of Toronto, Dominic had encountered many Roma on various local missions he and fellow post-grad students had participated in and he knew French Roma were largely Catholic—most deeply so. Like many countries, Canada had a large population of travelers, most of whom were peaceful people looking for work and security but finding little of either.

He had a thought. He doubted these people had much regard for police and other authorities, but if he was lucky, they might look differently on a priest.

He quickly changed into the black shirt and collar he kept in his backpack and hung his pectoral cross around his neck.

"Looking to make a few conversions, are you?" Hana said smiling.

"No, but I suspect there's a chance they may find more comfort with a priest than a cop." He shrugged his shoulders. "Couldn't hurt!"

Dominic, Hana, Dengler and Koehl got out of the van and approached the small group of men talking with Colombo.

"Father Dominic," Colombo said, "this is Gunari Lakatos, the *voivode*, or chieftain, of this commune. I told him we are looking for Ivan Gović, but they know nothing about him. He says the car was 'found abandoned' by his sons, Milosh and Shandor."

Dominic reached out to shake the man's hand, then said in fluent Romani, the gypsies' native tongue, "It is a great honor to meet you, *Voivode* Gunari. We seek only an object of sacred value to the Roman Church, something which has been stolen from us in France by this man we mentioned. Have you seen such an object?"

To a person, jaws fell as Dominic spoke the ancient language, clearly impressing the leader of the tribe.

The chief responded in kind. "No, Father, we have seen no such man. But if what you seek is inside this vehicle, you are welcome to it. We would, of course, prefer to keep the car..."

"We have no interest in the vehicle, Gunari, only the object within it. As far as we are concerned, we don't even see a car…" The chief smiled knowingly.

Dominic whispered his negotiation to Colombo in Italian, making sure this would be an acceptable arrangement, especially since he had already set the stage for it.

"Yes, Father, that is fine by me. I am sure Zharkov won't miss it, though I expect there will be hell to pay when he finds out Gović lost the reliquary if it is here. There is almost poetic justice in the very thought, no? Let's open the trunk and see what we have."

As Gunari instructed his people to stand back, Colombo tasked one of his agents to open the trunk. Doing so from the BMW's front seat, the trunk popped open—and there sat the black Pelican case.

Everyone breathed a sigh of relief. The long search was over.

"How do we open it now?" Hana asked.

Dieter Koehl stepped forward. "Allow me, mademoiselle."

Dengler reached into his pocket for his Swiss Army knife, extracted the tweezers tool and handed it to Dieter, who took out his own knife and swung out the toothpick. Both padlocks were opened in a minute or so.

And there sat the reliquary, safe and sound—but the map was missing.

Dominic took a deep breath, a look of sheer joy on his face as he hugged Hana in celebration.

"But where is the map?" Hana asked.

"Maybe Zharkov kept it," Dominic replied, disappointment in his voice. "That would be small enough to hide anywhere in his chalet."

Then, turning to Colombo, "Though we have the reliquary, I still want that map. It belongs in the Vatican, not in a private collection," he said with a bit more urgency in his voice than he'd intended. It echoed his guilt for having been the one to take the map from the sanctity of the Archives in the first place.

"Then we must again speak with Signor Zharkov," Colombo said. "But at least you now have the main prize."

Colonel Boucher of the Sûreté stepped forward. "Well, there is still the matter of rightful ownership we must deal with, since it was, in fact, found on French soil."

"I think my godfather may be able to help us with that," Hana said with a self-assured smile.

"Oh, mademoiselle? And who is your godfather?" Boucher asked smugly.

"His name is Pierre Valois. I believe you know him as president of the French Republic?"

Boucher was dumbstruck. "Ah, *mais oui*... Yes, I have heard the name," he said, blushing and smiling.

CHAPTER
SIXTY-THREE

T he long line of travelers with excessive luggage and screaming children wrapped around the coach-class queue of KLM Airlines at Genève Aéroport, but the first-class line was empty as Ivan Gov
ić approached the counter.

"A one-way ticket to Buenos Aires, please. First-class," he told the agent. He handed her his passport and the platinum Carte Maestro.

"Of course, monsieur, one-way to Buenos Aires." She processed the ticket, then handed it to him along with his passport. "Are you checking any luggage?"

"No, just what I have here." The agent looked at him oddly but continued her work. He realized his well-worn backpack likely didn't suit most of her first-class flyers. No matter. He'd soon carry Louis Vuitton luggage. He grinned.

"While waiting for your flight, please enjoy the complimentary comforts of our KLM Crown Lounge, Monsieur Gović. Once you pass through the priority lane at security, you'll find it close to your gate. You cannot miss it."

"Thank you," Govič said, heading toward the gates. He couldn't wait to board the jet, turning left into the first-class section for the first time in his life, then experience the privilege of having his own sleeping pod on the transatlantic flight. This is how it would be from now on—for the rest of his life, it would be first-class all the way.

There was plenty of time before his flight. Maybe he could even take a shower in the first-class lounge before boarding. God knows he could use one.

Approaching the Priority Lane at the security gate, he set his backpack and the Rolex in a plastic gray bin then walked through the body scanner. Fortunately, he had disposed of his Glock before reaching the airport.

But the scanning alarm went off anyway. The security agent asked him to walk through for a personal wand screening, which merely showed the BMW keys still in his pocket. The security guard let him through.

After clearing the scanner, three men, two of them in uniform and armed, walked up to Govič.

"Monsieur, will you accompany me, please?" the man in charge asked.

"Why? Is there a problem? I have a flight to catch!" Govič said adamantly, almost whining.

"It will take but a moment, monsieur. Please, this way."

Govič grabbed his Rolex then his backpack from the plastic bin, but one of the armed guards took that from him. They led him down a hall and through an unmarked door and into what appeared to be an interrogation room, leaving him alone and locking the door from the outside.

As Govič sat there, all manner of fears ran through his mind. Had Zharkov already discovered he hadn't shown up at the free port, and used his influence to have him detained? Had Tucci somehow turned him in, and if so, for what purpose? Could this be related to the bombing in France? But how would they have even known about his involvement at all? No one could have lived through that! Or had they?

Fifteen minutes later the door opened and two men walked in, the same man who was in charge before and one of the armed security guards.

"Monsieur Ivan Gović, I must inform you that pursuant to an Interpol Red Notice issued by Italian authorities, you are being placed under provisional arrest. You are the subject of a criminal investigation for illegal antiquities contraband and attempted murder. You have the right to remain silent and not to cooperate with police. You have the right to legal representation by a private or state-funded attorney. And you have the right to request the services of an interpreter.

"Do you understand these rights, monsieur?"

Gović's mouth fell open as if to say something, but no words came out.

"Monsieur? Do you understand your rights as I have explained them?"

"No, I do not understand!" Gović said, completely confused as to what was happening. Right now, he should be sitting in his first-class sleeping pod aboard KLM flight 1932 to Buenos Aires, enjoying a glass of champagne—not being arrested!

The man in charge sighed, then stepped back as the security agent pulled out a set of handcuffs. Still mystified, Gović stood up. The agent placed the cuffs on him, then escorted Gović to a holding cell, where the handcuffs were removed and the cell door was locked.

"Do I even get a phone call?" he asked.

"There will be time for that later," the man in charge said before walking away.

Time. Gović looked down at his shiny new Rolex, the only reminder of the good life he'd envisioned he'd be living for the rest of his days.

CHAPTER

SIXTY-FOUR

By the time Govíc had been arrested, it had been four hours since he had left Zharkov's chalet in Chamonix, and the Russian was not only worried but grew angrier by the minute. It was only a ninety-minute drive from there to Geneva, but the Croat never appeared at the free port. Where could he possibly be? Had Zharkov been betrayed? Perhaps Govíc got a better offer from someone else and was playing Zharkov as the fool. In which case, Govíc was a dead man.

As with many rich and powerful people, Zharkov had one person he could rely on for most anything he could not, or should not, do himself. Known in such circles as "fixers," these specialists carried out particular assignments or resolved situations too vulnerable, or simply too tedious, for their employers to handle, often involving shady or outright illicit elements in the task.

Véronique Dupont was such a person, a skilled French lawyer who had been on a generous retainer under the exclusive employ of Dmitry Zharkov for many years.

Véronique attended to such matters as providing counterfeit passports for Zharkov's friends who might need them, arranging for bail and legal assistance for the Russian's associates, representing him in court on any number of matters, and, when necessary, arranging for the elimination of any nuisances in Mr. Zharkov's life.

And Ivan Gović had become such a nuisance.

"Nikki," Zharkhov said after calling Véronique on the secure cell phone he had provided her exclusively for his calls, "I need you to find someone for me, and quickly."

He explained the situation with Gović and all relevant details—the BMW, a certain antiquity he had purchased, the Geneva Free Port, Tucci—enough to get her started on tracking him down.

On an educated hunch, Véronique first called a colleague in the Sûreté, to see if they might have any information on Gović. He might have been in an accident, in which case his name would be registered on the national police database. While she was waiting, she made a list of other places to call between Chamonix and Geneva: hospitals, hotels, airlines. She knew the drill.

When her colleague came back on the line, he had news: an Interpol Red Notice had been issued for Gović, and he had been provisionally arrested at Genève Aéroport while waiting to board a KLM flight to Buenos Aires.

As she was in Paris, Véronique couldn't immediately do anything in person, but she was not without influence or connections of her own.

Calling the Geneva office of Interpol, she reached Andreas Yoder, a close confidant whom she could count on to intercede in Gović's situation. Yoder, every bit the ardent Swiss mountain man, had long been smitten with

Véronique and would do anything for her—not to mention the money he knew she was attached to by way of Dmitry Zharkov.

"I am all yours, Nikki," Yoder said in his most disarming voice. "Tell me what it is you need."

A HALF-HOUR LATER A TALL, handsome man in a serious business suit walked into the security office at Genève Aéroport.

Presenting Interpol credentials with his photo—but a different name entirely—Andreas Yoder asked for the officer in charge. When the man appeared, Yoder instructed him to turn over Ivan Gović at once, that he would be taking him into custody.

A few minutes later the security agent produced Gović, again in handcuffs. Papers were signed using Yoder's concocted alias, and the two of them left the airport in the agent's black Mercedes.

With Gović handcuffed in the back seat, Yoder set the GPS navigation for a warehouse on the outskirts of Geneva. A warehouse owned by one Dmitry Zharkov.

SIXTY-FIVE

With the reliquary now safely in the trunk of the Rolls-Royce, Frederic drove everyone back to Saint-Clair's La Maison des Arbres château in Geneva. After discreet calls made to Pierre Valois, the President of the French Republic, the French police had relinquished custody of the Pelican case and its contents into the hands of Saint-Clair.

The cook had prepared lunch for the baron's guests, and as they sat around the large dining table overlooking Lake Geneva, the conversation turned to reacquiring the Vesconte map.

"Where would we begin to look?" Dengler asked. "Zharkov's home has got to be a fortress, if that's even where it is."

"I'd say it's the best bet," Hana said reassuringly. "Where else could it be, if it's not in the Pelican case with the reliquary?"

A thought came to her. "Michael, what if Gunari and his Roma boys are able to help us? They seem to be quick-witted in situations like this. Maybe they have ways we might not even consider, or...um...attempt."

Everyone at the table knew what Hana meant: a more felonious approach to the problem. But it was an astute analysis on her part.

"When I was in seminary, I never thought I'd be part of a criminal enterprise," Dominic said, laughing. "And look at me now!

"That's not a bad idea, Hana," he continued. "But how might we motivate them?"

"Michael," Saint-Clair said to the priest, "it's clear you will need certain resources with which to reacquire the map. Please allow me to assist. One never knows when one might require cash to incentivize others to act."

At this, Frederic produced a silver valise. Laying it on the table in front of Dominic, he opened it, revealing many packets of banded euros stacked neatly in the case.

"I should say fifty thousand euros should cover any expenses you might have, including airfare back to Rome when your mission here is complete. And what you don't use, consider as a donation to the Church, or put it away for a rainy day. You decide.

"And please, take the Maserati. It's my personal car when Frederic lets me drive on my own." He looked over at the chauffeur, who just rolled his eyes. It was obvious the two had a long and close bond. "Meanwhile, Hana and Dieter and I will head back to Rome and wait for you there."

"That's too generous of you, baron," Dominic said, considering the cash in the valise. "And, to be honest, I can't think of anything Gunari and his people need more than money. They're living in terrible squalor there, and this could certainly help them. Not to mention motivating them to help us."

"It's settled then," Saint-Clair said, slapping his hands on the table and standing up. "Frederic, please get the keys to the car for our guests. And of course, you'll stay here at the château in the meantime."

HANA and her grandfather gathered what they might need for a few days away, then went on to Genève Aéroport where Frederic loaded everything up in the Dassault Falcon for their trip to Rome.

Meanwhile, Dominic and Dengler stayed behind at the château, their only goal now being the recovery of the Vesconte map from Dmitry Zharkov. How they went about that might be a challenge for them.

But maybe not so much for the gypsies.

∾

ACCOMPANIED BY HIS SWISS COUNTERPART, Colombo appeared at the desk of the security chief at Genève Aéroport. "I am Agent Massimo Colombo from the Italian security agency," the man said, showing his credentials. "I am here to take Ivan Gović into custody."

The security chief looked at Colombo blankly. "But, monsieur, the agent from Interpol already picked up Gović, not even an hour ago!"

"*What?!*" Colombo shouted. "Interpol is not a law enforcement agency, you fool! They do not have powers of arrest, nor do they take people into custody. They are simply an informational entity. How do you not know this?! *Merda!*"

GARY MCAVOY

Duly chastised, the security chief simply shrugged his shoulders. "I am sorry, monsieur, but there is nothing more I can do about this. Gović is no longer here."

"Do you have the name of this Interpol agent?" Colombo demanded.

"*Oui*, one moment please." The man checked his logs and found the entry. "Here it is. The signature is very hard to read, but the printed name looks like 'Mr. Otto Graf.' Perhaps he is German?"

Colombo threw both palms to his head, slapping his cheeks. "*OTTO GRAF?!* You have got to be kidding! Is this a joke?!"

Now the man was hopelessly chagrined, not understanding the irony. He mumbled, "Agent Colombo, I am very sorry, but I must get back to work now. Au revoir." He scurried back to his office, leaving Colombo smoldering in the security lobby.

CHAPTER

SIXTY-SIX

E arly the next morning, Véronique DuPont's Air France jet landed at Genève Aéroport after a one-hour flight from Paris. With her sole client being in need of her services—and her retainer comprising certain expectations—her presence on the scene was presumed.

The first-class cabin was fairly empty, allowing her to make a series of private calls during the flight, tapping her extensive network to learn as much as she could about the situation and those involved. By the time she landed, she had a great deal to tell her employer.

Zharkov had sent a car to pick her up at the airport, and ninety minutes later she had arrived at his chalet in Chamonix. The boss was in a foul mood.

"*Privyet*, Nikki," Zharkov greeted her. "How was your flight?"

"Fine, Dmitry. Tell me more of what's going on." Véronique DuPont never minced words.

Beyond the brief particulars he had given her on the

phone the day before, Zharkov explained his introduction to the reliquary by Vincenzo Tucci in Rome, what little he knew about its acquisition, his payments to both Tucci and Govič, his giving Govič a BMW with the mission to deliver the reliquary to the Geneva Free Port, of being raided by the French Sûreté and Italian authorities here at his chalet, and Govič now having seemingly absconded with the reliquary and his money.

Véronique absorbed this with the efficiency of a lawyer accustomed to dealing with details. And she had much to add.

"It seems there are many others involved in this affair, Dmitry," she began. "A Vatican priest was the one to discover the reliquary in a cave in southern France. His name is Father Michael Dominic. He was accompanied by a Swiss journalist named Hana Sinclair—who also happens to be the sole heir of Banque Suisse de Saint-Clair in Geneva—and two Vatican Swiss Guard soldiers conscripted by Father Dominic. All of them were in the cave when Mr. Govič stole the reliquary from them, and then set off a bomb to seal them in. Apparently, he did this in retribution for his father's death the year before, blaming Father Dominic in particular.

"After the explosion, however, it appears they were all able to escape, and have presumably been after Govič seeking the return of the reliquary. Both the French Sûreté and the Italian AISI are now involved—as you obviously know from their raid here—and are assisting Father Dominic in recovering the stolen artifacts.

"My sources also tell me that Baron Armand de Saint-Clair, Hana's grandfather, flew them to Geneva from Rome and has been hosting them all at his château there, so we know they are in the area.

"We also discovered that Govic bought a Rolex in Chamonix, and shortly afterward rented a car, a Ford Fiesta, at a Europcar office in Chamonix yesterday, apparently soon after he left your chalet," she went on. "So, we must assume that the BMW you gave him may have been stolen or has been in an accident. The former is the more likely scenario."

Zharkov took all this in silently, impressed as ever by Véronique's mastery of facts and her breadth of connections to obtain such information.

"As for Mr. Govic," she continued, "Interpol had issued a Red Notice for his apprehension, and airport authorities in Geneva intercepted him waiting to board a flight to Buenos Aires. Fortunately, we now have him in our custody at your warehouse in Geneva. But the reliquary is missing. He has yet to be questioned. I thought it best to leave that to you."

"Yes, Nikki," Zharkov said darkly, "there will be many questions for young Mr. Govic. First, let me show you object that led them to reliquary."

Zharkov went to the wall of his office, swung back the large oil painting, opened the safe, and extracted the Vesconte map.

"This map was actually made as a puzzle by Italian mapmaker Pietro Vesconte..." he began, relating the rest of the story as told to him by Vincenzo Tucci. "On its own, it is a remarkable feat of engineering, especially for the thirteenth century." He proudly set it down on his desk, appreciating it as only an avid collector could.

Véronique looked at it as if it were simply another of the scores of, to her, meaningless baubles surrounding Zharkov here in his chalet and at his penthouse in Moscow, where she had often dined. Véronique DuPont cared little for historical objects. But she thrived on resolving bad situations.

"What shall we do with Mr. Gović when you are done with him, Dmitry?"

"The usual way these things turn out, I expect. I see no further use for him. I am more concerned with this priest and his friends. Perhaps they took reliquary back from Gović already. That might account for him wanting to flee country. Maybe they were ones who found BMW. Where do you suppose these people might be now?"

SIXTY-SEVEN

"How is it I get to drive so many cool cars lately?" Dengler asked rhetorically as the emerald-green Maserati Quattroporte sped toward Les Pèlerins and the gypsy camp.

Riding copilot in the stylish touring sedan, Dominic was thinking about how he might approach Gunari Lakatos for his help in recovering the Vesconte map. Whether buying or selling, he knew the Roma loved to negotiate, part of their tribal nature as they fought for the best deals when traveling from town to town.

And if Zharkov did have it in his chalet, how would they get past the resort's security? Would his guards or anyone else be there? What if it was locked away somewhere? These and more questions circled his mind as Dengler took the alpine curved roads with ease, the snow-covered landscape flying by while Dominic gripped the dashboard in front of him, only slightly alarmed at the high speed they were going.

Gratefully, the car began to slow as it entered the

village of Les Pèlerins and made its way through the forest road to the Roma encampment. The same scene as before greeted them: people huddled around fire bins talking, others chopping wood taken from the forest to keep them warm into the night.

All eyes turned to see the new arrivals in the Maserati. Milosh recognized Father Dominic—who was again wearing his priestly black shirt, white collar and black pants—from his prior visit when they found the reliquary inside the BMW. Milosh smiled at him as he called for his father.

Gunari Lakatos emerged from one of the central tents in the camp and made his way to where Dominic and Dengler were talking to his son. Dominic greeted him in his native language.

"Good morning, *Voivode*. It is good to see you again."

"It is my honor, Father. How can we help you today?"

"Gunari, we have another problem," Dominic began. "It seems the same scoundrel who stole our reliquary might have given another object that accompanied it—an ancient map of sorts—to a man named Dmitry Zharkov. We would like your help in recovering this map. But I must tell you, there may be danger involved."

"What kind of danger, Father?"

"From what I've been told by the police who raided his home, Zharkov lives in a well-protected chalet in Chamonix. There is a security gate to enter the resort, and he may have two bodyguards, perhaps other staff. We are not even sure this object is there, but we are fairly confident it is. We will pay handsomely for your assistance in retrieving this map."

Gunari looked directly into Dominic's eyes as he thought about his offer.

"You say there may be guards. Do you think they might be armed?"

"Most likely, yes."

Gunari looked down at the ground, then up to his sons Milosh and Shandor, who had joined the others gathered around the group. He instructed everyone but his sons to move away. Once the stragglers were gone, he gave his response.

"We can do this for you, Father. My two sons are the best ones to handle this type of work, but as there are many risks, it will require sacrifices from many."

Dominic understood what the chief meant.

"We are prepared to pay you five thousand euros cash, right now," he said firmly.

"Fifteen," the chief countered, a sly look in his eyes.

"Eight," Dominic said, matching the chief's gaze.

"Twelve," Gunari parried.

Dominic reached into his pocket and pulled out a banded packet of bills. "Ten thousand euros," he said, handing it to Gunari. No words could ever match the visual sight of a thick packet of freshly minted cash.

"We have a deal, Father Michael," Gunari said, smiling proudly at his superior negotiating skills and pocketing the money. "Now, come into my home and let us discuss the details."

CHAPTER

SIXTY-EIGHT

At the confluence of the Rhône River and Lake Geneva lies a seedy area known as the Paquis district, just northwest of the Port of Geneva. While the entire city itself is considered safe—as large European cities go—the Paquis is known for its rampant prostitution, drug dealers, strip bars, pickpockets, and the generally more bohemian population of Switzerland's second-largest city.

The Paquis was also home to Dmitry Zharkov's warehouse, a former shipping container storage site that now served whatever needs the oligarch's empire required in the way of maritime commerce.

It was also a conveniently secluded location to deal with nuisances like Ivan Gović.

At the moment, Gović was tied to a chair in the center of a large, vacant office. The only other person on the premises was Andreas Yoder. Both were waiting for the imminent arrival of Zharkov and his entourage.

"You know, I knew your father before his untimely

demise," Yoder said to the Croatian. "We both served the Ustasha proudly." He held up his Ehrenring in front of his captive's face.

Gović's despair quickly changed to hope. "Then you must free me! We are brothers, yes?! *Za dom-spremni!*"

"I'm afraid my first loyalty is to Mr. Zharkov, my friend. I don't know what got you into this mess. I only follow orders. But Zharkov is not one to cross, so here we shall remain until he decides what to do with you."

"But this is all a big mistake! My car was stolen, and—"

"—Yes, I heard your story in the car," Yoder interrupted sympathetically. "Still, we must wait. Maybe our employer will look upon your circumstances kindly, who knows?"

The sound of a door slamming shut echoed throughout the warehouse as several voices were heard approaching the office. Despite the cold weather and the dank air in the building, Gović was sweating profusely, terrified of what lay ahead.

The first person through the door was a tall, attractive woman in a black pantsuit wearing a dark sable coat, followed by Zharkov and his two henchmen. The Russian walked over to Gović and stood in front of him.

"Ivan," he said in a calm but chiding tone, "you have been naughty boy. *Where* is my reliquary?"

"Mr. Zharkov, the car was stolen when I stepped away from it for just a few minutes! I—"

"—Yes, we know you stopped to buy a Rolex in Chamonix, not exactly what I expected you to do while on such a simple errand. Couldn't it have waited until you completed your assignment? You would be twenty-five million euros richer, and not sitting here, waiting to die."

Gović burst into tears. Through his sobbing, he managed, "But this was not my fault! Can't you see?! I will do whatever you want. I will find the reliquary and punish those who took it. Anything, please!"

"I do not think we will see reliquary again, Ivan. By now it is probably on way to Rome. Do you know how this makes me feel? How humiliating this is?" His already dark mood escalated, Zharkov's voice got louder with each sentence.

Glancing at one of his men, Zharkov simply nodded. Yuri took off his jacket, laid it over the back of a nearby chair, and calmly walked toward Govíc. His left hand reached up and held the Croatian's chin for a moment, as his right arm thrust up and came down heavily on Govíc's face.

His nose broken, blood spattered across Govíc's face. His eyes started to swell as a second blow landed from the man's left fist in a roundhouse counterpunch. Govíc screamed in pain. Rivulets of tears mixed with blood trickled onto his chest. His body convulsed in agony.

Yuri then removed the Rolex from Govíc's wrist and handed it to Zharkov. The Russian looked at it admiringly, then twirled it around his index finger.

"I always wondered why these were so heavy," he said, as Govíc peered at the watch apprehensively through swollen eyes. Despite the pain and his escalating fear, all he could think of was: *All this for a fucking watch? Why? Why?!*

Zharkov held the Rolex closer for his captive to get a clearer look at. Then he bounced it off Govíc's sweating forehead a couple of times, held it up high, then let it fall to the cold concrete floor.

"Looks like you're out of time, Ivan."

Zharkov lifted his leg and brought his foot down on the

€24,000 Rolex, grinding it into pieces with his polished New & Lingwood Russian calf shoes.

Gović sat there trembling with a fear he had never known before. A dark wet stain appeared on his crotch. Grasping for any hope, he said, "But you have so much already, nearly everything. It was just some bones—"

"'Just some bones'?!" Zharkov shouted, his anger at a peak.

With that he reached into the jacket of one of his bodyguards, snatched the man's Glock 22 from its shoulder holster, aimed it at Gović's chest and pulled the trigger twice. The explosions rocked through the warehouse, startling Véronique and the others. Then the room fell quiet. Blood oozed from Gović's limp body, dripping onto the broken shards of the now worthless Rolex.

A few moments later, Véronique walked over to Zharkov and quietly said, "This could have gone another way, Dmitry. You should have let me handle it. At least I might have salvaged the twenty-five million you already gave him. Now that money is irretrievable, locked away in Gović's Swiss account."

Zharkov looked at her, now realizing the mistake his anger had cost him.

"You are right, Nikki. It was foolish of me. I must learn to control my temper. Oh well, what is done is done. Let's go home.

"Yuri, call our cleanup crew and make this go away. Now."

CHAPTER
SIXTY-NINE

Having gotten the address and layout of Zharkov's chalet from Colombo, Dominic, Dengler and the two gypsy boys—both hidden in the spacious trunk of the Maserati—headed out for Chamonix and Les Rives d'Argentière resort. The weather was brisk but not snowing, and the sun cast a near-blinding whiteness across the Argentière valley landscape.

Acting as chauffeur, Dengler drove the car while Dominic sat in the back seat beneath the expansive sunroof, his silver pectoral cross glinting in the bright sunlight.

As the vehicle approached the security gate, a guard emerged from the shack. *Lord*, Dominic prayed fervently, *forgive me this minor sin I am about to commit..."*

"*Oui*, monsieur?" the guard greeted Dengler. Dominic had rolled down his window to address the guard, who walked toward the rear of the car to address the priest.

"Good afternoon, monsieur," he said in fluent French. "I am Monsignor Dominic of the Diocese of Geneva. We are here as an advance team on behalf of the Vatican to inspect your premises for a possible visit by the pope later this year. I am advised your resort might provide most suitable accommodations for His Holiness, who, as you may not know, is an avid skier." Dominic winked at this as if passing on something of a highly personal nature to the guard, who—as with most people in Switzerland—was very likely Catholic. Dominic prayed he was, anyway.

"The Holy Father? *Here in Chamonix?! Mon Dieu!*" the guard said with wide-eyed astonishment. Dominic's instincts had paid off.

"We do not wish to meet with your management staff just yet, as our advance team relies on secrecy for obvious security reasons. We are only here to view various resorts and private residences in the area worthy of hosting His Holiness. May I have your word, monsieur, that our visit will remain between us for now? We only want to drive around the property for a while, assess its desirability, and send our report on to Rome. Would that be acceptable?"

"Ah, *mais oui*, Monsignor Dominic. You were never here." The guard winked back, then opened the wrought iron gates, allowing them to pass.

Dominic lifted his hand to make the sign of the cross, giving the man his blessing, then rolled his window up as the Maserati entered the property, heading toward Zharkov's chalet.

WITH ZHARKOV'S house on its own expansive property, there were no neighboring homes to contend with, no one else to see them lurking about. Dengler drove up the circular driveway and stopped the car in front of the entrance to the home. Dominic got out and walked up to the front door.

The plan was simple. He would knock on the door, and if anyone answered he would inquire if this was the home of a Madame Charbonneau, a lady who had called asking for a priest to visit her—in which case he would simply leave, and they would try another day.

Dominic's knocking, however, yielded no answer at all. He rang the doorbell to be sure. Still no response. He returned to the car.

There was a side driveway to the tradesmen's entrance behind the house, so Dengler drove around and parked the car where it couldn't be seen from the front.

He then opened the trunk and Milosh and Shandor leapt out of the vehicle, stretching to unknot themselves.

"No one seems to be home," Dominic said. "What do we do now?" he asked the gypsies.

Milosh stepped forward. "Leave this to me and Shandor, Father. We have done this many times before." He said this with both pride and slight embarrassment, since he was addressing a priest, after all. He would ask for forgiveness later.

Milosh and Shandor quickly tested many of the windows and doors of the large chalet, checking for signs of any security measures, peering through each to make sure the place was indeed empty. A high stack of cut wooden logs lay against an outside wall, next to which was a set of slanted cellar doors. Testing the latch, Milosh found it was unlocked, unsurprising since wood was probably brought in often for the chalet's many fireplaces.

Lifting open one of the two doors, Milosh led each of the men down into the dark cellar, where they stamped their boots to shake off the snow. From there they found the staircase leading up into the main part of the house.

They were in.

Entering through the kitchen, Dengler opened his phone and showed Milosh and Shandor photos of the object they were looking for, the Vesconte map. Each of them quickly fanned out to the various rooms in search of the object. Milosh and Shandor took the upstairs, while the others took the downstairs.

Moments later, Dengler and Dominic both entered the great room at the same time from different doors, having found nothing yet.

Pointing to the armory on the wall, Dengler was impressed and surprised. "Look, Michael! These halberds are nearly the same ones we were trained in using, and still use even today while guarding the Vatican. This is an amazing collection."

"We'll take the tour another time, Karl. Let's find this thing and get out of here. Our luck may not hold for long."

THE GUARD at the entrance to the resort was still enthralled at the thought of the Holy Father coming to visit his hometown when a black Mercedes SUV approached the gate. Recognizing Monsieur Zharkov and his men, he opened the gates and waved them in. The car drove slowly up the street, minutes away from the chalet.

ENTERING what appeared to be Zharkov's office, Dominic found more collectible arms on the walls here too, along with a vast collection of framed antique maps and architectural art. *This guy sure loves collecting things,* he thought, taking stock of every nook and cranny of the office for signs of the artifact.

And then he saw it—just sitting there on the desk! *Could it be any simpler?*

"Karl, I found it!" he whispered loudly, dropping the map into his backpack as he headed toward the door. He could hear someone running down the staircase, and a moment later Dengler appeared in the entryway. He was just about to say something to Michael when he heard a sound behind him.

The unmistakable sound of a key being inserted into a lock.

CHAPTER
SEVENTY

As Dengler scrambled toward Michael he pushed him back into the office. "They're here!" he whispered. "Someone's coming in the door!"

They looked around quickly, considering their options. There was only one door out of the office and that was the one they had just come through, leading into the foyer, where it was now clear Zharkov and a woman were assembling as they took off their coats and shook the snow off their boots.

They were trapped.

Voices caught their attention.

"Would you like something warm to drink, Nikki?" Zharkov asked his fixer. "Or perhaps nice brandy?"

"Sure, Dmitry. Brandy sounds perfect. It's freezing out there."

The sound of the voices diminished as they moved into the kitchen, away from the office. Looking around, Dengler eyed one of the halberds on the wall and went to fetch it, quietly removing it from its mounting bracket.

Dominic, feeling suddenly defenseless, grabbed an antique wooden Persian mace resting on a bookshelf, though it would be of little match if they were to face a gun. Still, it was better than nothing.

He wondered what Milosh and Shandor were doing. It should be obvious to them by now that they had company. They would probably try to escape from the upstairs windows. That was logical. Also logical was the probability of them filling their pockets with jewelry or other valuables they might have found, but right now all Dominic cared about was getting out of this predicament.

With their backs literally to the wall in the office, weapons in hand, they waited. As Dengler positioned himself in a better fighting stance, however, one of the oak floorboards creaked beneath his feet.

Both of them held their breath as they stood perfectly still.

When they thought things were quiet enough, they peered around the corner. The foyer was empty. They crept through the office door and quietly headed toward the front exit.

Just then Véronique walked around the corner from the kitchen. She had a small but lethal .357 derringer in her hand and waved it between Dominic and Dengler.

"Dmitry," she called out calmly, "it appears we have company."

At that moment one of Zharkov's bodyguards walked in through the front door, his eyes wide at the unexpected situation. He reached for the Glock inside his coat. Dengler, standing between the man and Véronique, slammed the halberd backward into the man's chest.

Véronique pointed the derringer at Dengler and pulled the trigger just as Dengler swung around. The bullet grazed Dengler's right shoulder, then hit the bodyguard directly in the face. Both of them went down.

Dominic jumped at the woman with the mace raised high above him and smacked it down hard on her collarbone. She hit the floor.

By that time Zharkov had run out of the kitchen and into the fray. He grabbed Dominic from behind in a ferocious bear hug. The Russian's unexpected strength overpowered the priest as a beefy right arm clamped around his throat in a forceful chokehold. As Dominic tried to shake free of the Russian, the grip only tightened. Dominic couldn't breathe.

Dengler scrambled to his feet, grabbed the mace and headed toward Zharkov—just as the other bodyguard rushed in the front door, his weapon drawn.

"Drop it! Now!" the man called to Dengler. Dominic was losing consciousness fast, and Karl was torn as to what to do.

From the stair landing above the guard, Milosh jumped over the banister and onto the back of the man, a wicked dagger in his hand. With both of them now on the floor, Milosh forcibly grabbed the man's hair and pulled his head back, the dagger arcing across the man's throat from left to right. Arterial blood gushed out as he fell, streams of dark red spurting out onto the floor with each beat of his dying heart.

Dengler swung himself behind Zharkov and brought the mace down heavily on the Russian's head as he held Dominic—once, twice, a third time.

Zharkov finally released his hold on the priest. Both of them fell to the floor.

Dengler rushed over to Dominic. The priest lay unconscious, his breathing shallow, too shallow. Dengler bent over him and started mouth-to-mouth resuscitation, ignoring the pain from his shoulder injury.

Meanwhile, Shandor raced down the stairs with his own dagger ready for battle. He and Milosh stood facing outward from where Dengler worked to revive Dominic, flanking them, prepared for more opponents. None came.

Dominic stirred and opened his eyes, then began coughing as Dengler ceased assistive breathing. He sat up, his eyes wavering as his mind emerged from the dark. Dengler helped him to his feet and then began assessing the situation.

Two dead, two unconscious. He decided to get them out of there before either Zharkov or the woman came to.

With Dominic still unsteady, Dengler grabbed his backpack and helped him out through the back door in the kitchen, then all four jumped into the Maserati.

"Milosh," Dengler said, "you and Shandor should get back into the trunk, so the guard doesn't get suspicious when we pass through the gate."

The two gypsies complied. Mostly recovered now, Dominic got into the back seat and straightened himself up, while Dengler—after wiping away the blood from his minor shoulder wound—started the car and drove down the driveway. A few minutes later they would reach the gate and be out of the resort.

REGAINING CONSCIOUSNESS, Zharkov pushed himself up from the floor and looked around, groaning in pain. His attackers appeared to be gone. His bodyguards looked to be dead. And Véronique lay unconscious on the floor next to him.

His first instinct was fury, and on its heels, revenge.

Unsteadily, he stood up and struggled over to the house phone. He dialed the number of the security gate.

THE MASERATI WAS JUST APPROACHING the closed iron gates when the guard came out of his shack, smiling at his important guests. Dominic rolled down his window.

The guard approached him. "So, monsignor, did you find our resort compatible for the Holy Father's visit?" he said hopefully.

"*Oui*, monsieur, this should do just fine. You have a beautiful location here."

Just then the telephone rang in the guard shack.

"Excuse me, Father, I will be just a moment."

"Actually," Dominic said urgently, "we are in a bit of a hurry and must return to the city quickly. Could you open the gate now, please?"

The guard, wanting to chat a bit more about the pope's visit, sighed.

"Of course, monsieur. *Bon voyage*." He pressed the button to open the iron gates. As the car passed through, the guard went into the shack to pick up the phone.

"*Oui?*" he answered.

"*Stop the priest from leaving!*" Zharkov shouted in a gasping rage.

Confused, the guard looked up. The Maserati was already out of sight, speeding away toward Geneva.

SEVENTY-ONE

O nce they were northeast of Chamonix, Dengler stopped the Maserati on a snowy shoulder of the road to free Milosh and Shandor from the trunk.

Dominic hugged them both gratefully as they emerged. "You guys helped us tremendously back there. I cannot express how grateful we are. There's no way Karl and I would have gotten out of that mess without you."

Adrenaline still coursed through Milosh from the fight. The young man's eyes danced with energy, even as guilt colored his words.

"Father, I truly regret having taken a life, but there was no time to think, and you both were in such great danger. I pray for God's forgiveness, and yours."

"I understand, Milosh. But as you say, things were happening fast. Those people had no regard for our lives, as the woman took a shot at Karl, and the Russian and his men would have killed us all. In my view, you acted in self-defense. If you are asking for absolution, I can grant that if you wish to make a confession. Let's get you home first. We can do it there."

Fifteen minutes later they pulled into the Roma camp in Les Pèlerins. Milosh raced out of the car to find his father and tell him of their adventure. Gunari approached Dominic and Dengler, thanking them for taking good care of his sons in what he now realized could have been a more harrowing situation.

"It is we who should be thanking you, Gunari," Dominic said. "You have two fine young men here who helped us retrieve an important artifact we can now take back to Rome. Without them, our lives would have been in great peril."

Reaching into his backpack, he pulled out another stack of ten thousand euros. "*Voivode*, please allow us to contribute to your community's well-being. Consider this a small gesture of goodwill for your valued help."

Gunari looked at the money with both allure and uncertainty.

"Father Michael, we Roma have a long and proud tradition. We do what we must to survive, but we do not seek charity. We prefer to earn our way through life, despite our sometimes unconventional methods.

"However," he added, an earnest glint in his eyes, "I might be obliged to accept this offering as an advance on some future assistance we might provide you. In other words, we would be in your debt. And I look forward to the day when we can repay it." He held out his left arm, and Dominic placed the packet in his hand. Both men smiled and shook hands.

"You have yourself a deal, Gunari," the priest said, "and my blessing.

"Speaking of which," he added, "Milosh and I need a

little time together. Is there somewhere we can have some privacy?"

Knowing his son had killed a man, and that it weighed heavily on Milosh when he had related it to his father, Gunari led them to his tent. "Take as long as you need, Father."

~

ONCE THEY WERE BACK at Saint-Clair's château in Geneva, Dominic and Dengler unpacked the Maserati and returned it to the garage.

Then Michael brought the Pelican case into the dining room from where Saint-Clair had secured it in a hidden cabinet and set it on the table in order to re-insert the puzzle map. They both looked at it with breathless anticipation, not only for what it contained but as a final reward for the days of struggle they'd endured seeking, then fighting, for it and the map's repossession.

The case itself had remained latched but unlocked since Dieter had opened it in the Roma camp after liberating it from the BMW. Dominic raised the case lid and lifted the reliquary out of its foam molding. Reaching for the skeleton key with shaking hands, he inserted it into the Egyptian ward lock, which emitted a creaky metal sound followed by a solid clunk as the key wards lined up with the grooves and the cylinder fell into place.

He held his breath and opened the lid.

The parchment, the skull and hand bones, the jewelry and the glass bottle of myrrh—all of it held their fascination as Dominic and Dengler gazed upon Sarah's remains.

Dominic clasped his hands together and began praying

for understanding and guidance on how to process the implications of such a discovery. Dengler followed his friend's lead, lowering his head in deference to the moment.

After making the sign of the cross, Dominic turned to Dengler.

"Karl, I'm not entirely sure what this will mean to the world, if the pope even permits it to be acknowledged. For all I know, you and I may be the last to see this. We should appreciate the moment."

Dengler nodded in silence.

THERE WERE two more things Dominic had to do before they called a taxi for their flight to Rome.

The first was to call Armand de Saint-Clair who was now in Rome. There was the problem of getting an ancient cultural antiquity through Customs, something the baron had stated he would help to facilitate when Michael was ready to return with it to Rome.

The second—another essential task the baron could facilitate—was to stop at Banque Suisse de Saint-Clair where Dominic could transfer some thirty thousand euros into his account at the Vatican Bank, since explaining that much cash to Customs personnel would most certainly present an unwelcome problem on its own.

CHAPTER
SEVENTY-TWO

A s passengers on Alitalia flight 575 from Geneva
disembarked at Rome's Leonardo da Vinci Airport,
Hana, Lukas and Dieter waited in the Customs
terminal, watching for Dominic and Dengler to appear.

After Dominic's earlier call from Geneva, Armand de
Saint-Clair, through his vast network, had promptly
arranged for an expedited Certificate of Free Circulation,
necessary documentation for such artifacts transiting
international borders. Having the proper paperwork—
with the requisite official stamps and colorful certificates
so beloved by Italian authorities—made the reliquary's
import into Italy an easier process than it might have been.

It was easy to spot Dominic's black shirt and white
collar notch among those arriving, and once they cleared
Customs and retrieved their baggage and the Pelican case,
their reunion was a flurry of hugs and happy faces over
their successful mission.

Hana held onto Michael for several long moments, then

looked deeply into his eyes. "I am so happy you're both back and in one piece. I can't wait to hear everything that happened."

With their things loaded up into Dengler's Jeep Wrangler, they drove on to the Vatican as Michael and Karl related the last few days' activities.

~

"AND THAT'S about the whole story, Rico," Dominic said to Cardinal Petrini as he summarized their adventures in France and Switzerland.

The unopened Pelican case sat on a nearby table. Petrini's eyes kept glancing at it from time to time as Dominic related the story, its tantalizing contents holding a seductive power in his imagination as he listened to every inconceivable word.

"I must say, Michael, I am overwhelmed by everything you've just told me. How you manage to get into these situations is a fascination on its own, but I learned long ago to trust your instincts. But this ... this is truly extraordinary.

"May I see the reliquary now?" he asked reverently.

"Of course!" Dominic replied. They both stood and walked over to the table. Dominic lifted the lid of the case and removed the reliquary, set it on the table, then opened it with the skeleton key.

He watched as Petrini relished the same sacred moment he had enjoyed earlier. After some time, the cardinal returned to his seat.

"You realize, Michael, that no one else may see this for now, or even learn of its existence. I must explain all of this to His Holiness, and as always in such cases, it will be his decision as to its disposition.

"Please ask your friends who are aware of it to abide by my request, will you? We do not wish to incur the frenzy of the media about something we know so very little of at this stage.

"And the pope may wish evaluation by select scholars and theologians. The implications of this are deep and far-reaching, as you can imagine. If Christ and Mary Magdalene did indeed have a child, it throws out much of what the Church was founded on. As with the document you discovered last year, such knowledge can be a dangerous thing to this institution, and to the faithful who depend on it."

Both men sat there in silence, pondering yet again the profound ramifications of withholding or releasing knowledge of the reliquary.

As with the Magdalene papyrus he had been instructed to conceal in the Vatican's Riserva last year, Dominic had conflicting feelings about the values of truth and transparency, of faith and fidelity. Though his own beliefs depended on more esoteric concepts, the power of devotion by the billion Catholic souls they served was far more predicated on certain established convictions. To undermine that foundation would cause turmoil and even more division in an already chaotic world.

But what about the truth? What about being honest to all Christians, not just those of the Catholic faith? Who held the moral high ground in these situations?

Such thoughts ran through his head as he balanced dissatisfaction with acceptance, anger over the fact that institutional preservation might again hold sway over the more enlightened prospect of historical revelation. He could easily envision years of scholarly debate over authenticity, but at least there would be an open discussion. But at what cost to the faithful, and to the Church?

Last summer he'd been tasked to hide the Magdalene papyrus, but Mendoza had discovered it. Truth was hard to hide. Michael Dominic felt gratified that he had preserved something so precious from the tainted hands of the greedy. Now it was out of his hands as well. The priest knew he may never see this reliquary or its contents again, never know its fate. He closed his eyes in silent prayer of acceptance and gratitude that the next decisions were not his to make.

CHAPTER
SEVENTY-THREE

T hough the air was brisk, the sun over Rome gave the Vatican gardens an especially warm luminance as Brother Mendoza and Father Dominic walked along the Stradone dei Giardini outside the Apostolic Library building.

Dominic had noticed for a few days now that his friend's countenance was more one of peace and comfort, unlike before he had left Rome, as if he had come to some resolution over what had been bothering him.

"Miguel, there is something I must say to you," he began as they walked beneath the old Mela Nesta apple trees. Dominic plucked two ripe fruits, and offered one to his companion.

"What is it, Cal?" he asked, as he took a crunchy bite.

Mendoza took the apple but held it, rolling it around in his hands as they walked.

"My friend, I was presented with a great challenge when I discovered the Magdalene papyrus in the Riserva. As I told you, my faith was shaken to its very core. I didn't sleep well for days and I ate practically nothing. I was in a moral abyss."

He stopped and looked into Dominic's eyes, smiling transcendently.

"But then, the Holy Spirit came to me, and I was reminded of something Saint Augustine said: 'Seek not to understand that you may believe, but believe that you may understand.'

"That manuscript may well be authentic, Miguel, but I choose to continue to believe that I may understand. It is all so clear to me now."

Dominic didn't say a word. This was his friend's moment of truth.

"But throughout these days of trial," Mendoza continued, "I have come to realize that it is time for me to retire. My faith is stronger than ever now, but I wish to be free of the responsibilities that come with my position here. I am soon to enter my eighties, Miguel, and I wish to spend what time I have left in simple contemplation. I will find a monastery in Tuscany, perhaps, where the food and wine are suitable for a man of my simple needs.

"There is something else," he added. "I want you to take my place. I am going to recommend you as the next Prefect of the Secret Archives. And since you are close to Cardinal Petrini, I think you may already have the job if you wish it. Will you accept my offer, Miguel?"

Dominic was dumbfounded. He looked at Mendoza, emotion suddenly clouding his eyes, then reached out to embrace the monk.

"Oh, dear Calvino. I'm flattered you hold me in such high regard. You have been a good friend and mentor since my arrival here, and you have taught me much more than I could ever repay. I would be incredibly honored to accept, if there are no others you feel are more suited to the task."

"Even though you haven't been here that long, Miguel, you have a quick mind and are an adept student of history. You have more devotion to your work than anyone else on our small staff, and I know Cardinal Petrini and the Holy Father will agree with me. It is an important role in the Church, and I believe you are ready to embrace its duties and responsibilities."

"Thank you, Cal. I'm so relieved to hear that you managed to evade the dark spirits haunting you over that Magdalene manuscript. I was quite worried for a while."

"As you can see, I have indeed come out the other side. Thank you for your concern, Miguel. It means a great deal to me."

The two men continued strolling the papal gardens in silence, taking in the rare warmth of an autumn sun.

～

AUTHOR'S NOTE

Dealing with issues of theology, religious beliefs, and the fictional treatment of historical biblical events can be a daunting affair.

I would ask all readers to view this story for what it is: a work of pure fiction, adapted from the seeds of many oral traditions and the historical record, at least as we know it today.

Apart from telling an engaging story I have no agenda here, and I respect those of all beliefs, from Agnosticism to Zoroastrianism and everything in between.

Many readers of *The Magdalene Chronicles* series have asked me to distinguish fact from fiction in my books. Generally, I like to take factual events and historical figures and build on them in creative ways—but much of what I do write is historically accurate. In this section, I'll review some of the chapters where questions may arise, with hopes that it may help those who are wondering.

AUTHOR'S NOTE

PROLOGUE

All characters featured in the Prologue— Raymond-Roger Trancavel, Viscount of Carcassonne; Raymond VI, Count of Toulouse; Godfroi de Bouillon, conqueror and first ruler of the Kingdom of Jerusalem; Raymond VII, Count of Toulouse; and Pietro Vesconte, the most renowned mapmaker of his time—were all real figures. The sacred reliquary passed among them is a fictional artifact.

The puzzle I describe later is actually the brainchild of a puzzle master living in Greece today.

CHAPTER 1

The mechanics of caving as described here are completely accurate, as generously provided to me by an expert British caver named Martin Hoff. Like Michael Dominic, tight spaces are not my favorite places to be in.

There is, in fact, a legend that the Cathars actually buried their "treasure" in one of the caves of the Languedoc region. There is nothing to distinguish *what* that treasure might have been.

CHAPTER 3

In Codice Ratio is an actual program of the Vatican's in which ancient manuscripts are being transcribed into machine-readable text using advanced optical character recognition.

CHAPTER 5

Guillaume de Sonnac, eighteenth Grand Master of the
Knights Templar, was a real historical figure, but his
journals have been contrived for this story.

CHAPTER 6

Though the original Croatian Ustasha was an actual fascist
organization, the "Novi" Ustasha is entirely fictional.

CHAPTER 7

The Vatican's Secret Archive (or what has recently been
renamed the Apostolic Archive) does in fact extend
beneath the expanse of the Pigna Courtyard and does
possess fifty-three linear miles of shelf space. Most of its
vast inventory has never been cataloged, nor has it been
seen by anyone living.

CHAPTER 9

As a foodie myself, I love feeding my characters what I
think they might enjoy. The meals I use in my stories are
all from authentic menus at the real restaurants I mention
—in this case, from the Michelin-rated La Pergola in Rome.

CHAPTER 13

The folding plate puzzle used here is, in fact, a real device,
used with the generous permission of its ingenious creator,
Pantazis the Megistian. Using similar elements of Rubik's

puzzles, it does actually transform from its unusual original shape to one of a square tower.

CHAPTER 24

The simplistic DNA sequencing description I provide here is more or less accurate, although much more is actually involved. But the basics provided are used in actual practice.

CHAPTER 34

The story of Mary Magdalene, her siblings and several disciples, and a young "maid" named Sarah—all cast adrift in an oarless boat on the Mediterranean—is based on actual oral tradition.

CHAPTER 35

The *tombaroli* or tomb raiders of Rome are an actual group, and their leader is called the *capo zona*, regional chief. Not surprisingly, Rome has a massive black market trade in antiquities, keeping the also-real Italian Art Squad very busy.

CHAPTER 43

The description of carbon-14 dating is as accurate as I could describe without being overly complex. As longtime readers know, I favor passing along knowledge of things I've always wanted to know myself, reducing them to simpler explanations.

CHAPTER 51

The Geneva Free Port is the real deal, filled with the works of art, bottles of wine, and other high-value collectibles exactly as I describe them here. It is also a bane to Customs authorities since sales and purchases can be made on the property, all tax-free, while still retained on-site in the ultra-secure facility.

CHAPTER 54

As I mentioned in the Author's Note for *The Magdalene Deception*, Apple's AirTags are actual products that perform as described in the book. I make note of this only because—given a solid tip by insiders—I wrote about them (with fingers crossed) a good eighteen months before they were released, so many readers assumed I made them up.

CHAPTER 61

The mechanism for unlocking cars remotely using a relay scanner is a fact, as described.

~

Thank you for reading *The Magdalene Reliquary*. I hope you enjoyed it as much as I enjoyed writing it. Would you please consider leaving a review? Even just a few words would help others decide if the book is right for them.

I've made it super simple: just click the link below and you'll travel to the Amazon review page for this book where you can leave your review.

www.amazon.com / review / create-review?
asin=B08P61ZNFK

And if you'd like to learn more about my other books—
especially if you haven't read the prequel to this book, *The
Magdalene Deception* or the final book in the series, *The
Magdalene Veil* —I invite you to visit my website at www.
garymcavoy.com.

With best regards,

Gary McAvoy

YOUR FREE BOOK IS WAITING

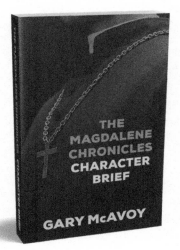

Download your free copy now of **The Magdalene Chronicles Character Brief**, containing brief backgrounds and other biographical details of all the main characters in *The Magdalene Deception, The Magdalene Reliquary,* and *The Magdalene Veil*—with my compliments as a loyal reader!

www.garymcavoy.com/character-brief/

ACKNOWLEDGMENTS

Many of the scenes in this book would not have been as well conceived without the invaluable help of Greg McDonald, whose logical thinking is only rivaled by that of Mr. Spock's—and even that may be debatable.

To Pantazis Houlis on the Greek island of Kastellorizo, thank you so much for the use of your ingenious folding puzzle concept. Thanks also to Martin Hoff, an accomplished caver in the U.K. who expertly guided me through the dark caverns of France.

Thanks as well to the unrelated Kent Gray and Brad Gray for their expertise in ordnance and explosives, and for keeping me safe from literary injuries.

In the end it all came together under the capable hands of my longtime editor, Sandra Haven, to whom I am forever grateful, along with John Burgess, whose vision for my books' covers is always inspired.

And finally, to my launch team, whose review and feedback were gratefully appreciated: Kim Cheel, Rob Conway, Kathleen Costello, Michelle Harden, Jim Harris, Jeanne Jabour, Fran Libra Koenigsdorf, Yale Lewis and Carolyn Walsh.

Credit for the Cave Map: "Map From www.gozzys.com (CC BY-SA 4.0)."

Made in United States
Orlando, FL
14 August 2022

21023454R20221